Missing But
Not Missed

J WILCOX

Grosvenor House
Publishing Limited

All rights reserved
Copyright © J Wilcox, 2024

The right of J Wilcox to be identified as the author of this
work has been asserted in accordance with Section 78
of the Copyright, Designs and Patents Act 1988

The book cover is copyright to J Wilcox

This book is published by
Grosvenor House Publishing Ltd
Link House
140 The Broadway, Tolworth, Surrey, KT6 7HT.
www.grosvenorhousepublishing.co.uk

This book is sold subject to the conditions that it shall not, by way of
trade or otherwise, be lent, resold, hired out or otherwise circulated
without the author's or publisher's prior consent in any form of
binding or cover other than that in which it is published and
without a similar condition including this condition being
imposed on the subsequent purchaser.

This book is a work of fiction. Any resemblance to
people or events, past or present, is purely coincidental.

A CIP record for this book
is available from the British Library

ISBN 978-1-80381-963-1

For Mum

Acknowledgements

Thank you to everyone who has helped with this book. To Jonathan for reviewing the drafts and giving encouragement; to Lynne for reviewing and for culinary and crossword contributions; to Mary for her superb artwork and for her patience with the process; to Phil for the original photograph; to Jasmine for helping with the publication process, and to Harry who has proved to be a most irresistible salesman!

1

"If you lean over the balcony, you can see the cliff where she plunged to her death," said Valerie Marsden, bending so far over the railing she looked as though she might perform a reconstruction of the tragedy. Stretching even further, she pointed towards the ill-fated spot several hundred yards away, beyond the gently sloping hotel gardens. "Over there!" she said.

Leslie, who was not fond of heights, winced. Bennett also winced but this was because, looking up from his book, he had caught a most unflattering rear view of the lady. He raised an eyebrow and returned his eyes to the page.

"It was exactly a year ago this week," she continued, turning round and leaning her well-upholstered hip more safely on the railing. "June the tenth; a date I'll never forget as long as I live. Sometimes I can still hardly believe it happened.

"The cliff isn't part of my property, thankfully, and we were completely exonerated at the inquest. The verdict was accidental death. Mercifully, even in this day and age, you can't be held accountable if a silly woman runs over the edge of a cliff after a hat that's blown away. I mean, really, fancy dying in the cause of a hat!"

Leslie felt weary. Val Marsden was nearly as garrulous as her cousin, Gloria, who had arranged this holiday for them. They were here to recuperate, Leslie from an accident which had concussed him and dislocated his shoulder, and Bennett, rather belatedly, from a heart attack earlier in the year. It was supposed to be a restful break.

They had arrived two days ago, on the Saturday, and found everything just as Gloria had described it: the neat Georgian country house, the sweeping gravel driveway, the elegant terrace and landscaped gardens, and the stunning sea views. The suite where he and Bennett were accommodated was on the first floor of the newly restored coach house, situated in the gardens to the rear of the main building, and it was furnished with every possible luxury. The location of the hotel on this part of the South Devon coast was also perfect, standing high above a rust-coloured sandy cove which was notched into the rugged coastline, and close to some pretty little villages but well away from the main seaside resorts. Even the weather was delightful; a sea breeze had obligingly sprung up to keep them comfortable in what would otherwise have been scorching weather. Leslie knew he ought to be perfectly content.

"Well, hark at me depressing you with stories of doom and gloom while you're supposed to be convalescing," laughed Val. "I really came to tell you that I've just had a call from Gloria, and guess what? She's coming down to stay, arriving today!"

"Gloria? Today?" Leslie tried to sound enthusiastic. Like Val, Gloria's friendliness and good humour could not be faulted, but sometimes the dose could be too much.

It was a relief when Val added, "Yes, but I don't know how much you'll see of her as she's coming down to join the creative writing course for the week."

Leslie cast an involuntary glance at Bennett, but he was intent on his book. They had been warned that a residential writing course was to take place at the hotel during their stay and Bennett had expressed some sardonic opinions.

"The guests, or delegates as they like to be called, will be arriving from about three o'clock this afternoon, and they'll be here until Friday morning," continued Val. "Actually, we've never had any other guests resident while the course is running. That way, they can have full use of the lounge and the conservatory for their classes and their readings and whatnot."

"We'll try not to get in their way," said Leslie with sincerity. He was not feeling equal to encountering a group of aspiring poets.

"Don't you worry about that," said Val. "You won't be in anyone's way, and I'm glad to be able to have you. I was so pleased we had this new suite ready, and I could put you in here where you can have plenty of peace and quiet."

Peace and quiet was not, however, to be their portion for the moment. The coach house restoration was a project of which Val Marsden was rightly proud and on which she seized every opportunity to discourse at length. She explained in depth the complexities of gaining planning permission for a listed building, the difficulties of finding suitable craftsmen and, in particular, the delights of designing and furnishing the interior. Leslie, by nature genial, would normally have listened with tolerance, and even some interest, as Val chattered on and on about portieres and dormer rods, skirted valances and Persian pouffes. But right at this moment he felt the urge to rush across and tip her backwards over the balcony.

"The main house is really much too small," she continued cheerfully, oblivious to her imaginary fate. "It's all well and good being a boutique hotel, but it's galling to turn business away. Restoring this building has been my dream. I budgeted on taking the extra bookings in here from the start of the main season in July, and I never expected that we would have one of the suites ready by now. That's how I was able to take you at short notice when Gloria told me about your accident and your need to convalesce. I'm usually booked out."

"We're really very grateful," said Leslie. "But talking of Gloria, when did she decide to join this writing course? She drove us down here, as you know, and she didn't mention that she was even thinking about it."

"It was a spur of the moment thing, but that's Gloria for you. She often pops down here for a few days, and it's always at a moment's notice. She happened to be here last year when the writing course was on and, just between you and me, I think she was a bit taken with Jeremy, the chap in charge of the course. All the women are. He's run his writing course here for the last three summers and it's always women who sign up for it. He's a right charmer. You know the type: tall, blond, sun-tanned."

This seemed even more reason to keep out of the way.

"Well, I can't stand here chatting all day; masses to do before the guests—I mean delegates—arrive," said Val, and she stepped from the balcony into the sitting room.

There she turned and, after a further ten minutes of uninterrupted talk, she left them to recover.

***

An hour or so later, Leslie was picking his way cautiously along the narrow pavement of the nearby village of Alemouth, hampered by a shopping bag in one hand and his other arm still awkwardly supported in a collar and cuff sling. The street was full of charm, flanked on both sides by an interesting selection of shops, and sloping steeply down to a small pebbly bay which was busy with a mixture of fishing boats and pleasure craft. On the previous day, Leslie had spent a pleasant couple of hours pottering about and watching the comings and goings in the harbour. His enjoyment had only been marred by the nebulous sense of anxiety that had plagued him since his accident, and the disappointment that Bennett had declined to join him on the walk. Leslie had allowed himself to hope that things might be different on holiday, but it was futile; Bennett was content to remain inside their suite, reading and working, eschewing all attempts to entice him out.

Today, Leslie had no intention of lingering, anxious to complete his shopping and get back to their rooms before the writing group started to arrive. His destination now was the chemist shop to procure an indigestion remedy, as the change of diet was taking its toll on his insides. The food, so highly recommended on the hotel's website, and personally by Gloria, had been an unexpected disappointment. Cooking was Leslie's hobby, and he knew he could be overly critical, but he had overheard complaints from some of the other guests who were there over the weekend. Val Marsden had confided in him that they had a new chef in the kitchen and the team had not quite 'shaken down' yet. Leslie massaged his abdomen; the same could be said of his greasy breakfast.

The chemist shop was at the top of the street and Leslie paused outside its crooked bay window to catch his breath after the climb. The pavement was narrow but that had not stopped the shopkeeper from placing a metal carousel cluttered with sale items, and a tub of novelty walking sticks, outside. While he regained his breath, Leslie glanced casually at the posters in the window, always of interest in a new place. There were adverts for a sale of agricultural machinery and a farmer's market, a list of forthcoming WI meetings, and a traffic notice warning that the high street was to be closed to vehicles on Wednesday for filming. Leslie looked down the picturesque street; it was certainly perfect for a film location. He was speculating on what costume drama or historical thriller was to be set there as he turned back towards the low, dark doorway of the shop, when a man came barging out past him.

Taken by surprise, and instinctively protecting his immobilised arm, Leslie sprung backwards, out of the way. There was a great crash and clatter as the tub of walking sticks knocked into the metal display unit which overturned, spilling its contents into the road. Dismayed, Leslie immediately dropped his bag and made a cautious, one-handed attempt to retrieve the cans and bottles bouncing about on the ground. Making no effort to help him, the man whose thoughtless behaviour had caused this, stepped across the scattered items as though nothing untoward had happened and made his way down the hill without looking back.

A middle-aged woman, obviously the shopkeeper, appeared from the doorway, and her expression turned from annoyance to sympathy when she saw Leslie's plight and heard his apologetic explanation.

"We don't half get 'em here at this time of year, m' dear," she said, righting the display stand and stooping to gather up the escaped items. Fortunately, the cobbles prevented anything from rolling too far. "They come here on their holidays and think they own the place. I wouldn't mind but they don't even support the local businesses. They drive out to the supermarket at Burnsbridge for their shopping. A box of corn plasters and a packet of blackcurrant pastilles, that's all he bought—I ask you—and then gives us all this trouble."

The shopkeeper bent down to retrieve the final stray item, a garish green shower gel, and, satisfied that everything was in its place, went back into the shop with Leslie following meekly behind. He quickly obtained the medicines he had gone there for and, to make up for all the other parsimonious holidaymakers, added some toothpaste, shampoo and shaving foam that he did not need.

There was a choice of three ways to walk back from the village. Leslie rejected the road, for although it was the quickest, he had discovered the previous day that there was a long stretch with blind bends and no footpath. There was, apparently, a walk along the beach if the tide was right, but he had been told it involved negotiating sand and rocks to a place well beyond their hotel above, then ascending a steep climb of slippery stone steps up the cliff side before walking back to the hotel. This was clearly not suitable for a one-armed man carrying a bag of shopping and wearing summer sandals, so Leslie took the third option, the route he had earlier used to walk down to the village. This was the cliff path, and although there was an initial steep climb, the magnificent views and welcome sea breeze would be ample recompense for the effort. This route had the added advantage of leading into the bottom of the hotel grounds which would reduce the chances of being detained by Val Marsden or encountering any delegates who may have arrived prematurely.

The walk was everything Leslie had anticipated. The first part was strenuous, and all his attention was on a thoughtfully placed bench at the summit of the climb. After that, it was easier, and the rugged coastline, the birds wheeling and calling, and the yachts gliding along on the sparkling sea could be fully appreciated. Thankfully, the path was set at a comfortable distance from the cliff edge, sometimes well inland, so that Leslie could enjoy the walk with his nerves intact. At last he arrived, feeling weary but virtuous, at a division in the pathway where to the left was a neatly painted sign which announced: 'Private, Alemouth Lodge Residents Only'. Following this path for a few yards, he came to the tall, ivy-covered brick wall which bounded the hotel grounds, and into which was set an arched, verdigris-coloured wooden door. The quaint 'secret garden' effect was somewhat marred by a warning notice to any would-be trespassers and a security keypad which permitted Leslie to enter as he swiped his hotel card.

Taking a shortcut to the coach house, Leslie started out across the grass, passing behind a large outbuilding, but to his dismay he discovered his plan to avoid encountering anyone had backfired. Two newcomers had already arrived and were deep in discussion, standing close to the wall of the building. Leslie sensed straightaway that this was a private conversation and stepped back into the shadows, but not before he had seen the woman pull her arm away from the man's grasp.

"No," she said in a low voice but with urgency, "I keep telling you it's different this year."

The man, who had his back to Leslie, said something Leslie could not hear, but the woman's reply, though quiet, was clearly audible:

"We can't, not this year. Absolutely not," and Leslie heard her footsteps padding away across the lawn.

The man now turned round to pick up a small black shoulder bag that had been at his feet, and Leslie could see he matched Val's description of Jeremy, the writing course leader. Leslie took a step back to avoid being seen. As he did so, his foot caught some tiles which were stacked on the ground behind him, and the man swung round with a look of alarm on his face. Leslie stepped forwards with exaggerated nonchalance, hoping to look as though he had only just appeared, but he was never good at dissembling and guessed that his greeting was too full of explanations for belief. However, the man quickly recovered, introduced himself with a smooth and courteous manner that betrayed nothing, and the two men walked up the garden making polite small talk.

***

On the balcony, over lunch, Leslie described it all to Bennett. "It was most embarrassing," he said. "It's hard not to put the obvious construction on what Jeremy was after."

"It doesn't sound like they were talking about iambic pentameters," agreed Bennett.

"Although I couldn't hear what he said, his tone sounded rather desperate, and when he turned round, I thought he looked sort of anxious and guilty." Leslie took another bite of his sandwich and munched thoughtfully. "But I could be making that up. It's easy to start imagining lurid things, and it might all have a completely different interpretation. She must be one of the delegates, I suppose."

Bennett examined a plate on the low table between them and selected beef and horseradish in crusty white bread.

"As to that bag he was carrying," continued Leslie, "it wasn't large, but it looked quite heavy. What on earth would he need to carry around the hotel grounds with him?"

"Curious," said Bennett. "Perhaps it was poetry books, after all."

Leslie laughed and then winced and rubbed at his midriff. He stood up in search of his newly acquired medicines. "This isn't doing anything to help my digestive system," he sighed. "I felt as though I'd walked in on the unfolding plot of a cheap TV drama."

2

Dinner was an interesting affair. Leslie and Bennett went across to the dining room at six-thirty to find the other tables already occupied and well into the main course. The creative writers were evidently early diners. At their entrance, the animated chatter stopped abruptly and there was silence, broken only by Bennett who chose this moment to strike up the *Aida Triumphal Entry* quietly but audibly under his breath.

In contrast to the glacial reception of the main party, Gloria leapt from her chair with a squeal of delight and embraced them both warmly, only remembering Leslie's injured shoulder at the last minute, as he had bravely abandoned the sling. The lady was clad in a voluminous crimson and orange striped dress with a necklace of glass beads decorating her ample bosom, and Leslie was involuntarily put in mind of a circus marquee strung with coloured lights. She returned to her food with a promise to catch up with them both afterwards, and they settled themselves at the table they had occupied on the two previous evenings. The delegates were not to be kept from their food or conversation for long, and eating and talking soon resumed.

Leslie had a good view of the two tables at which their companions sat. At one, Jeremy was holding court, under the admiring gaze of the four women who shared his table. Leslie guessed that Jeremy was in his early forties, and the ladies were all at least a decade older. One of them was so transfixed, sauce was dripping onto her plate from the piece of meat she held motionless on her fork. There was such a similarity in mannerisms and appearance between her and the lady to her right that Leslie decided they were sisters. Next to her, and with her back to Leslie, was a woman of medium height and build who had long auburn hair of an unnaturally vivid shade tied up with a chiffon scarf. The fourth lady at the table, who was of ample build, had her attention divided between fascination with Jeremy and interest in her food, which involved many loud comments and enquiries about the ingredients. The words gluten, lactose and allergen were mentioned frequently.

Gloria was at the second table, with four more women. One, who looked in her forties, was seated beside an older woman of what Leslie would describe as 'young retired' age, which was how he liked to think of himself. The third lady was older again, and she was wearing wrist braces and moved very stiffly. She also had elbow crutches which clattered from the back of her chair to the floor more than once and had to be retrieved by her neighbour. The person of most interest to Leslie, however, was the woman he had seen earlier with Jeremy. She looked in her late-thirties with short blonde hair and, although Leslie already knew she was tall, he could now see she had quite an athletic physique. There was something rather imposing about her, and Leslie thought, with some relief, she looked equal to warding off any unwanted attentions from Jeremy. Interestingly, unlike the other women who all frequently glanced across at Jeremy, this lady showed no interest in him, but throughout the meal Leslie noticed Jeremy stealing quick and furtive glances at her.

The hotel provided only a table d'hôte menu and so the choice was limited, and it was, as it had been on the previous two evenings, unsuitable for the sweltering weather. When Leslie enquired politely if he might have a fruit juice for starter instead of the vegetable broth or deep-fried brie on offer, the waitress, Sadie, a woman of mature years who had earlier been in to clean their room, said, "Don't fancy the soup or fried cheese? I don't blame you, duck."

Bennett selected the fish and chips for the main course and, on trying it, wearily declared it to be 'the piece of cod that passeth all understanding' and compared the cooking unfavourably to Leslie's. This would normally have been a welcome comment as flattery rarely came his way from Bennett. But indigestion and a dull ache in his unsupported shoulder were making him tetchy, and tonight the comments irritated him as much as if Bennett had come right out with it and said, "I told you we should never have come away on holiday."

This was entirely unjustified, for although Bennett had refused to convalesce after his heart attack, he had only offered a token resistance following Leslie's accident and had not complained once since they had arrived. Annoyingly, it was Leslie himself who, having pressed so long for a holiday, was now finding it impossible to relax. Still, it was early days; it was a fortnight's holiday and they had only been there since Saturday. But nearly two more weeks of this food! It was more than Leslie could bear to contemplate, so he distracted himself by creating the menu he considered suitable for the weather and was transiently consoled by thoughts of melon and Parma ham, chicken, salmon and crab, rice and linguine, and sorbets, mousses and meringues.

True to her word, as soon as she had finished her meal, Gloria joined the men at their table, bringing her coffee with her. "We're having a little introductory session in the lounge in a minute," she said eagerly. "But do let's have a walk around the grounds after that. There's sure to be time with these long evenings. I adore this hot weather, and the view across the sea is simply marvellous in the evening light. Sometimes the colours—"

Her eulogy was interrupted at this point, as Jeremy had risen to his feet and was inviting the delegates to join him in the lounge for 'a little drink on the house', and an icebreaker. With a quick, "Well, see you later, then," Gloria took up her unfinished coffee and joined the others as they followed their mentor in eager obedience.

***

It had been at about eight-thirty that evening when Leslie heard his name you-hoo'd from below the balcony, and now it was an hour later, and they were admiring the sea view from a seat beyond the picket fence which marked the boundary of the hotel grounds. The bench was in memory of Denise Brown, the poor lady who had fallen to her doom the previous year, though of course there was no mention of the unfortunate event on the neat bronze plaque. To the west, a fiery crimson globe of a sun was going down. This was more than could be said for Leslie's dinner which was still lying heavily in his stomach. Bennett had resolutely declined to join them on the walk, but Leslie had been glad enough to stretch his legs outside, though he knew that Gloria could be an exhausting companion with no one else to dilute her effusive enthusiasm. She had taken Leslie on a tour of the grounds which, of course, he had already familiarised himself with over the previous two days. However, he had been happy to meander through the scented garden and among the rose beds, hear the history behind an unusual sundial, and discover a badger sett by a little copse of trees, which he had not noticed before. The sculpture trail still left him cold, however, and the biography of the local sculptor who was responsible for the metal monstrosities, which Gloria imparted in detail, did not win Leslie over.

For all Gloria's alleged interest in the grounds of her cousin's hotel, it transpired that her main object was to show Leslie the exact spot where the tragedy had occurred the previous year, and which was now marked by a 'Beware: cliff edge' sign. A quick glance at the disastrous place was enough. Leslie retreated to the bench which, fortunately, was far enough from the spot for him to marvel at the colours of the sky and sea while he was obliged to hear Gloria's narrative of the disaster. As she had been staying at the hotel at the time, she was able to supply more details than Leslie's vertigo could comfortably tolerate.

"It was windy, you see—blowing quite a gale. Not a bit like this," she explained. The earlier breeze had gone, leaving the evening oppressively still, the air hot and thick, and the horizon a dark amber smudge. Leslie removed his collar and cuff sling, which was now more trouble than it was worth, and mopped the back of his neck with a handkerchief. Gloria rummaged through her capacious bag and brought out a large oriental fan which she wafted about to little effect. "A gust took her sunhat away and she ran after it. Straight over the edge she went, and she plunged into the sea; that drop is well over one hundred feet. No one knows how it happened as there was nothing to obscure the edge. They ruled out suicide or foul play at the inquest and in the end put it down to her bifocals, which were new."

"How shocking," said Leslie, trying hard not to picture the event.

"Mercifully, I didn't see it, but three of the other ladies witnessed the whole thing. Two of them are on the course again this year; one of them was so badly affected—quite hysterical—that I'm surprised she could bear to come back."

"Perhaps she needs to put the ghost to rest, so to speak?" said Leslie. "Which one is she?"

"She was sitting opposite me at dinner. I don't know if you noticed her? A small, mousey lady in a frilly pink top. She seems to be a bag of nerves, poor soul. She's called Ann and she's brought a friend with her this year—that older woman who was next to her. I guess it's for moral support as the friend doesn't seem a bit interested in the writing course itself. When we were all asked to say why we had come, she said in the coldest voice, 'Because Ann invited me'. That was it, nothing more. It was a bit embarrassing really as everyone else had given in-depth answers; some of them had told half their life story."

Leslie could well imagine.

"Barbara—that's the name of the friend. Well, after Barbara had said her few words, there was an awkward silence, so Jeremy quickly moved on to the next person. He's very good at that sort of thing, keeping everything upbeat. There's been no mention of the tragedy and I get the impression it's a closed subject. I can see why. The only people who were on the course last year, apart from Jeremy himself, were Ann and Susan, the two ladies who witnessed it. Ann, I've just told you about. Susan was next to me at dinner, the one wearing the blue top and the harem pants."

"Yes, I saw her earlier when she'd just arrived. She was talking to Jeremy in the grounds." Leslie restrained himself from disclosing the details of the encounter although he was itching for more information.

Gloria dropped her voice to a conspiratorial whisper, quite unnecessarily given their seclusion. "I say, that is interesting," she said, unwittingly gratifying Leslie's curiosity. "You see, last year it looked as though there was something between Jeremy and Susan—not officially, but everyone noticed it—and there were rumours about them being seen coming out of each other's bedrooms in the night." Gloria's face had turned a shade more crimson, and she fanned it energetically. "I don't know how true the bedroom stuff was; I don't stay in the main house when I'm here as Valerie puts me up in her annexe. But anyway, the interesting thing is that so far this year it's been completely different. You wouldn't think they'd ever met before; not so much as a word between them at the meal or in the icebreaker session. I was wondering if it had just been a holiday fling and they've decided to behave as though it never happened. From what you've just said, though, it looks like Jeremy thinks it best not to be seen in a relationship with one of the delegates, and so they are going to make out they don't know each other."

With laudable self-restraint, Leslie forbore to reveal the little drama he had witnessed between the couple. "Do you think they knew each other before the writing course last year?" he asked. "Or did it all start up during the week?"

"They all know Jeremy before they come," explained Gloria. "He runs creative writing workshops throughout the year, mostly along the south coast: Bournemouth, Milford, Christchurch, the Dorset area. That's where he recruits for this residential week. Not me, of course, I just happened to be here last year when it was running, and I knew from Valerie it was booked again for this week. Why don't you join it as you're here? I do think it's going to be a lot of fun, and I'm sure Jeremy would squeeze you in if I asked him."

"No thank you, really," said Leslie emphatically. Before she could try to persuade him, he added, "I'm supposed to be resting, don't forget. But tell me, who are the others on the course?"

"Well, you saw the big woman at Jeremy's table. Now what's her name? Carol, that's it. She's a receptionist at a GP practice and, goodness me, what a long list of ailments she seems to have. Enough for a whole waiting room full of patients. She told us more about her digestive system than anyone should have to hear. That's exactly what comes of surrounding yourself with illness all the time."

Gloria, who ran a natural health shop, had strong views on the limitations of traditional healthcare and took any opportunity to promote her products and ideas. Before she could set off down this avenue, Leslie said, "There were two particular ladies at Jeremy's table. I said to Bennett I bet they're sisters. Am I right?"

"I say, you are a clever old thing," Gloria chirruped. "They certainly are. And they are both retired, but from doing what I can't remember. Both unmarried, they live next door to each other, and they finish each other's sentences. One is called Deborah and the other is Dee, though I'm blessed if I know which is which."

Gloria was counting the delegates off on her fingers. "Then there's the other woman from that table, with all the hair. She calls herself Cassandra, which is quite a name, don't you think? She seems to have a lot to say for herself. You know the type—whatever anyone says, she can go one better."

Gloria held up seven fingers.

"Then there's me, of course." She added an eighth finger. "It's like the seven dwarfs, you can never remember all of them, only there are nine of us. Who have I said? Susan, Barbara, Ann, Carol, the two sisters Dee and Deborah, Cassandra and myself."

"It's the old lady with the crutches," said Leslie, feeling guilty as soon as he had spoken that he had defined the poor woman like this.

"That's it! Thelma with arthritis; just the sort of person who always gets forgotten," declared Gloria, compounding the felony. "I'm going to see if she's tried the clove and ginger diet. It's had some miraculous results."

Disinclined to hear details of this or any other purported remedy, Leslie picked up his sling and started rising to his feet. They strolled back towards the house, and as they passed through the gate in the picket fence, Leslie turned and indicated the land sloping down to the fateful cliff edge. "If the hotel grounds only come to the fence here, then who is responsible for that area?"

"The council. They offered to sell it to Valerie for next to nothing when she first bought the hotel. I don't suppose they want the trouble of maintaining it, and there is no access to it except from the hotel grounds. She said then that she didn't want responsibility for a cliff, and she was right, wasn't she?"

They walked slowly up the sloping path towards the house, past the well-tended and watered flowerbeds, and across the manicured lawn.

"Even though Val was completely vindicated at the inquest, she was worried about adverse publicity, as you can well imagine," confided Gloria. "In actual fact it had the opposite effect. Not one person cancelled their holiday booking, and the bar was full all season with people wanting a first-hand account. Very ghoulish, but good for trade. As for this year, it's as though it never happened; yesterday's news."

"Val said it's the anniversary of the tragedy this week. I wonder if the lady's family will be coming to lay flowers there."

"I shouldn't think so; she didn't really have anyone," said Gloria. "Just a couple of distant relatives who came and collected her things. Valerie thinks that a lot of the women who come on the writing course are like that: lonely people who don't have anyone else to go on holiday with. Valerie put the bench there with the plaque on it herself."

They had reached the coach house and stopped by the entrance.

"One of the worst things about it," Gloria continued, "was that the poor woman's body wasn't recovered until ages later. The tide was just on the turn when she fell, and the water was very choppy. The coastguard said that the currents are so strong along this stretch that the body might never be found, but it did wash up eventually, miles down the coast. By that time, of course, the corpse—"

"I'd better be getting in now," Leslie interrupted. He'd had more than enough of both the oppressive heat and the gruesome topic.

"But you are coming across to the lounge for a night cap?" said Gloria. "And be sure to drag Bennett out of that room."

Gloria would not be contented until Leslie had agreed, despite professing fatigue and his insistence that nothing would budge Bennett. Even though he and Bennett had spent the last two evenings in the lounge sampling the wide selection of spirits available at the bar, he was certain that nothing would induce Bennett to mingle with the new incumbents. At last, Leslie tore himself away and went upstairs to the suite, in eager anticipation of its air conditioning and ice-making machine, in the forlorn hope that Gloria would forget about his promise when he did not appear later.

3

Bennett, sitting on the settee with his laptop balanced on his knees, looked up from the screen as Leslie came in. "He stands by the sea," he said. "Five letters."

"You're not still working, are you?" said Leslie. "You should have come out for a stroll. Mind you, it's baking hot out there." He took a couple of tall glasses, clattered in a generous helping of ice-cubes from the icemaker and filled them with water. "What was it again?" he asked, passing one glass to Bennett and taking a long drink from his own.

Bennett repeated the clue.

After a moment Leslie said, "Is it 'Cliff'?"

"Too easy," said Bennett with a disgruntled snort.

"It's a bit like one of those what-do-you-call-a man-with-a-seagull-on-his-head jokes," said Leslie. "But I might not have got it so quickly if I hadn't been hearing about cliffs all evening." He recounted everything Gloria had told him about the previous year's tragedy, and then enlightened Bennett about all the delegates, especially the rumours about Jeremy and Susan. "They'll all be in the bar this evening. I told Gloria I'd go across later, but I'm not keen."

"I've no great desire to view the inmates, either,' said Bennett, in a resigned tone. "But I suppose we could finish the evening off in the bar again if you don't want a scolding from Gloria. And Val really does keep an excellent selection of whiskies."

Leslie sighed; Bennett was exasperating. He was impossible to predict, and Leslie could only attribute it to innate contrariness. For a second, he felt like refusing to go, but his desire to uproot Bennett from the room was greater than his instinct for revenge, so he put aside his chagrin, and his genuine weariness, and agreed. At least he was guaranteed some amusement as Bennett would be sure to keep up a commentary of wry and witty, and undoubtedly uncomplimentary, observations.

He was thwarted in this too, however, for as soon as they set foot in the lounge, Gloria pounced on them and seized Bennett's arm, steering him across the room.

"Oh, Bennett, I knew you would come across, and what perfect timing. You must come and be introduced to Barbara. She's a chess player, just like you, and I know she'll want a game. I believe she is quite an expert."

They had arrived beside the lady in question who, though shunning the compliment, greeted Gloria's suggestion with enthusiasm. Leslie remembered this was the reluctant delegate who, according to Gloria, had come on the holiday as a companion for her friend, Ann. Barbara's general demeanour certainly suggested she was more suited to putting her mind to a game of chess than pouring out her soul into blank verse.

"And such a coincidence," said Gloria. "I've just found out that Barbara lives in the same village as my daughter, Gina. It's such a pretty place in the New Forest and I've been there hundreds of times. Just fancy! What a small world it is."

Leslie excused himself and went over to the bar in quest of a much-needed drink. Susan and Cassandra were already there, standing together, and as he was being served, Leslie could not help overhearing their conversation. Cassandra was saying, in a supercilious drawl:

"...when I was up at Oxford. I read literature, of course."

She seemed oblivious to the look of rank boredom on Susan's face.

"'Happiest days of my life when I was up at the varsity,'" she went on.

Surely no one had spoken like that for more than a century, if ever. Cassandra was boasting now of her sporting achievements which sounded as unlikely as the language she was using to describe them. "It's such an honour, you know, to represent the varsity," she said, drawing breath at last.

Leslie remembered what Gloria had said about Cassandra's one-upmanship. But it seemed Susan was not to be bested.

"I know," she said, with disdain. "I rowed for Cambridge—in a crew that won the Oxford and Cambridge women's boat race."

"Really?" said Cassandra, unabashed and with an unmistakable tone of disbelief. "What year?"

"Oh, it was a long time ago," said Susan and, turning abruptly, she walked to the other end of the bar. It looked for all the world as though she wanted to drop the subject, but it was probably just a response to Cassandra's want of manners.

The young man serving drinks caught Leslie's eye and shook his head in derision, before stifling a yawn. Apart from this lapse in professionalism, he was good behind the bar, much better than in the kitchen, for he was also the new and incompetent chef. Leslie could not help but feel some sympathy for him, even though the man was responsible, single-handedly, for the worst bout of indigestion Leslie had experienced for years. He must have been on duty since before breakfast time and he seemed to work these long hours every day, an unenviable lot, especially in this heat.

Cassandra had taken her glass over to the table where the two sisters and the lady with arthritis were talking together. As far as Leslie could see, she had joined them without invitation and was now monopolising the conversation.

Leslie took Barbara and Bennett their drinks, but they were silently engrossed. Leslie was not a chess player but sensed that Barbara was good, as Bennett, who was quite capable of winning a chess game in less than ten minutes, was obviously proceeding with caution.

Leslie looked round for somewhere to sit. Gloria was seated with Ann, Barbara's friend who had witnessed the tragedy the previous year, and also the lady described by Gloria as 'the big woman with the many ailments'. They were absorbed by something on the table that Gloria was showing them. The only other people in the bar were two middle-aged men who Leslie hadn't seen before and must be non-residents calling in for an evening drink. The hotel bar attracted a small but steady stream of outside customers, mostly on the reputation of the whiskies.

And there was Susan, of course, alone at the end of the bar. Leslie hesitated; he hated to see someone on their own and rarely found it hard to make the sort of small talk needed on such an occasion. But there was something rather aloof about Susan that deterred him from approaching her. Jeremy was nowhere to be seen, and she did not seem to be looking out for anyone.

Feeling slightly abandoned and rather irritable, Leslie went to join Gloria's table, even though he had no desire to butt in on the three ladies. Gloria had a small silk bag in her hand which made a rather pleasant rattling sound as she jiggled it about. He seated himself slightly apart but where he could see what was going on. Gloria's carrying voice was easy to hear.

"As I was saying," she said, "I'm still a beginner at this, a complete novice. I've had quite a lot of success using crystals for healing, but I've only just begun to use them for guidance. It's called scrying, or divination, and it's very exciting."

"Healing!" exclaimed Carol, shifting her large bulk further back into the chair. "It's a miracle I need for my IBS, not crystals. But who knows, they may provide some relief. Perhaps you could—"

She was interrupted by Ann, who had been hanging on Gloria's every word. "Do tell us how it works for guidance," she said. "I'm sure I could do with some of that. I've always been interested in this kind of thing, but most people laugh at it." Leslie saw her cast an anxious glance across the room at Barbara, who was just moving a bishop diagonally across the board.

"Oh, I take no notice of the sceptics," declared Gloria confidently. "It's their loss, I say. Now, the method I'm working on at the moment involves drawing out stones from a bag and interpreting their significance. There are lots of different ways to do it. I'll show you with the single stone method. Like this," and with eyes shut and a rapt expression on her face, she thrust her hand into the bag, swirling her fingers among the stones. Opening her eyes, she withdrew a large, oval opalescent stone. She placed it reverently on a beer mat on the table where it shimmered its blue and white and purple colours.

"Oh, I say," said Gloria, her florid complexion blushing to a deeper shade of red. "That's the opal. It's for love and passion and... you know. I can't think—"

"Oh, may I have a try?" interrupted Ann. "I don't suppose I'll get another chance." Again, she looked across towards her friend at the chess board.

"So long as you understand that I'm not yet proficient. My interpretations may not be accurate, though I must say I do feel I have a gift for this. I'm hoping that, with a little experience, I could become quite an expert."

Ann, her eyes bulging with excitement, eagerly brushed aside all Gloria's disclaimers and drew her chair closer.

"First, we must cleanse our hands of all impurities. I forgot to do that just now; that explains the opal, I suppose." She drew out a small bottle and squirted a liquid into her own and Ann's hands. "Next, you must cleanse your mind of anything that will contaminate the process; any doubts or negative thoughts."

Ann closed her eyes and adopted an expression of beatific serenity.

"Let's try with two stones this time," hissed Gloria, as near to a whisper as her strident voice would allow. "Reach into the bag. Run your fingers through the stones and let them speak to you."

Ann's face now took on an expression of holy rapture as she swirled her hand about in the silk pouch, and there was a satisfying clunking and tinkling as the stones of different sizes and materials rattled together.

"When you are ready,"—Gloria's voice was lower still—"select two crystals that feel right for you, the stones with a significance." The last words were spoken with great meaning.

There was an awestruck silence at the table and, after an interminable wait, a smooth, grey stone was drawn out followed by one which was small and knobbly.

"Roll them on the table," Gloria urged eagerly, exclaiming suddenly, "Hang on a minute, I forgot to put the scrying cloth down." There was a breathless pause while Gloria conjured a piece of black velvet from her bag and, with a flourish, spread it on the table before her expectant audience. "Now, cast them down gently."

The two little stones landed beside each other on the cloth and Gloria leant forwards, her eyes screwed up in concentration.

She tilted her head this way and that. "It looks like a cat," she declared at last.

Ann stared at her in bafflement.

"No, hang on a minute," said Gloria rummaging in her bag and producing a pamphlet. She rifled through the pages and said, "No, no, I was quite mistaken. I believe it's an unexpected visitor."

"Perhaps you're going to get an unexpected visit from a cat," said Carol. "I'm glad it's not me. I have a terrible allergy to cat dander, it makes me—"

"I can't see how I'll get an unexpected visitor here," Ann interrupted. "But perhaps it means when I get home. I hope it won't be someone bringing bad news."

"Are you sure you had no negative thoughts or doubts?" asked Gloria.

"Well, I'll be honest,"—Ann's voice was so low Leslie had to strain to hear—"I couldn't help thinking Barbara wouldn't approve of this. She hates this sort of thing. She tells me off even if I have a little peep at the horoscopes. She's one of those very logical people; she was a chemist, a pharmacist actually, and she can't bear anything that goes against science."

"Oh, don't worry about her," said Gloria. "She's completely engrossed in her chess game. Have another go, why don't you."

Tiring of this chicanery, Leslie looked across to the table where Barbara and Bennett, silent and studious, were studying the chequered board. It was not often Bennett found a player his equal.

Susan was still standing on her own at the bar, beyond Bennett's table and, just at that moment, Leslie saw her look towards the door. A sudden expression of alarm crossed her face. Following her gaze, Leslie saw a man entering the room. He was a wiry man of medium height with a weather-beaten face and dark beard. Leslie recognised him straightaway as the unpleasant person who had knocked into him coming out of the chemist shop. But rather than looking sullen and surly as he had then, the man was gazing directly at Susan with an expression of complete self-satisfaction, even triumph. For several seconds

Susan was frozen in an attitude of horror, and he was motionless in apparent victory.

He started towards the bar and Susan, who had regained her composure, picked up her drink and walked past him and out the door. However, as she passed the man, she paused and there was the briefest exchange of conversation. He carried on to the bar and was soon ordering a beer.

Pondering on this very odd incident, Leslie turned his attention back to his own table where Ann's second attempt at divination seemed to have had a satisfactory outcome, for she was looking quite animated as Gloria returned two small purple stones to the bag. Carol declined a turn and Leslie wondered, unkindly, if she was worried that the crystals might foresee a cure for her complaints. Soon, both Ann and Carol retired for the night and, as they departed, Ann went to say goodnight to Barbara while Carol could be heard describing, to anyone who would listen, her peculiar susceptibility to fatigue.

"Not bad, but I think I need a little more practice," sighed Gloria to Leslie, who had taken Ann's seat. She absentmindedly plunged her hand into the bag of crystals and stirred them noisily.

"Who is that man, there?" asked Leslie, indicating the newcomer at the bar. He was now standing exactly where Susan had been, holding his pint glass. "Do you know him?"

"No, I've never seen him before," replied Gloria, looking at the man and withdrawing her hand from the bag of crystals. Opening her fingers, she gave a gasp. Lying on her palm was an iridescent black gemstone.

"What's the matter?" asked Leslie.

"That's the black diamond," she said. "It's a bad omen."

Gloria was uncharacteristically subdued by this portentous sign and took herself off to bed soon after. The chess game was still in progress and so Leslie made his way back to the coach house alone, mulling over the encounter between Susan and the stranger. Once inside, he put the kettle on and made a cup of camomile tea in an effort to relax, but his mind was buzzing like a machine. First, there had been the encounter between Susan and

Jeremy, and now this one with the bearded stranger. It was all very intriguing.

He took his drink out onto the balcony and stood quietly in the darkness. Leslie had always been fascinated by the night sky and enjoyed picking out the constellations. As his eyes adjusted, he could make out The Plough, high in the sky and, just to the west, Gemini, little diamonds sewn onto the velvet curtain of the night.

It was very peaceful with just the faint sounds from the hotel in the background: the thrumming of a generator, the distant shutting of a door. But then came footsteps moving closer; a man's, he thought, soft and unhurried but purposeful. It was not Bennett, Leslie was sure of that, and he wondered with some curiosity who else would be coming out to the back of the hotel at this time of night. The footsteps stopped just beyond the balcony and Leslie was surprised to hear a woman's voice. She spoke very quietly, but despite this Leslie recognised it as Susan's. She must have been waiting beneath Leslie's balcony all the time.

"I'll give you five minutes," she said in a low voice, "but not here. Come on, down the garden."

"Like that, is it?" said the man in a mocking tone.

It was not a voice Leslie recognised—not Jeremy's—so it must surely be the man who had come into the bar.

They were already walking away, and Leslie heard nothing more except two ominous words from Susan: "...pestering me."

Leslie moved to the railings as quietly as he could and looked down, but they had already gone and, in the darkness, there would have been little to see anyway. Leslie toyed briefly with the idea of trying to follow them in case Susan was in danger, but decided this was a ridiculous over-reaction and an unwarranted intrusion into a private affair. All that could be done was for Leslie to remain, silent and unseen, on the balcony and hope they both returned. Sure enough, in a few minutes Leslie heard their footsteps again. They were silent until they parted when Leslie heard Susan say, "On Wednesday, then," and the man grunted an inaudible reply.

Bennett was characteristically indifferent when Leslie described the incident to him half an hour later when he returned to the room.

"It can only have been that chap who came into the bar," said Leslie, and described Susan's reaction.

"The sailor, do you mean?" said Bennett.

"Sailor? What makes you say that?"

"Didn't you see his keys? He got them out when he was paying for his drink, and they were attached to a damn great cork. And he was wearing boating shoes."

"I do believe you're right," said Leslie, thinking also of the man's weather-beaten complexion. "Trust you to notice that while engrossed in your chess game."

Bennett made no reply, and Leslie added thoughtfully, "I wonder what he's doing here, and what his business is with Susan."

4

Stifled with the heat, Leslie could stay in bed no longer. His mind would not rest and his shoulder, though nearly mended, refused to allow him to get comfortable. He'd been tossing and turning without sleep for the last two hours and the room was suffocating. It had been a mistake to turn off the air conditioning; its irritating drone could not disturb his sleep more than this heat. Bennett had kicked off the cover, but slept, as he always did, uninterrupted by any of the inconveniences or discomforts guaranteed to keep Leslie in a state of fretful wakefulness.

Leslie got up and cautiously felt his way through the bedroom doorway and into the living room, where he found and switched on first the light and then the air conditioning control. He filled a tall glass with ice and water and held it to his forehead before taking a long draft. He made for the balcony, hastily switching off the light behind him because a huge moth, which seemed to be the size of a small bat, was hurling itself against the glass sliding door.

There was still no discernible breeze, but at least it was a few degrees cooler on the balcony and Leslie felt he was no longer suffocating. He was wide awake as if it was the middle of the afternoon, and his mind was racing. He scolded himself for his preoccupation with Susan and the intriguing exchanges he had overheard with both Jeremy and the stranger. It was nothing more than shameful nosiness on his part, no doubt the result of having retired to a small village where gossip was the currency of everyday life. This turned his thoughts to home, and he realised quite suddenly that his restlessness on this holiday was less to do with indigestion or the heat or his recent accident, and more a case of simple boredom. He missed his house and garden, the village life, the mundane routine, and he was not used to having nothing to do. This was a mortifying revelation; he had badgered Bennett over and over to go on holiday after the heart attack, and now that they were here, Leslie was fit to snap with tension while Bennett was as languidly composed as he was anywhere. He felt an unreasonable indignation at Bennett, and knew it was unreasonable, neither of which improved his mood.

To distract himself from these vexatious feelings, Leslie was about to fetch his book to read, when he realised that putting on a light would make him visible. Although the coach house was angled away from the main building, so that by daylight the balcony afforded a magnificent view of the sea across the gardens, it was still in full view of the rear of the hotel and its courtyard terrace. He did not relish being seen in nothing but his pyjama shorts by another insomniac who might glance out of their bedroom window.

Just then, Leslie was distracted from his fretting by the quietest of sounds. It was unmistakably the distant click of a door being opened and then, very quietly, closed again. The cautious quietness of the action itself made it suspicious. Someone was very anxious not to be heard. The night had that intense darkness to which one's eyes would never adjust but, even so, Leslie leant forwards in his chair and peered across the balcony rails. His curiosity was assuaged with alarming suddenness as a blazing light unexpectedly illuminated the hotel courtyard. A security lamp had been triggered revealing Jeremy, standing outside one of the courtyard bedroom doors, shielding his eyes with his forearm against the dazzling beam. To Leslie's consternation, the security lamp was in a direct line with his balcony, so that Jeremy was facing towards him, and he was seized with embarrassment until he realised with relief that Jeremy could see nothing behind the blinding light. In contrast, Leslie had an excellent view of Jeremy who was wearing a short dressing gown over bare legs and, bizarrely, carrying the same bag Leslie had seen him with earlier.

Jeremy looked like an animal trapped in a pen, for the small private patio outside each courtyard room was enclosed by a high fence to provide privacy at ground level. He was, of course, quite visible to Leslie from his balcony in this new coach house development. After only a few seconds' hesitation, Jeremy passed quietly through the gate at the end and, with the same stealth, opened what was evidently his own gate and the door to his room and slipped inside. Without any knowledge of where anyone was accommodated in the hotel, the obvious supposition was that Jeremy had been coming from Susan's room. It was none of his business, but it was impossible for Leslie not to recall the earlier discussion with Gloria about the relationship between Susan and Jeremy the previous year, nor could he forget the enigmatic encounter he had earlier witnessed between the two. Leslie sat pondering, long after the security light had switched off and plunged the world back into darkness.

***

In consequence of his disturbed night, Leslie slept late the following morning and by the time the two men went down to breakfast, the writing group delegates were nearly finished. They were spared the deathly hush of the previous day's entrance as all attention was on Jeremy who was addressing the group as they went in.

"And have you all signed up for your individual tutorial?" He held aloft a sheet of paper and cast a winning smile around the group. His eye alighted momentarily on Barbara and he added quickly, "Those of you who want to, of course."

There was a general buzz of assent.

"That's great; awesome, in fact," Jeremy enthused. "I can't wait to get started. We'll convene in the conservatory at ten sharp. Don't forget to bring your writing pack with you, and your muse, of course!"

Dazzling them with one final flash of perfect teeth, he took himself off, though not before Leslie noticed his eyes flick towards Susan. She was busy pouring from a cafetiere and did not return his glance. The delegates gradually drifted away from the tables in ones and twos, leaving the greasy detritus of breakfast behind. Carol's plate, Leslie noticed, was the only empty one, and he saw her skilfully conceal her neighbour's uneaten croissant, gluten and all, in a serviette and slip it into her bag as she left.

It was the young waitress-housekeeper, Lauren, who was on duty this morning. She seemed relieved when the two men declined the cooked breakfast, and she slouched off to the kitchen where Leslie heard her giggling with the chef when he went to help himself to fruit and cereal from the counter.

She returned eventually with the tea and coffee, and a message. "Val says you're not to go back to your room until she's had a word with you." She sounded, to Leslie, as though she was expecting Val to give them detention. "I dunno what it's about, but she said it's important and I wasn't to forget to tell you." She plonked their cups unceremoniously on the table.

"Service with a smile," Bennett remarked as she departed back to the kitchen.

"I wouldn't say that she's found her vocation," Leslie replied. "But I wonder what Val wants."

They ate their breakfasts at a leisurely pace, and Lauren grudgingly replenished the teapot and cafetiere, but there was no sign of their hostess.

"Do you think Val has forgotten she wanted to speak to us?" said Leslie. "I think I'll see if I can root her out. Maybe Lauren got the message wrong and she's expecting us to go and find her in her office. I wonder what it's about."

"She'll come and find us in our rooms if it's that important," Bennett replied, getting up to go.

"That's what I'm worried about." Leslie lowered his voice. "You know how long that would take."

"Good point. But I'll leave you to it, anyway."

"Thanks very much," said Leslie to Bennett's departing back, and made for the reception area in quest of the elusive manageress. There was no one at the counter, but the office door behind was open and Val, telephone to her ear, saw him straightaway and made a gesture eloquent of I'm-so-sorry-something-urgent-has-cropped-up-but-wait-there-I'll-be-with-you-in-a-minute.

Leslie amused himself by leafing through the visitors' book, discovering that previous guests had come from as far away as New Zealand, and as near as Lymeford which was the neighbouring town to Leslie and Bennett's home in Dartonleigh. That person had given their full address and Leslie could picture the very row of houses along the main street. He observed that the comments were unanimously and effusively positive, but this always seemed to be the case in a hotel visitors' book; discontented people probably waited until they returned to the safety of their own home and then left an unfavourable online review instead. As he was considering this, Val appeared, overflowing with apologies for keeping him waiting. It had been one of those mornings.

"The Wi-Fi has gone down again—that's what I was caught up with."

Val started to give a verbatim report of the issue, but Leslie managed to cut in with a reminder that she had wanted to speak to him.

"Oh yes, of course, how could I forget?" She lowered her voice, though there was no one within earshot. "It's what got the day off to a bad start. I had Jeremy here at reception at the crack of dawn, demanding to have the new security light switched off."

Leslie made a small exclamation before he could stop himself, which Val fortunately took to be his reaction at such a request.

"You may well be surprised; I was myself. It seems that the light came on in the early hours and shone into his room, waking him up. I suggested, politely of course, that he makes sure the curtains are shut properly, but he insisted they were. They couldn't have been, they're proper blackout curtains, which I paid a fortune for incidentally, but I could hardly call him a liar, could I?"

Leslie tut-tutted sympathetically but forbore to disclose the real circumstances behind Jeremy's demand to have the light disabled. Who knew what Pandora's Box could be opened if he mentioned that?

"But he was adamant about that light and, just between you and me," she continued in a whisper, "I saw his other side. He's not always Prince Charming, you know. He's a bit of a Jekyll and Hyde on the quiet. He came down last month about some last-minute arrangements—not that he's ever done that before—and he made quite a fuss when he saw that the coach house was being done up and that I hadn't informed him. I don't know what business it is of his. He calmed down when I said that it wouldn't be occupied when the course was on, so you can imagine he had something to say about it when he arrived and found you and Bennett in situ."

For a moment, half uncomfortable and half hopeful, Leslie wondered if Val was going to ask them to vacate and go home, but it seemed she was leading up to a different point.

"Anyway, I must try to keep him sweet, so I've had a word with Mike who does my maintenance, and he's going to temporarily disable the lights, just while Jeremy is here. And unfortunately, one of the sensors is on the underside of your balcony, so I'm afraid we will have to disturb you this afternoon."

Before Leslie could dismiss the inconvenience, Val continued:

"So, you must both have afternoon tea with me here while it's being fixed, by way of compensation. I won't take no for an answer. And don't worry, I'm getting Sadie to do it; she does a lovely tea. I'd like you to see what our catering should be like. Believe me, as soon as I can get a replacement chef that Lee will be out of the door before his lazy feet can touch the ground. I took him on as an assistant chef and then the head chef left at short notice, so he's had to work on his own and he's just not up to it. If he made a bit more of an effort it would help but he hasn't shown the slightest enthusiasm since he first walked through the door. The trouble I've had with staff this year! But you're on holiday and you don't want to hear about that. You'll be wanting to get on with your day."

Despite this, it was some time before Leslie could disengage himself without being rude and, as he departed, Val said darkly, "What a morning. First the security light, then the Wi-Fi. Problems always come in threes. What will be next?"

Passing through the back of the hotel on his way to the coach house, Leslie unexpectedly encountered the writing group who had now assembled on the terrace in a semi-circle of chairs. One of the sisters was reading out what sounded like an extravagant description of last night's sunset while Jeremy beamed and nodded encouragingly, and the group listened politely.

"Helios, my god; red as blood, and to my blood he spoke," she crooned. "Setting a fire burning in my soul; scorching the anger, regret and despair of years gone by, and leaving behind at last the smouldering embers of peace."

Leslie hurriedly veered across the grass to avoid disturbing the group or attracting any attention to himself, but not before he had noticed, yet again, Jeremy casting a furtive glance towards Susan. She was seated with her back to Leslie, but judging by the way her head was inclined towards the current orator, it looked as though she was giving him as little attention as usual.

"Dear heavens, I wouldn't care to sit through five minutes of that let alone five days," said Leslie, joining Bennett on the balcony. They could see the terrace, where it looked as though 'feedback' was now being given. Leslie described the recitation which was being given as he passed. "Purple prose, I think they call it."

"Positively heliotrope, by the sound of it," Bennett replied.

Leslie then went on to relate his conversation with Val. Naturally he had already told Bennett all about Jeremy's apparent nocturnal philandering, and when Leslie described Jeremy's complaint about the security light, Bennett said:

"He means to repeat the adventure, by the sound of it. You didn't give him away, did you?"

"Of course not, what do you take me for? It's none of my business what he gets up to, and I wish I hadn't seen him; I felt like a voyeur. Val was completely taken in by his story, so his secret is safe."

***

"Entice a former partner with a three-quarter length coat," Bennett said, and bit into a peach. They had decided to forgo their usual sandwich lunch in anticipation of the afternoon tea and Val had supplied them with a bowl of fruit. "Four letters," he spluttered; it was a particularly juicy piece of fruit.

"Four letters," Leslie mused, passing Bennett a serviette. "The short ones are often the hardest. You get a great long clue and then a fiddling number of letters to make into an answer. What was it again?"

Bennett obliging repeated the clue and Leslie frowned with concentration.

"Former partner will be an ex, I suppose?"

Bennett made no reply, but this may have been because he was busy with the peach.

"I can't think of many four-letter words with ex in them." Leslie put down his apple and took up a pen and Bennett's pad of paper. Muttering, he wrote, *Exam. Text. Next. Flex.* "None of them have anything to do with enticing and three-quarter length coats. I give in."

"Coax," said Bennett.

Leslie wrote the word down and thought for a moment. "Oh, I get it! That's a good one. I don't know how you think of them."

This last remark was a casual comment, but Bennett said, enigmatically, "Perhaps I had ex-partners on my mind."

Before the conversation could go any further though, they heard a familiar yoo-hoo and Leslie stepped out onto the balcony. Gloria was beaming up at him and as he peered cautiously down over the railing, she clapped one hand to her ample breast and extended the other up towards him, fingers wide. "Romeo, Romeo, wherefore art thou, Romeo?" She gave a peal of laughter to rival the bells of Notre Dame. "I couldn't resist it," she added, still laughing.

"I think we might be the wrong way round," said Leslie, smiling.

"In more ways than one," observed Bennett, joining Leslie on the balcony.

"Hello there, Bennett, dear," she called up. "I just came to persuade you both to come for a quick walk down into the village with me. I'm playing hooky from the course this afternoon. Actually, we've been set a little writing task which I did in five minutes, so I'm not being quite as naughty as it sounds. There are one or two things that Valerie needs from Alemouth, so I said I'd pop down for her. It's for the afternoon tea. She's driven over to Burnsbridge for most of the shopping, but she insists we have the local clotted cream and a few other bits from the village." Gloria sighed deeply, as if anticipating gastronomic rapture.

Bennett would not be persuaded to walk down at any price, but Leslie was pleased to have the diversion, and ten minutes later they were passing through the door in the garden wall and strolling along the clifftop path.

"I'll have to keep my eye on the time," said Gloria, ambling along at a leisurely pace. "I said I'd help Sadie with the sandwiches and everything. That Lee who Val's got in the kitchen at the moment is a hopeless creature. He spends most of his time making eyes at Lauren; that's about all he can make. And she's a dozy thing, too. They're a right pair! Val's got her work cut out this summer. She lost both her regular chefs earlier this year; one moved away and the other's on maternity leave. She could normally get by with one chef temporarily, if they were any good, as Sadie can help in the kitchen; everyone must be able to do everything in a little hotel like this. Boutique they call it nowadays."

Bennett had raised a cynical eyebrow at the term 'boutique' when they had first seen it applied to the description of Alemouth Lodge and had wondered aloud how this differed from 'small'. Since their arrival, Leslie observed that, in this case, it seemed to comprise knick-knacks everywhere with a lively nautical theme. Though Leslie rather liked the cheerful decor, Bennett's first action on arriving in the suite had been to remove a handkerchief from his case and make a ceremony of covering the bust of a jolly pirate to which he had taken an immediate dislike.

Leslie returned his wandering attention to Gloria who had not changed topic.

"But Lee is hopeless," she was saying. "I don't believe he's ever worked anywhere near a kitchen before; anyone can fake a reference."

"Sadie is the older lady who helps, isn't she?" asked Leslie. "She seems very good."

"Oh yes, Sadie's marvellous. An absolute treasure, that's what Valerie calls her. She's been with Val since she took over the hotel and she can do the work of twenty Lees or Laurens. She can turn her hand to anything around the place, but the trouble is, her ancient mother's just been taken ill so she's very limited in the hours she can do at the moment. She's coming in when she can but it's all very uncertain."

Gloria elaborated at length on Val's staffing difficulties, and Leslie listened with half an ear, while at the same time watching the gulls, cormorants, terns and possibly a fulmar swooping and plunging over the sea far below. Dolphins and porpoises had recently been seen along this stretch of water, so he kept an eye out for these, though he knew from long experience that such sightings only came when you were not looking for them. It was an idyllic afternoon, the sun high in the cloudless sky, a gentle breeze, and the vast, rugged curve of the coastline stretching far ahead. Leslie amused himself as they walked, by trying to make out which seaside resorts he could see in the hazy distance and by attempting to identify the various peninsulas jutting out into the sea. Before long they were making the steep descent to the village.

"I hope you and Bennett both like shrimps," said Gloria, and looked pleased when Leslie said that they loved them. "Valerie insists we have fresh shrimp sandwiches this afternoon and believe me, they'll be heavenly."

She led the way from the cliff path and down a steeply sloping slipway towards the fresh fish stand and Leslie followed very cautiously. He was without his sling now but naturally he trod warily on the uneven surface which was slimy in places.

As Gloria chatted familiarly to the fishmonger, Leslie had time to run his eye across the inviting, if pungent, produce. There were trays displaying cod, mackerel, dace, pollock and whiting, all just waiting to be turned into stews, chowders, fish cakes and kedgerees or simply seared in a hot frying pan and served with some new potatoes and a crisp multi-coloured salad or some buttery asparagus. There were little pots of glistening cockles, rubbery whelks and whiskery prawns; big tubs of crabs, whole and dressed, and a pile of impressively clawed lobsters. By the time Gloria had completed her purchases, Leslie had already prepared and cooked half a dozen fantasy meals.

In search of the acclaimed clotted cream, they made next for the general store.

"Are you down for long, Gloria, my dear?" the shopkeeper asked as Gloria selected a large carton from the cold cabinet. Leslie had noticed that everyone seemed to know Gloria by name.

"Only until Friday," she replied and explained the reason for her visit. "The course finishes Friday after breakfast."

"And are you coming down to see the filming tomorrow?" The shopkeeper indicated the notice displayed at the counter, which was the same one Leslie had seen in the chemist window on the previous afternoon.

Gloria peered at it with exaggerated interest and the lady leant across the counter whispering, as though it were a state secret, "It's *Trevallion Cove.*"

Leslie had watched only the first episode of this popular peak-time drama, but he was familiar with several of the actors who the shopkeeper was now assuring Gloria, in hushed tones, would be in Alemouth.

"The story's set in Cornwall, isn't it?" said Leslie. "I suppose the bay and the village do have quite a Cornish look about them." He immediately wondered if this was a tactless comment, recalling what he had heard about the traditional rivalry between the two counties. However, the shopkeeper simply remarked that it was amazing what deception they could perform with cameras these days.

As they left the shop, Gloria said, "Thank goodness I didn't sign up for my tutorial with Jeremy for tomorrow. *Trevallion Cove*, I say! I haven't missed a single episode. You wait until I tell my daughter, Gina. She'll be green with envy."

The newsagent next door was Gloria's final destination, to pick up 'a few little bits' for herself. Leslie was well acquainted with Gloria's sweet tooth, so he tactfully crossed the road instead, to the antique shop, and spent a pleasant couple of minutes browsing the crammed shelves. He had explored this shop on an earlier expedition, hoping to find an addition to his milk jug collection, but had been disappointed. He had no expectation of success so soon after his previous visit, but it was a good excuse to escape discussing the filming all over again in the newsagents, and to avoid being persuaded into buying sweets by Gloria, to assuage her own conscience.

As they met up again and wandered back down the street, Gloria paused by one of the several tearooms along the parade and looked longingly through the window. "This is my very favourite shop in Alemouth. You simply must try the éclairs and the ice cream while you are down here. What a shame we don't have time to stop today," she said, and added with a sigh, "So many tasty things, and so little time to enjoy them!"

As they moved on, a familiar figure appeared through the door of an off-licence ahead of them. It was the sailor, Susan's visitor, and he stomped past them, seemingly oblivious, forcing them to step from the narrow pavement into the road to avoid his bulky bag which was clearly full of cans and bottles.

"Really!" said Leslie, under his breath, but Gloria, who had nearly collided with a cyclist, said at full volume:

"I told you he was a bad omen."

They made their way back to the hotel and, as soon as Gloria could recover her breath from the steep ascent, she returned to the thrilling subject of *Trevallion Cove*, which occupied them for the rest of the walk.

***

Leslie had fully expected that Bennett would refuse to join the afternoon tea party, but to his surprise Bennett got himself ready to go at the appointed hour. Leslie's delight that he would not have to make embarrassing apologies for Bennett's absence, and also that Bennett was prising himself away from the room and into company again, was tinged by slight misgivings, as it was just the sort of setting where Bennett's eccentricities could be the most conspicuous. Fortunately, Gloria treated everything that Bennett said and did as a hilarious joke, and Leslie hoped that Val was sufficiently alike her cousin to do the same.

Gloria was waiting for them in the hotel reception. Although she had parted from Leslie less than an hour earlier, she greeted the men with a lavish embrace as though she had not seen them for a month, and led them through to Val's private apartments. "Isn't it beautiful?" she said, airily throwing open the doors to Val's bathroom and bedroom as they went along, to reveal rooms which, though small, were all luxurious and tastefully decorated. "You're not allowed to see this one, though. That's my bedroom and you wouldn't believe what a mess one person could make in just a few days."

Gloria insisted they stepped into the kitchen, which looked as modern and chic as an advertisement, and Sadie, who was busy with the kettle, assured them that everything was ready. Finally, they came into the living room, also attractively decorated, and he observed that the apartment was far less twee than the main hotel.

Val was already there, putting the finishing touches to the magnificent display of food. They took their places around a circular dining table and helped themselves to the freshly made finger sandwiches, including the recently bought shrimps to which had been added a light, creamy dressing. Leslie asked Val for the recipe.

"You'll have to speak to Sadie about that in a minute when she comes back in with the cakes. It's her recipe," she replied, adding ruefully, "I'm afraid I'm hopeless in the kitchen. How I've regretted it this year—that I can't step in and take over. But I've never had to before as I've always had a brilliant kitchen team; a couple of first-rate chefs I could rely on. But one's on maternity leave and the other had a lot of family problems out in Italy and had to go back home at short notice. Sadie has always covered days off and holiday in the kitchen as an assistant but she's not really a chef, and now that her mother is poorly, she can only help out as and when. Everyone round here has had problems recruiting kitchen staff this season, it's just one of those years. I took Lee on as an assistant to cover the maternity leave. I knew he didn't have the experience, but I hoped he'd be OK working with Marco. I couldn't have known that a week later Marco would give notice. The agency couldn't even send me anyone temporary, hence the disastrous catering."

She poured more tea as Leslie and Gloria made sympathetic responses.

"I feel jinxed at the moment," she continued, well into her stride. "Lousy chef, Sadie having to see to her mother, Wi-Fi coming and going, and I didn't tell you about the to-do with Lauren this morning. I told you there would be something else, didn't I?" she said addressing Leslie. "This must go absolutely no further, you understand, but I know from Gloria that you can both keep a confidence. The trouble kicked off at about half past eleven this morning, or thereabouts, when I was accosted by one of the women on the course. It was Cassandra. Do you know who I mean?" They all did, so Val continued. "She was livid, absolutely incandescent. In all the time I've been running the hotel I don't think I've ever seen anyone so annoyed, though to be honest I can't remember the last time we ever had a complaint, other than the Wi-Fi going off, and Jeremy this morning. Oh yes, and the awful catering at the moment."

She paused again, this time to insist that everyone topped up their plates. "Cassandra had gone back to her room to fetch something or other, and she found Lauren looking through one of her drawers. To be more precise, looking into the drawer; I established that she wasn't actually touching anything. Apparently, when she challenged her, Lauren just said she 'wasn't doing no harm' and left the room, without so much as a sorry. You can see why Cassandra was annoyed, although she did go right over the top. I had the devil of a job to placate her. I've promised to see to her room myself for the rest of her stay."

"What was Lauren's side of the story?" asked Leslie.

"I can't make her out," said Val, standing up to refill everyone's teacups. "She behaved as though she'd done nothing wrong. She said she often looked at the guests' belongings as they had nice things, and what was the harm in looking? She said she never touched anything, and she seemed to think it was only a problem if you got caught. She looked blank when I said it was intruding into the guests' privacy and, when I added that it might seem as though she was looking for things to steal, she went off on one, and demanded to know if anyone had ever complained of missing anything. What do you make of that?"

"Has anything gone missing since she has been here?" asked Bennett.

"Nothing that I'm aware of," Val replied, "but she hasn't been here very long so perhaps she hasn't seen anything to take her fancy yet. I don't know what to think. I ought to get rid of her straightaway, but getting housekeeping staff is as bad as getting kitchen staff this year. As soon as I can replace her, I'll give her notice; Lee too, as soon as I can get another chef. They're both still on probation so I only need pay them a week's notice, and that will be cheap at the price. Heaven knows what they'll both have cost me in damage to the hotel's reputation, though. It only takes a couple of bad reviews."

"I did my best to stand up for Valerie when Cassandra came storming back into the group," said Gloria, to Leslie and Bennett. "She was trying to whip them all up, but I said very firmly that I was certain Valerie would sort it all out. Those two old spinster sisters started saying that it was all very well for me as I wasn't staying in the main house so my personal belongings wouldn't have been touched. They've got a point, of course, I wouldn't like anyone looking through my things."

Leslie was glad, for once, that Bennett had kept vigil in their room. Leslie had nothing to hide but some of Bennett's worn-out clothes which he refused to discard and had packed despite having perfectly good alternatives at home, were shameful. Leslie thought about Gloria's earlier visit to the sweetshop and guessed her secrets were probably of the edible variety.

"But I wasn't going to admit anything to those miserable old biddies," Gloria went on. "That's not the first time they've had a dig at me for staying in here with Valerie. Isn't it strange what some people get jealous about? Anyway, some of the others started fussing, and telling Jeremy that they were going back to their rooms to check that nothing had been stolen. But then, luckily, Barbara sided with me and said she'd locked her handbag in the room safe, as recommended, and she had nothing else in the room worth looking at. She added, rather scathingly I thought, that anyone who brought valuables on holiday and then left them unlocked in their room in any hotel, anywhere in the world, wanted their heads testing, and that in a really top hotel the guests would think nothing of a drawer being opened as they expected the maids to put their clothes away for them."

"How did they react to that?" asked Leslie.

"Well," continued Gloria, "Jeremy handled it really rather well, I thought. He said that we'd lost the flow of what we were doing in group, and he would give us what he called a breakout exercise; we were to go and find a 'creative space' and capture our emotions in a 'word net'. Something like that, I can't remember exactly. Of course, the point was that it gave everyone the chance to go back to their rooms if they wanted to, without having to make an issue out of it. I don't know what happened after that as I came to find Valerie straightaway. They were all still talking about it over lunch though unfortunately."

"It's hardly surprising," said Val gloomily. "To be honest, they were a miserable enough bunch before this happened. Apart from the raging Cassandra, there are the two sisters who look as though their faces would crack if they smiled, and Carol, with all those eating fads and supposed health issues. I know Barbara took sides with you today, Gloria, but she's not exactly a bundle of fun, and as for her poor friend, Ann, who saw the accident last year, she looks like she's expecting another tragedy at any moment. Why she came back this year if she's still so upset about it, is a mystery. Then there's the po-faced Susan and the disabled lady, poor dear, hobbling about on her crutches, not that she's given any trouble."

Val stood up to clear away the now empty sandwich platter. "Last year's group was much easier, even considering the disaster that occurred. Gloria, do you remember that sweet lady who came with Susan? It's a shame she didn't return. She was a dear, so grateful for anything anybody did for her, and she said she'd definitely be back this year. I was very surprised she wasn't among the number."

"Yes, I overheard Ann asking Susan about her," said Gloria, "but Susan said the woman had moved house and that she'd lost touch with her."

"That seems odd," Val replied, "I was sure they came together, and I thought they were close friends, but perhaps I got the wrong impression. Oh well, I hope nothing has happened to her, she was such a nice person. Jean Rook: there, her name's just come back to me! Now, Susan's name, Susan Gunner, is easy to remember as I was at school with a Susan Gunner in Torquay. She was a most peculiar girl, which is why the name has stuck with me, I suppose. Not the same person as this Susan Gunner, of course; even if it's not a common name I expect there are lots of Susan Gunners in the world!"

Val's chatter was suspended as Sadie came in bearing a tiered cake stand, replete with mini éclairs, tiny brandy snaps, macaroons and other delicious-looking items of patisserie, along with scones, jam and the clotted cream which Gloria had bought earlier. Everyone was busy for a while and the conversation diverted to a discussion on the fine distinctions between Devon and Cornish cream teas, with such variations as Devon splits, Chudleighs and cutrounds, and punctuated by exclamations of rapture as the luxurious treats were sampled.

"Do you put on an afternoon tea for the writing group?" asked Leslie. When Val replied in the negative, he said, "They'd forget every complaint they'd ever had after a tea like this, I'm quite certain."

"Leslie believes that good food solves everything," said Bennett, licking strawberry jam off his fingers. "He's quite right, of course."

"I'll give that some thought," said Val. "It would make a hole in my profit margin as it's not a cheap do. Not that I mind doing it for you, of course, I didn't mean that. But it might be worth it. It could pay for itself in avoiding reputational damage."

"Two afternoon teas in one week; what joy," said Gloria gleefully, popping another éclair into her mouth. "Leslie's always so clever at solving things. Why don't you announce the tea at the quiz night tonight, Valerie?"

"The quiz night!" exclaimed Val, "thank goodness you reminded me; I quite forgot about it for a moment. I have a marvellous little book of quizzes, but I do hate being the quizmaster. I'm always so worried that I'll pronounce something wrongly and make a complete ass of myself. I got the book out last night, but what with all the problems today I haven't had a chance to choose any questions."

She went to the sideboard and picked up a fat red book decorated with question marks.

"Fancy that!" Leslie exclaimed with a laugh. "Bennett, look; it's one of yours. Bennett writes quizzes and puzzles," he said to the two mystified women. "Mostly crosswords and the sort of puzzles you get in newspapers, but he's contributed to quite a lot of quiz books, too. I've got copies of all of them at home."

"I say, is this true, Bennett?" squealed Gloria in delight. "What a dark horse you are."

Bennett inclined his head and said gravely, "I'm afraid it seems I must be excused taking part tonight. It would be against the rules."

"No such thing!" Val thrust the book at him. "Behold our quizmaster; you have about four hours to choose the questions for tonight."

Bennett accepted the book with a deep sigh of resignation as Val declared her delight in being relieved of the task.

"Now all I have to worry about," she said, "is that they don't all pack their bags and go home before I've had the chance to seduce them with my sandwiches and scones."

5

The quiz was a triumph and, despite the earlier ill-feeling in the group, everyone except Jeremy turned up and joined in enthusiastically. Apparently, he never participated in the quiz night, claiming that it was his only chance for 'a little downtime', but Val whispered to Leslie that she thought 'that poser' was afraid of displaying his ignorance. With Leslie, Val and Sadie joining in, there were to be four teams of three. This was supposed to be decided by lot, but when the two sisters refused to be separated, Val gave up and let them all make their own teams.

Bennett was well practiced as a quizmaster. Dartonleigh, their home village, had innumerable clubs and societies, and each one had its own quiz nights. Bennett's occupation as a quiz and puzzle-maker was no secret—Leslie was too proud of him to allow that—so his services were called upon regularly. Although normally very reserved, on such occasions Bennett adopted the public persona he had refined in three decades of university lecturing before his retirement, and he was extremely entertaining.

As with most accomplishments, Bennett's skills were the result of considerable hard work over the years. While strictly objective when setting pub quizzes, especially where there would be visitors and strangers, he took a very different approach for local groups and had refined the art of assembling exactly the right combination of questions for the particular attendees. His real flair lay in the knack of choosing questions that, by the end of the evening, had each participant feeling that they had been clever on at least one occasion. This was relatively easy in a village where everyone's background and peculiar interests were known and where a percentage of the answers could rely on knowledge of an obscure fact, likely to be known only to one or two individuals present. It was only necessary to know who was attending, which was easy in Dartonleigh, as the same people went to everything. Now, with only four hours to prepare a quiz for strangers, Bennett had to fall back on everything he had observed, or heard from Leslie, in the last two days, and he worked without interruption, except for black coffee, until the time of the quiz.

The evening was a great success. Heads together, excited whispers and hastily scribbled notes told that Bennett had succeeded as usual. Thelma showed a surprising competitive streak, ignoring her fallen crutches as she leant forward in her chair to hiss urgently to her colleagues. Susan too seemed to supply a constant flow of answers and looked far more genuinely engaged in the quiz than she had in the literary activities during the day. It seemed that Bennett had succeeded, as usual, in choosing questions that gave everyone a chance to shine, which was especially obvious in the quick-fire round, when the team was rewarded if someone answered without conferring. Thelma, whose late husband had been a clergyman, was delighted to show off her liturgical knowledge; the two sisters were experts in wildflowers, and Susan's instant answer on a question about rowing seemed to support her earlier boast to Cassandra. An obscure question on the periodic table was answered without hesitation by Barbara while Ann knew without a second's thought that Gemini was the star sign for the twentieth of June.

Barbara, Ann and Sadie's team were the overall victors, winning a box of chocolates which they generously shared with the whole group, and the mood was so upbeat that Leslie wondered if Val would go ahead with arranging the afternoon tea. However, as soon as the prize had been awarded, and Bennett given a bottle of red wine for his role in the evening's entertainment, which he showed no signs of sharing with anyone, Val announced the special treat that was to go ahead on Thursday. The rapturous response confirmed that full atonement had been made for the failings earlier in the day, and Val went to sort out the evening refreshments looking relieved.

Bennett took himself and his bottle back to the suite soon after the quiz and Leslie found himself sitting with Barbara, Ann and Thelma. There was a pleasant murmur of conversation as the guests chatted in groups, though Susan, as usual, had resumed her look of detachment, rather as though she was present in body but not in spirit.

As Leslie was observing this, Thelma said, "That lady, Susan, there. Don't you think she's elegant? I wish I had her height and could wear those lovely flowing clothes. Those loose trousers would look like pyjamas on me."

Leslie was rather surprised that Thelma should make such a comment but, before he had the chance to examine his conjecture, Ann reacted in an even more surprising way.

"I don't know about elegant," she said sharply. "At least she's decent this year, I suppose. Last year she went about in a tiny little skirt or shorts, flashing her legs at you-know-who at every opportunity. Ridiculous in a woman of her age."

There was a shocked silence at the table at this outburst, then Barbara said with a forced laugh, "Your glass is nearly empty, Ann. Why not drink up and turn in for the night? I think we're all tired after our victory in the quiz."

But Ann was not to be distracted. "She must easily be the same age as Cassandra or Val, and you couldn't imagine either of them making a fool of themselves like that," she said, far too loudly. Leslie realised that she had probably had considerably more to drink than she was used to.

"Well, she seems to have thought better of it this year," Thelma replied, equably.

"I asked her about it, actually," said Ann. "She told me that she'd had a skin cancer scare and had been advised to cover up. But I think it's because it didn't get her anywhere. There's obviously nothing going on between them."

Thelma, who'd probably spent years dealing with awkward parishioners, commented pleasantly, "I might make a move myself. It takes me so long to get to bed these days and I'd like to be fresh for the morning." She turned stiffly to retrieve her crutches which someone had kindly replaced on the back of her chair.

Barbara looked grateful, and when Ann got up to leave the room, her unsteady gait endorsed Leslie's suspicions and he guessed that she would never have spoken so boldly if sober. Leslie looked around and saw that Susan had also gone.

***

"It was rather embarrassing," said Leslie, describing Ann's outburst to Bennett later.

"They say a drunken man's words are a sober man's thoughts," said Bennett, looking up from his book. "Try some of this red wine. It's rather good."

"Well, you did it again, Bennett." Leslie took the glass of wine that Bennett had poured him. "It really was a great quiz. It was easy to predict that Carol would know those medical terms, but did you actually know that Sadie was a connoisseur of old films, or was it just a good guess?"

"Don't forget that Sadie comes in to clean the room while you are out gallivanting, and she likes to talk."

"Ah yes. But Cassandra was caught out, wasn't she? I knew she couldn't have been at Oxford by the stupid way she was talking yesterday. Surely anyone who had been there would have identified the Bodleian Library. I guessed it myself, but she obviously hadn't got a clue. It was rather embarrassing," said Leslie reproachfully.

"I had no intentions of humiliating the woman," said Bennett, but without the least hint of remorse in his voice.

"At least she redeemed herself by recognising that quote from *Sense and Sensibility*. Perhaps she really did study English literature, but not at Oxford."

"I doubt it," said Bennett. "She's probably just a Jane Austen fan. I wonder what she's really called."

"What do you mean?"

"Don't you remember? Jane Austen's sister was a Cassandra."

"Our Cassandra was probably christened Mary or Joan," laughed Leslie.

"What's in a name?" said Bennett, and he drained his glass. "The rest of the quote doesn't seem to apply," he added wryly as he stood up and headed for the bedroom.

***

Whether it was the wine or exhaustion from the previous bad night's sleep but, even with the whirring of the air conditioning, Leslie dropped off to sleep straight away, unhindered by anxiety, indigestion, shoulder pain, or any other goblins of insomnia. This blissful state was only to last for a few hours though, for shortly after three o'clock Leslie was wrenched from the depths of slumber by an agonising pain in his right calf. He sat up with a loud groan, clutching at his leg. Without turning over, Bennett mumbled:

"What is it? Cramp?"

"Yes, sod it," gasped Leslie.

"Get up and walk it off," advised Bennett from his recumbent position.

With much huffing and puffing, Leslie eased himself out of bed and into a standing position and then limped cautiously across the dark room. He was seized with this nocturnal affliction at least once a month and knew that the excruciating pain would pass in a few moments so long as he got walking, as Bennett had prompted, but it didn't make the task a pleasant one. In the sitting room, he put the light on and hobbled painfully around the room until the knot in his calf muscle relaxed itself and he could walk normally again. He knew from experience that it was no use going straight back to bed—unless he kept moving for a while the cramp would return—so he poured himself a glass of water and went out onto the balcony, switching off the light as he went.

It was another warm, clear and still night, and the star-speckled sky was intensely black, but for once Leslie was in no mood for appreciating the wonders of nature. How infuriating it was that having been relieved of the other pestilences that had kept him awake on previous nights, this infernal cramp had now dragged him from a perfect sleep. Disturbing snatches of an elusive dream half surfaced and disappeared and, as he sat in the wicker chair on the balcony, circling his foot slowly round and round to keep the muscle from seizing up, Leslie was filled with a grim sense of foreboding, as though he was waiting for something dreadful to occur. He was being ridiculous, of course; this was just the disquietude of being awake when one should rightly be asleep, and probably some evolutionary response to send humans scurrying back into their beds during the unwholesome hours of darkness. Having rationalised his feelings Leslie felt a little better, but he was still sufficiently on edge to jump at a faint rustling and movement in the garden; a fox or badger no doubt, or some other nocturnal animal, going about its business.

Just as Leslie had decided that the cramp had safely passed and he could return to the comfort of his bed, there was a sound from the direction of the house. It was the same click of a door being cautiously opened and shut again that he had heard the previous night, and just as quiet as before. Leslie automatically froze, half expecting the security light to come on again, but the lamp had been successfully disabled and all remained in darkness. Despite this, Leslie felt in little doubt that it was Jeremy, indulging in his night-time pursuits again with Susan and, recalling again the conversation he had accidentally intruded on shortly after their arrival, he hoped that she was a willing recipient of these attentions. Resolutely dismissing the subject from his mind, Leslie made his way back to bed.

***

Once again, Leslie's disturbed night meant that the two men were late to breakfast the next day, arriving in time to hear Carol insisting that Val be summonsed to confirm her toast was gluten free. Val duly appeared, bearing the packaging which Carol subjected to quite unnecessary scrutiny, since even from his table, Leslie could clearly read the legend: Gluten free bread.

"I can't understand it," complained Carol loudly. "I was convinced it was the toast yesterday morning. Such gas all day—"

Val interrupted hastily, saying very firmly, "It was definitely gluten free toast yesterday, as well."

Carol leant back with a look of disbelief, rubbing her enormous frontage.

"I supervise any special food requests myself," Val continued, "and there is a separate area in the kitchen so that nothing can get contaminated."

"Yeast!" declared Carol with satisfaction. "I must be yeast intolerant as well. I've suspected it for some time."

"Shall I take this toast away, then, and bring some gluten free crackers instead?" said Val, with a patience and politeness she could not possibly have felt. "I'm sure the crackers won't contain any yeast, but I can bring the box and you can check for yourself."

"No, no," Carol replied, taking firm hold of the toast rack. "Don't trouble yourself. I'll make no changes to my diet until I've consulted my doctor when I get home."

Before she could add anything else, Val escaped, and Carol subjected her companions to an exposition on her food allergies. Ann affected interest and sympathy, but Barbara absorbed herself with the remains of her breakfast, having made a cursory remark or two to Susan who was the other occupant at the table. Leslie could see Susan clearly from where he was seated and he observed her thoughtfully, trying to make out what it was about her that he could not quite put his finger on.

"How's Susan today?" asked Bennett, who had his back to the room. "Looking any the worse for wear?"

Leslie had, of course, related the night-time goings on, but Bennett surprised him by asking him to describe what he'd heard, again.

"Why are you so interested? And how did you know it was her I was looking at?" asked Leslie, averting his gaze from Susan in case anyone else noticed that he'd been staring at her.

Bennett's only response was to fish out a couple of pips from the fruit salad before him, tapping them onto his side plate.

"She looks like she usually does, only more so, perhaps," said Leslie taking a spoonful of the fruit salad and making a face. "The grapefruit in this cocktail has gone a bit fizzy, don't you think? I'm sticking with the cereal and toast this morning." Returning from the breakfast bar with a bowl of muesli, Leslie continued with his observations of Susan. "I'm not quite sure what it is that puzzles me about her," said Leslie.

"Other than her apparent fascination, possibly unreciprocated, to two men."

"Well, that obviously drew my attention to her. But don't you think that something about her manner is rather odd, anyway? She sits with the others, and she speaks as much as Barbara, if not more, but she's distinctly aloof. It's as though she's mentally somewhere else all the time. She does look particularly distracted this morning, in a non-specific sort of way, but perhaps she's just tired. She must have had a very late night," he added wryly.

He paused to eat some of his cereal then said, "But I'm probably exaggerating it, and if it hadn't been for those odd encounters with Jeremy and the sailor, I don't suppose I'd have noticed her manner at all. I'm probably doing that thing where as soon as you believe something, you start to make everything else fit your theory. I can't remember what it's called."

"Confirmation bias," supplied Bennett.

"That's the one," said Leslie. "I suppose most people do it to some extent all the time. And, as I was saying, if I hadn't seen those strange incidents, I don't suppose I'd have thought Susan was stranger than anyone else. Everyone here seems pretty odd, after all. Present company excepted, of course."

Bennett looked up and smiled at him, and the happiness that Leslie had been seeking in the holiday was, just for the moment, within his grasp. They were interrupted by Jeremy standing up to give the arrangements for the morning's session which seemed to be entitled: Creating word nets to capture the elusive spirits of the soul.

"And this afternoon's tutorial," he consulted a sheet of paper, "is with Dee and Deborah. Is that still on, ladies?" He flashed them a fulsome smile and they responded in simultaneous agreement. The group started to drift away from the dining room.

Gloria, who until now had confined herself to waving her napkin at them, now hurried over. She put both hands on the table and leaned forward, her necklace chiming tunefully against Bennett's coffee pot. "You will come into Alemouth this afternoon with me, won't you?" she said confidentially. "It's the filming, remember, and I do so want to see if I can get some photos for Gina. She's desperate for me to get a picture of what's-his-name, that chap who plays Sir Clem Penhallan. Do come down with me."

Leslie had no very great interest in the programme or any of the actors but, in the absence of anything else planned, he happily agreed. Bennett made no answer, which was taken as a tacit decline, and neither of them tried to persuade him.

***

"I wonder whereabouts they'll be filming," said Gloria, as they walked towards Alemouth village after lunch. "I asked around but no one at the hotel seemed to know. We're supposed to be doing another little writing task this afternoon for Jeremy, but it's easy enough to bluff; no one would know if you were making it up on the spot. I happen to know that Ann, Carol and Cassandra are coming down to see the filming as well, but I managed to escape from them."

When they reached the main street, they discovered it had been blocked to traffic and was lined with onlookers, kept back by temporary barriers on the narrow pavement.

"Look over there," said Leslie. "There's Carol and Cassandra, but I can't see Ann with them."

"Quick, let's go this way," said Gloria, doubling back and heading along an alleyway. "It looks to me as though they're filming down on the beach."

"I'm sure I just spotted Dee and Deborah in the crowd, too. Weren't they supposed to be at Jeremy's tutorial this afternoon? I wonder how he'll feel about being stood up."

"Perhaps he'll have a secret rendezvous with Susan instead," Gloria replied mischievously. "I've seen him sneaking a crafty look at her, but she doesn't give anything away!"

Leslie was spared replying, for the alley had become so narrow he had to drop behind and Gloria was forging ahead. They soon reappeared onto the street, lower down and much nearer to the beach, but barriers and crowds here too made it impossible to catch any sight of the filming. Undaunted, Gloria set off purposefully back to the start of the cliff path which they had just come down by. Before long they reached a gate, which Leslie hadn't noticed before, bearing the sign: Bay View Cottage.

"Tom and Maggie are great friends of Valerie," Gloria said as they passed through the gate and round the side of a pretty, whitewashed cottage. "I do hope they're in. Yoo-hoo! Maggie! Tom! Anyone home?"

"Is that you, Gloria? Come on down," came the reply and a red-faced and smiling woman appeared. "I heard from Val that you were here, and I wondered if I'd see you. Tom's in the summerhouse watching them filming on the beach. Go round while I put the kettle on."

The view from the cottage garden was spectacular, and a perfect spot to spend the afternoon. It was high enough to command a far-reaching view along the rugged coastline, and it overlooked the bay directly so that they could watch all the action from the comfort of the summerhouse.

"That one there, just getting into the boat," said Gloria, peering through the binoculars she had produced from her bag. "That's Sir Clem. I'm sure of it."

"Are you certain, Gloria, love?" replied Tom, focussing his own binoculars on the same spot. "I think it's t'other one."

Leslie was appealed to for an opinion but would not have known even if he had been standing on the beach with them. Maggie returned with a tray of tea and biscuits and agreed quite positively first with Gloria and then with her husband. As the afternoon and the filming progressed, each character and actor was identified with the same degree of confidence. Gloria took photograph after photograph even though one would need a paparazzi lens to take an identifiable shot at that distance. They could, however, easily make out Carol, Cassandra and the two sisters crowded on the pavement in the village, where they could not possibly see anything, and Gloria did not attempt to hide her pleasure as she revelled in their own good luck.

After a while, Leslie begged permission to investigate the garden and spent an enjoyable time strolling between the beautifully kept flower borders, bursting with foxgloves, delphiniums, sweet William and many other cottage garden flowers. There was a well-stocked kitchen garden and a large pond edged with a neat rockery. This side of the garden faced away from the bay with its transient film set and looked along the coast in the direction from which they had come. Try as he might though he could see no sign of Alemouth

Lodge or its grounds from this point, as the part of the cliff on which the hotel was situated was cut sharply inland and obscured by the landscape between.

The garden sloped down to the cliff edge which, fortunately, was not a sheer drop, allowing Leslie to enjoy the view below without his usual qualms. Two small jetties protruded into the sea, with a dozen or so boats moored to each, and it obviously made an ideal viewing point for the filming, judging by the crowd of boat owners with their families and friends, all busy with their cameras. This must be where Susan's sailor acquaintance had moored up, but there was no sign of a dark-bearded man on either of the little piers.

"It looks like they're finishing for the day," said Gloria when Leslie returned at last. "Do you think I ought to run down to try to get an autograph or a selfie as they're leaving?"

"I wouldn't bother," Tom replied. "They've got their cars parked right down on the slipway and they didn't so much as acknowledge the crowd when they arrived. I bet they drive straight out without stopping."

"I won't waste my time, then." Gloria sounded relieved. "We ought to be making our way back to the hotel, anyway. I like to give Valerie a bit of a hand before dinner."

After a further ten minutes' discussion about Val's current staffing woes, they took their leave, arriving back at the hotel to see Ann and Jeremy having a tête-à-tête on the terrace.

"Oh, I say," said Gloria. "Jeremy didn't get his afternoon off after all. It looks like Ann's taken the tutorial slot vacated by the sisters. Greedy thing: she had her tutorial yesterday. Between you and me, I think she's rather sweet on Jeremy, and I bet she saw her chance and took it."

From what Leslie had seen, all the women on the course, except Barbara and Susan, were rather smitten with their leader, including Gloria in her own way. But there could be no doubt from Ann's adoring gaze that she was utterly besotted with the man. It hardly presented Ann in a very positive light, but far less so Jeremy, to tolerate or even court such wretched admiration.

"They didn't have these tutorials last year; Jeremy said he'd introduced them because of popular demand. Since Ann and Susan were the only ones here last year, I think we can guess which one requested the individual tutorials, and why," laughed Gloria.

Finding it rather embarrassing, Leslie curtailed any further discussion and headed straight back to the coach house and Bennett.

***

In the dining room that evening, it was no surprise that the filming dominated the conversation, with Carol, Cassandra and the two sisters covertly trying to outdo each other in who and what they'd seen. Of course Leslie, who could hear their remarks quite clearly from his table, knew that none of them could have seen a quarter of what they were describing.

Thelma struggled into a seat at the table where Ann and Barbara were sitting, hooking her crutch over the edge of the table from where it was destined to crash to the ground at least once during the meal. "I love the series, especially the beautiful costumes and scenery, and I should like to have seen the filming. But even if I could have got down there, I can't stand for long these days. But never mind, I had a pleasant afternoon in the lounge. Didn't you two go down?"

"Not my cup of tea, I'm afraid," said Barbara. "I'm not much of a one for celebrities. I had a peaceful afternoon in my room with a book."

"I was going to go with Carol and Cassandra," said Ann. She cast an apologetic look towards Barbara. "But when Dee and Deborah dropped out of the tutorial right at the last minute, Jeremy came and found me and insisted I had another session this afternoon." She flushed and giggled. "How could I refuse? We went on for ever so long, as well. I only just had time to go and wash my hands before coming in here."

Barbara's expression was a mixture of embarrassment and exasperation, but she said nothing, and Ann extolled Jeremy's praises until the man himself came in and, after a brief survey of the room, honoured them with his presence at their table. Leslie thought that the look on Barbara's face would have been enough to repel anyone without exceptional hubris, but Jeremy took his seat with his usual conspicuous self-assurance. Or was it? Leslie had a good view of Jeremy's face, and he fancied that despite the smiling countenance, there was an odd look in his eyes; a determinedly fixed focus on those at his table.

"There's something peculiar about Jeremy," said Leslie in a low voice.

"I thought we already knew that."

"Perhaps it's just that he's not looking across at Susan every five seconds." There was a short pause as Leslie glanced round the room. "And that's because she hasn't come in yet. I suppose he noticed that she's not here when he came in; when he was deciding where to sit."

But this was contradicted a moment later by Jeremy rising to ask, "Are we all present?"

Leslie was momentarily transported back to school, and half expected Jeremy to say the grace, but instead of remarking on this to Bennett, he said quietly, "He knows Susan's not here, I'd swear to it. There's something funny going on between them, I'll be bound."

Someone pointed out Susan's absence and Cassandra went off to knock on her door. While she was gone it was agreed that she was never late but perhaps she had lost track of the time, or even dropped off to sleep. Cassandra returned with the news that Susan did not seem to be in her room; there was no answer at her door.

"I hope there's nothing wrong," said Ann, with a slightly indignant note in her voice. "I remember now that she said she was feeling a bit under the weather earlier. She told me she's being investigated for a heart complaint. She shouldn't have gone off on her own if she wasn't feeling well. I hope she hasn't been taken ill somewhere. Perhaps I should have—"

"It's easy to lose track of the time sitting outside on a nice evening like this," interrupted Val who had come into the dining room by now, having been alerted by Sadie, who was serving them this evening. "But I'll check her room, myself, just to be on the safe side."

"If she's not there, someone should check Lantern Cove," said Thelma as Val started towards the door. "She passed me on her way there, earlier on, as I was going into the lounge. I'm sure she said she was going down there to do her writing task. She had her bag with her, the big straw one she keeps her writing things in."

"She went down to the cove yesterday afternoon as well," volunteered Gloria. "Don't you remember, she mentioned it when she was reading out her piece this morning?"

There were general murmurs of agreement.

"She'll miss her dinner if she's down there now," said Val. "The tide will be right in. She'll have to sit up on the rocks or at the back of the cave until it goes out again and she can get along to the steps." As she passed Gloria she added in a lower voice, "I do wish they'd heed my warnings. I make sure everyone knows that Lantern gets cut off at high tide. I'll go and check her room first, anyway; she might be asleep in there."

"Look on the bright side," said Gloria, to Val's departing back. "She must have been feeling better. She wouldn't have taken herself all that way to Lantern Cove if she was feeling groggy. It's a good twenty minutes' walk there and a most exhausting climb back up those steps again."

"Has Susan messaged anyone?" asked Jeremy suddenly, getting his own phone out of his pocket.

There were some general murmurings and, just as it had been confirmed that no one had exchanged contact details with the absent lady, Val returned with the news that Susan's room was empty.

"I'm sure there's no need for any alarm," said Jeremy.

Leslie thought that his usual suave manner was tinged with anxiety, as well it might be having had a disaster on the previous year's course.

"Let's not hold up dinner any longer," Jeremy continued. "I'll give her a call and see where she's got to." He moved a discreet distance from the tables while he found and rang the number, but it was soon obvious that there had been no reply. "I'll go and see if she's down in the cove."

"But you won't be able to get to Lantern Cove, sir," said Sadie. "It's completely cut off when the tide's in."

"Yes, I know that," replied Jeremy. "I'm only going as far as the clifftop. I can look down into the cove from there and she might be able to hear me if I shout. If she's trapped, there's a chance she may be able to call back up. Valerie, do get started with dinner, please."

"Why don't we all split up and search the grounds?" suggested Cassandra, standing up. "Just in case she's collapsed somewhere."

"No, there's no call for that, I'm sure. At least, not until after dinner if she hasn't appeared by then," said Jeremy firmly, but again Leslie could see unease in his manner. Indeed, he felt that a strange sense of foreboding had pervaded the whole group.

"It will be most embarrassing for Susan," went on Jeremy briskly, "if it turns out she's just got so immersed in her work that she's lost all track of time. I'm sure she'd be quite put out to think that dinner had been ruined on her account. But if I could perhaps have one volunteer to join me."

Ann was on her feet and at Jeremy's side before the sentence was out of his mouth.

"No," said Barbara, also jumping up. "Not with your nerves, Ann."

But to everyone's astonishment and discomfiture, especially Jeremy's judging by the look of aversion which passed fleetingly across his face, Ann thrust her arm through his and said, "I'm coming with you and no one's stopping me."

"Ah, very well," said Jeremy, and he made a swift exit, presumably to avoid a scene, politely disengaging his arm as he went.

"Dear God," groaned Barbara under her breath, and followed them out.

"I still think we should all go," said Cassandra, but by this time their starter was arriving, and she had no support for the idea.

Sadie came over to Leslie and Bennett's table to take their order. Unlike the writing group who pre-ordered their evening meal at breakfast, the two men made their selection at the mealtime, in the usual way. "If I were you," she said confidentially, "I'd have the mushrooms for starter and the lasagne for mains.

There's plenty already made, and you'll get served quicker. I've got a feeling that things are going to go from bad to worse and you might as well get your dinner down you before we all have to join a search party. That Susan's never late in for a meal and I don't see how she could have let the tide come in and cut her off without noticing it. Something's up, you mark my words." She headed off for the kitchen without checking that her suggested menu choice was to their liking.

"I wonder if Susan changed her mind and went down to see the filming after all," said Leslie, "and something in the village has held her up."

"She certainly set off across the garden in the direction of the cliff," said Bennett. "I saw her from the balcony. I didn't see her return, but I did go inside once or twice during the afternoon, so I can't be certain that she didn't come back."

"She could have fallen asleep in the cove." Leslie lowered his voice. "I don't like to be vulgar, but if she was at it with Jeremy until three o'clock this morning, and the night before, it would be no wonder if she'd nodded off."

Sadie appeared at that moment with the promised mushrooms and, at the sight of a pool of glistening oil, Leslie immediately knew he should have chosen fruit juice again. He raised his hand politely to signal to Sadie who had moved to the next table, when a sound outside caught his attention and he turned towards the window.

He looked out, half expecting to see a gull screeching above the garden, or perhaps the gardener with some sort of high-pitched cutting tool; there was nothing to be seen and yet the sound was getting closer. Everyone was looking out now and there was something sinister about the noise that made Leslie's blood run cold. A moment later, a figure came into view, running up the garden towards the house. It was Ann, and she was screaming and screaming and screaming.

6

Everyone was on their feet and most of the group were on the terrace before Ann reached the house. As they surrounded her, the screaming changed to uncontrollable sobbing, and she was completely incoherent. By this time Barbara, who had been following, reached the group, panting for breath.

"Someone take her in the house and give her some brandy," she gasped. "She's had a terrible shock. I'm afraid you're all in for a shock. Can we go inside?"

Sadie had taken charge of the inconsolable Ann and, casting a meaningful look in Leslie's direction, she led her inside and into the lounge. Everyone else went back into the dining room and gathered round Barbara who had been ushered into a chair by Gloria.

"I don't know how to tell you this," she said in a voice of stony self-control. "I'm afraid there's a body in the sea, and there's no doubt it's her—it's Susan."

A cacophony of questions, cries and exclamations burst forth but, speaking over them all, Barbara explained that as soon as the three of them reached the cliff edge, they had seen the figure, floating face down and about fifty metres out to sea, fully clothed and bobbing about in the waves in a way that left no doubt about her condition. Jeremy had stayed at the cliff and was calling the emergency services.

Val now did her best to take control of the situation. She begged everyone to go through to the lounge and help themselves to whatever drinks they needed but, apart from Ann and Sadie who were already there, and Thelma who obediently hobbled through to join them, everyone surged from the house, across the garden, through the picket gate and towards the clifftop.

As they hurried along, Leslie felt someone clutch his arm and turned to see Gloria beside him, her face unusually pale, despite the heat and exertion.

"That omen's come to pass," she said. "My crystals. Terrible for Susan, of course, but it's poor Valerie I can't help thinking about."

"I was thinking that, too," said Leslie. "I can't believe it; it all seems unreal."

They had reached the clifftop where Jeremy had turned to meet them, but the horrible sight that they were bracing themselves to see was not there.

"I'm afraid," he said in a grave voice, "she disappeared a few minutes ago. Just after Ann and Barbara left, there was a particularly big wave. This is the first time I've taken my eyes off the sea but I'm afraid she hasn't come back up."

"Where did you see her last?" It was a man's voice that no one recognised, and they all turned in surprise to see that Lee, the chef, had joined them.

Jeremy indicated a direction vaguely towards their right, but without any landmarks in the sea it was hard for him to explain.

"I'll go out and see if I can find her," he said.

"But what can you do?" said Jeremy looking concerned. "It takes ages to get round to the steps from here and the sea looks very dangerous to me. We don't want another casualty."

Several others joined in with protests and warnings.

"Rubbish," said Lee confidently. "I was with the lifeguards at Torquay all last summer. It's always worth a try. I've got my motorbike; I can get round to the lane at the top of the path leading down to the steps and be in the sea in five minutes. It's worth a go."

As it was obvious that Lee was determined, Jeremy tried to explain with more accuracy where he had last seen poor Susan's body and the direction in which it was moving, but Lee was anxious to be off and Jeremy had to pursue him up the garden, clutching at his arm, with the last of his directions.

Once Lee had departed, Barbara went back up to the house to join her friend, but everyone else was rooted to the clifftop. Every few moments someone would see something that could be an object in the sea, but each time it was only a trick of the waves. The steps down to the sea, into what the locals called Steps Bay, were not visible from this point, nor the road leading that way, so there was no way of judging Lee's progress, and they looked out to the empty ocean in vain. Leslie, who was not at his best on a clifftop even in normal circumstances, stood close to Bennett and was immeasurably grateful when Bennett linked his arm through his, a gesture as welcome as it was rare. They stood together in silent vigil.

They waited about helplessly for what seemed to Leslie like an hour but was really only minutes, then everything happened all at once. The inshore rescue boat came into view; the coastguard helicopter appeared above them, terrifyingly low and loud, and the police arrived at the hotel. Amid all this noisy confusion someone spotted a figure swimming vigorously out to sea and, although there were some fleeting and desperate hopes that it was Susan, it was confirmed to be Lee when a pair of binoculars was produced by Val who had brought them down with her. A couple of policemen were at the clifftop by now and, shouting above the noise of the helicopter, Val explained the identity of the person in the sea, and they radioed through the message as both the helicopter and lifeboat must have seen the figure too.

Everyone was ushered up to the hotel and they all gathered in the lounge, thankful to be inside and away from the noise and blast of the helicopter and the unhappy, ill-fated place. An ambulance, closely followed by a rapid response vehicle, had also arrived and three redundant paramedics were lurking about in the reception area.

The presence of the police had an inhibiting effect on the gathering. Ann, still supported by Sadie, was pale and silent, and the rest of the party were calm and quiet, speaking only when they had an answer to the various questions posed by the policemen. Gradually, it was established that Susan had admitted to feeling unwell that morning, though no symptoms more specific than 'peaky' and 'off-colour' had been given. She had previously told both Ann and Carol that she was being investigated for a heart complaint, and Leslie was impressed by the way the police officer managed, very politely, to foil Carol's attempt to introduce the subject of her own medical history. Susan had not given many details, but Carol said that she'd mentioned palpitations, and Ann thought she had referred to fainting attacks. Thelma confirmed that Susan had said she was on her way down to Lantern Cove, and there was a general agreement that she had also gone to the cove the previous day to carry out the afternoon's writing exercise. Bennett, it seemed, was the last person to have seen her on her way through the garden, in the direction of the cliff from where, it was surmised, she had walked along the top to the steps, down into Steps Bay and back into Lantern Cove.

It was established that no one had seen Susan since then.

"I didn't see her at all after lunchtime," volunteered Gloria. "Leslie and I went down to the village. They were filming an episode of—"

The officer, very courteously, cut Gloria short. Yes, he knew all about the filming.

"Cassandra, Carol, Dee and Deborah were there too," she went on, and the ladies all murmured assent.

"I didn't see her either," said Barbara. "I went up to my room to read for the afternoon. It was too hot for me outside; the rooms have air conditioning, it's much more comfortable."

Ann and Jeremy had stayed on the terrace, Thelma spent the afternoon in the lounge, Bennett in the coach house, and Val and the staff were working in the hotel. No one had had any reason or inclination to walk down to the clifftop and from there watch Susan collapse on the sand and be washed into the sea, as everyone was now imagining, though not quite putting into words.

The events leading up to Jeremy, Ann and Barbara seeing Susan's fully clothed but lifeless body being tossed about in the sea were described, and the policemen waited patiently while Ann, amid a fresh flood of tears, recalled the tragedy she had witnessed the previous year, an incident the officers appeared to know about. No one had much information about Susan's personal circumstances and none about her next of kin.

"She was divorced and had no children," announced Gloria. "I asked her directly, and that's what she told me. But I got the impression she didn't like talking about it, if you know what

I mean, so I could hardly press the subject. I wondered if it was a sore topic."

The policeman asked if anyone knew if she had a job.

"Oh yes," said Gloria again, adding unapologetically, "I seem to be the nosey one of the group, officer. I asked her if she worked and she said she was a personal finance advisor, self-employed, but that she hadn't worked much recently. She didn't volunteer any more information about that either and I didn't like to sound as though I was prying. Perhaps it was her health that stopped her, though you wouldn't have thought there was a thing wrong with her to look at her."

Leslie had been thinking the same thing; anyone would have taken Susan to be the fittest person in the group. No one else had anything to add to Gloria's knowledge. Val said she had none of Susan's personal details as this was a group booking and she'd taken only a list of the guests' names.

"I won't make that mistake again," she said grimly. "Jeremy has all the delegates' details, but just imagine if something had happened to him as well."

Jeremy, looking rather disconcerted at this suggestion, confirmed that he did have everyone's 'data'. "On the application forms for the course. I'll go now and have a look."

As he went out, the officers stood up too and made a few comments, obviously intended to be reassuring, to the effect that this was still a rescue operation and that things may not be as bad as they seemed. Leslie did not think anyone would really feel reassured by this, but the kindly intention was appreciated.

"I don't think there's anything more any of us can do for the moment, is there?" Val asked, correctly interpreting that the police had finished with them. She turned to the guests. "Well, in that case, I think we should go back through to the dining room, and I'll see what I can do about dinner. We're all very upset, I know, but no one will feel any better if they're fading away with hunger." And in an aside to Gloria, who was standing next to Leslie, she added quietly, "I don't want anyone outside, getting in the way of the search. Or witnessing anything unpleasant if they find... you know."

Gloria took the hint and, gathering up those around her, led the way back into the dining room. Surprisingly, though perhaps because there was nothing else to be done under the circumstances, everyone followed without demur.

Leslie and Bennett dropped back to allow the ladies to pass, and so were still in the lounge when Jeremy returned carrying his open laptop. Bennett went on through to the dining room but Leslie, victim to his insatiable curiosity, perched himself on a chair in an unobtrusive spot near to the door and, quite unnecessarily, re-buckled his sandals.

"Here we are," Jeremy said to the policeman, and read out a Sussex address and a date of birth that, Leslie calculated, indicated Susan was thirty-eight. "But unfortunately, I don't seem to have a next of kin for her. She didn't fill it in on the application and I'm afraid I didn't notice. I didn't expect to need it, of course," he added, defensively.

"You can't give us any clues?" asked the policeman. "Do you know if she had any family? Parents still living? Brothers or sisters?"

Without pausing, Jeremy shook his head. "I don't know any more about her than anyone else on the course," he said, closing the laptop. "But if I do remember anything, I'll certainly let you know."

"Hopefully we'll find something in her belongings to help us," said the officer.

Jeremy disappeared in the direction of his room and Leslie hurried through to Bennett in the dining room and, in a whisper, related the conversation he had overheard.

"I don't believe it," Leslie said. "The man was her lover, for goodness sake, he must know something about her. I can't understand it."

Before Bennett could reply, if he was going to, Val and Sadie came in to clear away half eaten starters and begin over again, with some adjustments to the menu so that everyone could be served quickly.

"As I was saying," said Leslie when they had moved out of earshot, "Jeremy must surely know something about Susan's family; I can't believe he doesn't know if she has or hasn't got living friends or relatives. He doesn't have to disclose his relationship with Susan to the police—if that's what's bothering him—to let them have information that might help them locate her family or friends."

"That is supposing she has any family or friends," said Bennett.

Leslie shook his head gloomily, oppressed by the melancholy idea of a person having no kith or kin, at Jeremy's puzzling response to the police, and by the dreadful drama they found themselves a part of. At the neighbouring table, Barbara sat in grim silence, while Ann gazed tearfully at Jeremy who had edged his chair as far from her as the table would allow. Gloria had joined them, and even she was more subdued than usual. At the other table conversation was more animated, though clearly about the only subject anyone could think about, and appetites seemed undiminished. The meal was accompanied throughout by the sound, and sometimes the sight, of the helicopter searching the sea, and a few personnel from the coastguard and the police could be seen passing up and down the garden. The paramedics were sitting out on the terrace drinking coffee kindly supplied by Val. Lesley commented to Bennett that their presence was surely a formality, or perhaps as a precaution in case of injury to the rescuers, as hopes of finding Susan in a condition to benefit from their ministrations were surely vanishingly small.

After desserts had been cleared away, Jeremy announced that coffee would be in the lounge in half an hour as scheduled. They would use the evening session to 'debrief', though of course attendance was optional and if anyone would prefer not to— At this moment, he ceased to be the centre of his devotees' attention. Those facing the door were the first to see Lee coming in, wrapped in a foil blanket and hair still wet, and their reaction caused the others to turn, and everyone jumped to their feet with cheers and clapping.

They clustered round him, the hero of the moment, and Leslie overheard Val say to Gloria under her breath, "How can I get rid of him after this? I'll be stuck with him all bloody summer, now." After a pause she added, "That's if the hotel's not finished after this disaster."

7

The two men were back in the coach house, having declined an invitation, initiated by Gloria, to join the debriefing session. Leslie paced about, going over the events and all the details which were tormenting him, while Bennett sat in silence, occupied with the half bottle of brandy he had carried over from the bar.

"On the face of it," said Leslie, at last, "it's very simple. Susan went down to the cove to do her writing, as she did yesterday, had a heart attack or something of the sort, and was washed out to sea by the tide and currents. She had a medical condition, and wasn't feeling very well, so that should explain it." He paused and looked at Bennett who, infuriatingly, did not pick up the cue and ask for the caveat to this neat scenario.

Instead, Bennett offered him a small tumbler containing an inch of the golden liquid and said, "Here, drink this before you have a heart attack yourself."

"But I'm convinced there's been some foul play in it," said Leslie, pointedly ignoring the comment and the proffered drink, though making sure he sat down within reach of the glass. "For starters, there's Jeremy's behaviour. Everything suggests that they were in a relationship but keeping it quiet, for whatever reason. There was that strange encounter I accidentally gate-crashed when they first arrived, and it seems that Jeremy visited Susan's room both nights. To say nothing of the gossip about last year's course." Leslie took a slow drink of the brandy, and still Bennett made no comment.

"Susan and Jeremy were secret lovers," Leslie reiterated. "Nothing out of the ordinary in that. But it's all wrong now." He stood up, walked out to the balcony, stared out towards the sea where the helicopter had been joined by a second one in the search, and came back in again. "If Jeremy was her lover, you'd expect him to be stunned, distraught, and utterly pole-axed by this. Even if he was trying to keep up the secrecy, even as the leader of the group. His reaction is all wrong."

"Lovers aren't always in love with each other," observed Bennett.

"Yes, I know that," said Leslie impatiently, "but I think that Jeremy was. Well, I don't know if he was actually in love with Susan, but I'm certain he had feelings for her of some sort: strong ones. You must have seen Jeremy looking at Susan furtively; he does it all the time, in a way that he never does to anyone else. But maybe I've got it wrong." Leslie took another sip of the brandy and thought for a while. "Perhaps it was just lust, and perhaps lust can make you fixated with someone when they are alive but not unduly upset when they suddenly die. Is that possible? But how do you account for Jeremy not divulging any information about Susan to the police? Can it be possible to have a relationship with someone, however superficial, and really to know nothing about them at all?" He sat back down again and held his glass out to Bennett for a top up. "And I've just remembered something else. Didn't I say that Jeremy's manner was odd when he came into the dining room? I think he already knew something was amiss."

"Supposing there is incongruity in Jeremy's behaviour," said Bennett as he replenished both their glasses. "That doesn't inevitably mean he's involved in foul play. As you've already pointed out, there could be other explanations for all those things."

"Maybe, but those aren't the only things that are wrong." Leslie took another drink of the brandy as he tried to unknot the tangled string of events. "There's the chap we call the sailor as well; I haven't got to him yet. There was no mistaking that there was a problem between him and Susan. The meeting in the bar upset her, and she doesn't look like a woman who's easily upset. Then later that evening I overheard her more or less accusing him of pestering her; that's what it sounded like."

"You didn't actually see that it was the sailor she was talking to at that point, did you?"

"I suppose not," admitted Leslie, "but who else could it have been? And, goodness, I've just remembered what else she said to him: 'See you Wednesday'. No, that's wrong. Her words were 'on

Wednesday, then'. That could mean she was planning to see him again on Wednesday, and that's today. What if he met her in the cove?" Leslie started pacing about again with fresh anxiety. "I think I ought to go and tell the police. She might have been murdered."

"Who are you planning to accuse?" asked Bennett. "Jeremy or the sailor? Or were they in league together?"

"Laugh at me if you like," said Leslie, crossly. "I'm convinced there's something amiss, but it's just like you to sit there saying nothing until you can find something amusing to come out with."

"I'm not laughing at you," said Bennett with irritating detachment. "I'm only suggesting you think it through before speaking to the police."

"That's exactly what I'm trying to do—think it through," said Leslie, exasperated. "I wish you'd be more helpful. A poor woman's dead, no one saw it happen, and some odd, if not downright suspicious, things happened in the preceding days. I can't just ignore it and say nothing."

Bennett swilled round his tumbler thoughtfully without replying. Leslie was recalling previous occasions when he had reported things to the police; he always, for some reason, ended up saying something foolish. He resented being reminded of it now, even if that had not been Bennett's intention.

"There's not much I can do at this time of night," he said grumpily. "I'll decide in the morning. Perhaps by then they'll have found the poor woman's body, and then we might get a clue about what really happened to her. I wish Ridgeway was around; I could speak to him about it, however stupid it sounds."

But Detective Chief Inspector Charles Ridgeway was miles away across the Atlantic taking a holiday with his family in Canada. A previous escapade had brought the men together, and a passion for chess, not to mention a fondness for Leslie's baking, had cemented a friendship between them all. Alemouth was within Ridgeway's jurisdiction and Leslie suddenly felt irrationally annoyed with the man for taking a vacation when they needed his help.

At this moment, an unusually restrained 'Hello there,' from below the balcony, announced Gloria's presence, inviting them to come across to the lounge where drinks were being served 'on the house'. Bennett would not be persuaded, but Leslie was glad of something to do and wandered across with Gloria, whose usual ebullience was, not surprisingly, somewhat subdued.

As they went into the lounge it was obvious that the tragedy had brought everyone together, as misfortune does. Sitting among Jeremy and the delegates were Sadie, Lee and Lauren, while Val was on her feet, serving the drinks. Ann was speaking as they entered and it sounded, from the sympathetic responses, as though she had been reliving the experience of discovering Susan's body.

"I was the only one who knew Susan from last year. Apart from Jeremy," she added, looking longingly at him across the room. Jeremy was seated as far away from her as was possible and made no response to this reference to himself. "I've been racking my brain to see if I could remember anything Susan said then that might help trace any friends or relatives. Then I suddenly realised we didn't tell the police about that friend she was with last year; Jean, she was called. What a pity Susan didn't have a friend with her today..."

"But Susan said the woman had moved away and she'd lost touch with her," interrupted Barbara before Ann could pursue this useless speculation.

"Didn't the police find anything in her room to identify her relatives?" asked Cassandra.

"I'm afraid not," said Val. "She must have taken her phone with her down to the cove, and there wasn't anything like bank cards or her driving licence or letters in her belongings. They were looking for her house keys, but they couldn't find those, either. I guess they were all in that big bag she carried about."

She refilled glasses and coffee cups, obstinately refusing Sadie's help. Leslie noted that Lauren didn't offer any assistance and appeared to be enjoying the novelty of being waited on by her employer.

"I've just remembered something about Susan," said Cassandra. "She told me she was up at Cambridge, and rowed for them, too. But I can't see how that would help."

Since no one knew which college Susan was at, or which years, except that it must have been about twenty years ago, it was agreed that it probably wasn't much use, and the conversation broke up into smaller groups.

Having just imbibed a quantity of brandy, Leslie confined himself to coffee and he sat back to observe the reactions of the assembled company. Jeremy was the model of a concerned and caring group leader, although there was a look in his eyes and a restlessness that convinced Leslie he was ill at ease. Although this was hardly unexpected, his manner reinforced again Leslie's view that even if he was troubled, he was not behaving like a bereaved lover. In fact, now that the initial shock was wearing off, no one looked particularly upset, but perhaps that was not surprising given how little any of them had been acquainted with Susan, other than Jeremy. Ann was easily the most distressed person in the room, but this seemed to be from the horror of seeing the body, and from reliving the previous year's tragedy, rather than sorrow at Susan's demise.

Beside her on the settee was Sadie who, having failed to persuade Val to let her help serve drinks, had thrown herself into the role of chief comforter. On the other side of Ann, seated in a high-backed armchair, Barbara's reaction was quite different. She was silent, her face masked with an inscrutable expression. The two sisters had bagged the chairs either side of Jeremy and were making the most of his company, while Lee had moved on from the story of today's adventures to captivate Cassandra, Thelma, Carol and Lauren with his exploits as a lifeguard in Torquay the previous year.

Gloria, who had been giving Val a hand with the drinks, now came and sat beside Leslie. "I'll let Valerie get on with it," she said under her breath. "I know she wants to keep busy at the moment."

Leslie made a suitably sympathetic response and Gloria continued, still speaking more quietly than usual. "I wish there was some hope of finding Susan alive, but you can see that everyone's resigned to the worst." She looked across at Jeremy, in conversation with the sisters, and then whispered, "I'm not sure there was anything going on between Susan and Jeremy after all, are you? I'd thought that there was, and they were keeping it secret. After you mentioned that you saw them talking in the garden on the first day, I did notice him looking at her. But now he doesn't seem particularly upset."

"I know what you mean," agreed Leslie evasively. "But no one does, do they? How melancholy: no one knows a thing about her and, although the business has been upsetting in a general kind of way, no one seems very sad at her loss."

"Well, she was such a cold fish," Gloria replied. She picked up her glass and looked across at Jeremy again. "I'm blessed if I can understand what, if anything, was going on. Half of me thinks that there was something between them and half thinks there wasn't."

It was very tempting to confide what he knew about Susan and Jeremy—the full details of that encounter on the first day, their nocturnal rendezvous, and all his concerns—but Leslie resisted. His suspicions about Susan's death were mere conjecture. Gloria would undoubtedly receive the information with gratifying interest, but really it would amount to little more than the cheap gossip he complained about in the village.

"Unfortunately, it looks as though it's all history now, anyway," replied Leslie, "sadly, for the poor lady."

"Yes, of course," sighed Gloria, "but isn't it so unexpected!" She looked around the room at her creative writing colleagues. "Susan was the last one you'd expect to drop dead like that, wasn't she? You'd have thought she was the healthiest person in the world."

"I thought the same," agreed Leslie, "but it's often the most unexpected people who succumb." He was thinking now of Bennett's heart attack earlier in the year. If Bennett, who didn't carry an ounce of fat and was so imperturbable, could be struck down, he knew that it could happen to anyone.

Leslie was suddenly seized by the heart-lurching panic that used to ambush him hourly in the weeks after Bennett's illness, when he'd lived under the perpetual terror that Bennett would have a second, and fatal, heart attack the minute he was left on his own. It was a fear that had denied Leslie a second's peace of mind and had robbed him of sleep for weeks. It had only been gradually relinquished and it was still apt to recur with little prompting, as now. Forgetting Susan, Jeremy and everything else, Leslie was suddenly impatient to get back to the coach house and, without worrying about being impolite, he left his coffee and said goodnight.

As he hurried across the terrace, Leslie was dismayed to see the coach house in pitch darkness, although dusk was falling. By the time he had ascended the stairs and fumbled with the door, he was gripped by a terrible sense of dread. He flung open the door into the unlit and empty sitting room, shouting, "Bennett, Bennett!" in panic. There was no reply. The bedroom was likewise in silence and darkness, and he hastily switched on the light, calling out again. The room was empty, but he moved slowly round to look behind the other side of the bed, his heart thundering.

The shower room door opened, and Bennett appeared, dripping wet and holding a towel. "What's to do?" he said, head cocked on one side.

"Oh, Bennett, I thought you were dead," exclaimed Leslie and then added, with unreasonable irritation, "What do you mean by leaving all the lights off and frightening me like that?"

"I've been sitting out on the balcony," said Bennett, simply. "Then I came in and had a shower. It does seem to be going dark," he conceded, and stepped back into the shower room, shutting the door.

Leslie, overwhelmed by the events of the day, stomped out into the sitting room. He threw himself on the sofa, wishing that just for once Bennett would behave like a normal person and say that he was sorry for worrying him, even though he was not at fault. His nonchalance was so provoking, and Leslie felt his annoyance escalating. At home on occasions like this, there was the kitchen to escape to and a hundred and one things to distract himself with, but here on holiday there was no hiding place.

In a state of agitation, he got up and went out onto the balcony, though with little hope that the oppressive evening air would lift his mood. However, no sooner had he slid the balcony door shut behind him and lowered himself moodily into the wicker chair, than something caught his attention and distracted him entirely from his woes. He saw a light go on in Jeremy's room and saw the man's silhouette at the window as he closed the curtains. A moment later, Jeremy came out of his door and into the small, enclosed courtyard outside his suite. It was not yet completely dark, and he was clearly visible to Leslie, even without the assistance of a security light. Keeping close to the house where he could be overlooked by no one except Leslie on his balcony, he paced up and down restlessly, repeatedly checking his phone. After a few minutes he looked at his phone again, sat down quickly and bent over the device as if sending a message. That done, he went back inside, leaving Leslie with the impression reinforced of a man who was frantically worried but not stricken with grief.

***

They had all woken to the sound of the helicopter the next morning, but it did not stay for long, although the police officer who arrived during breakfast assured them that the search was continuing. He made a little speech to them all, reminding them to try to remember anything that could help them identify any family or friends of Susan, and hinting that good news was less likely with the passing of time. This was hardly necessary as, although Ann gave a little squeal of dismay in response to his words, everyone knew that the best they could expect now was for a body to be found.

It was the final full day of the creative writing course and Jeremy announced that he had changed the itinerary; the whole morning was to be group work on the theme of 'Language as our anchor in the storms of life'. Bennett raised an eyebrow.

Leslie observed with distaste Jeremy's smooth, unctuous manner and the rapt expressions of his devotees and, turning to Bennett, hissed, "What a charlatan. Everything about him is phoney. All that concern he's expressing is just words; I don't believe he cares about anyone but himself. Before this happened, I just thought him rather nauseating. But, in the light of Susan's death, he now strikes me as a sinister and dangerous man."

There was no chance for Bennett to respond, if he had been going to, as Val, who was more visible than usual this morning, came to offer more tea and coffee and toast. By the time she returned to their table with the fresh drinks, the delegates had all left and she said, "I've told Jeremy he's to keep them all indoors today. I don't want them anywhere near the search, and I don't want any of them talking to reporters. We haven't had the press here yet but it's only a matter of time and I haven't forgotten what it was like having them crawling all over the place last year."

"We won't speak to anyone about it, I promise," said Leslie earnestly.

"I know you won't," said Val, gathering up the side plates and cutlery into a neat pile. "It wasn't a hint to you. But I can't risk it with that lot. Goodness knows if we'll survive this disaster, but I'm going to do my best to limit the damage. What else can I do?"

Leslie muttered a sympathetic response, but Val was in full flow.

"Fortunately, we've got the afternoon tea today. At first when the calamity happened, I was annoyed that I'd bothered organising it; everyone's forgotten all about Lauren nosing around in Cassandra's things. There's nothing like a tragic death for overshadowing everything else. But now I can see it's the perfect opportunity to keep everyone in the house for the afternoon, and I'm hoping I can have a bit of influence on them so that the hotel comes out of this in a positive light. You can't believe how influential reviews are and, in a small hotel like this, they can make or break you."

"No one can blame you for Susan's death, and you've done everything you possibly could to support everyone," said Leslie. "I'm sure it will be fine."

"I just hope you're right. I must sound awful even thinking about the hotel at a terrible time like this, but it's my livelihood, and if my business goes under it won't bring Susan back. The poor woman has gone, we all know that, and I don't want to be a victim of the tragedy too. I got away with it last year—in fact trade was brisker than ever afterwards, there are so many morbid people about—but I don't dare to think what effect a second death connected with the hotel will have if it gets out."

Bennett looked up. "You could always change the name of the establishment to something catchy like Death-top Lodge," he suggested, "and run guided walks from Lethal Cliff to Corpse Cove."

Leslie put his face in his hands, but Val Marsden burst into laughter. "Gloria's always saying what a wicked sense of humour you have," she said. "And it's not as though any of us knew the poor dead woman." With that, she gathered up a few more items from a neighbouring table and made her way back to the kitchen, still smiling to herself.

As the men stood up to leave, one of the policemen passed by the window outside and Leslie breathed out a long, involuntary sigh. Bennett raised an enquiring eyebrow.

"I won't be easy until I've voiced my concerns about Susan," said Leslie gloomily, "even though I've got nothing to report except some unrelated incidents concerning what seem to be unconnected people. I know I'll end up feeling a complete idiot, but I suppose it has to be done."

He'd woken early that morning fretting about the whole business and struggling to compose a coherent account of his concerns. There was the possibility that the sailor had met Susan in the cove and killed her, though in the cold light of day this seemed more melodramatic than ever. But Leslie's instincts against Jeremy were stronger, even though they seemed to have even less logical foundation. It was almost certain that Jeremy could have had no direct part in Susan's death for, assuming Ann was to be believed, he had been up at the hotel all the afternoon of the tragedy. And everything else Leslie had observed might be explained by them being secret lovers, which was quite obviously no crime; everything that is except for Jeremy's behaviour since Susan's death. In the absence of any proper evidence, Leslie could hardly expect the police to take his suspicions seriously.

It was another glorious day, hot but not yet oppressive, and as they made their way out onto the sunny terrace, Leslie saw the policeman sitting alone at one of the outdoor tables, looking out towards that ill-fated sea.

"I'm going to have a word before I change my mind," Leslie said to Bennett. "At least he's on his own and I can speak to him informally."

"An opportunity has no tail," responded Bennett blandly and continued across the garden to the coach house.

Leslie walked across to join the officer, with a growing conviction that he was about to make a monumental fool of himself. However, he was cordially invited by the officer to sit down beside him and explain whatever it was that was concerning him.

"I'm probably making something out of nothing," said Leslie, "but I was wondering if Susan's death is all it seems. I know you haven't found her body yet, at least I presume not; we're all expecting the worst, of course."

Leslie ground to a halt and the policeman, exhibiting laudable patience, asked Leslie for his name, introduced himself as Sergeant Payne, and then said kindly, "What is it that's worrying you, sir?"

"There are two people I think might be a bit... fishy. They said odd things, and their behaviour to Susan was, I thought, suspicious. But I may be mistaken of course, and I don't want to make any accusations. I just thought I'd better mention it. Just in case."

"If you have any information that might be helpful, I'd be obliged if you'd tell me. And don't worry, we're quite capable of judging what to do with the information you give us."

It seemed that the officer was doing his best to be pleasant, but Leslie's past experiences made it impossible for him not to feel that he was being patronised.

"First there's the sailor," Leslie said.

"The sailor?"

"Yes," he went on courageously, and started to describe the meeting in the bar and the words he overheard from the balcony, though admitting he could not see the speakers at the time.

Leslie was getting into the swing of his narrative at last when Gloria unexpectedly appeared, carrying a laden tray. She had approached with surprising stealth from behind and she was at Leslie's elbow before either of them was aware of her presence.

Leslie knew that Gloria had abandoned the writing group for the day to give Val moral support, but he had not expected her to appear at that moment.

"I was bringing out a pot of tea for the officer here," she said, "and then I saw you talking to him, so I went back and got a mug for you, too. I took the liberty of adding one for myself, but I think perhaps you're having a private conversation."

By this time Gloria had placed the teapot and all three mugs on the table, making it awkward to send her away, though Leslie would far rather have spoken to the policeman alone.

"There's no need to go, but please don't repeat a word of it to anyone," said Leslie, making a lily-livered compromise. "If that's all right with the sergeant, of course."

The sergeant began to make a non-committal gesture and before he could object, if he was going to, Gloria said brightly, "Mum's the word! Talking of which, I'll be mother and pour the tea. I'm afraid I couldn't help overhearing you were talking about that obnoxious sailor chap."

With some difficulty Leslie completed the tale and, before Sergeant Payne had a chance to ask any questions Gloria said, "I told Leslie from the start he was a bad lot. I'm not a bit surprised if he did away with her. I knew it from my crystals, you see."

"Your crystals?" The sergeant looked worried.

"Oh yes, the stones told me clearly. Just after Leslie and I had seen that man, I drew out a black diamond and that's a bad omen."

"I do think I would have been concerned about him without the crystals," said Leslie unhappily. He had not the courage to dismiss Gloria's beliefs to her face but was very anxious to distance himself from them in the presence of this policeman.

"Oh, I know that," said Gloria, her manner cheerful. Turning to Sergeant Payne she added, "Leslie is wonderful at investigating. Did you know he solved a murder? Only a couple of months ago and quite locally, in Dartonleigh. You must have heard about it." Gloria prattled on, giving a lively account of the incident, with Leslie interrupting whenever he could to insist she was exaggerating his role, and Gloria insisting with even greater vehemence that she was not.

The policeman's face registered nothing but polite interest, but Leslie groaned inwardly as he imagined Sergeant Payne entertaining his colleagues back at the station later with his encounter at Alemouth Lodge with Sherlock Holmes and Marie Castello.

Gloria eventually drew breath, and the policeman could speak. Without referring to anything that Gloria had said, he turned to Leslie. "You said there were two people you were concerned about. You've told me about the man you call the sailor. How about the second person?"

Leslie had been hoping that Sergeant Payne would have forgotten this as, wishing he'd never begun the conversation, he was hoping to wind it up as quickly as possible and melt away. What he had to say about Jeremy was already weak enough, even if the interview had not deteriorated into this farce. And, as he had never mentioned any of his negative concerns about Jeremy to Gloria, her reaction to this revelation was impossible to predict. However, there was nothing for it but to go on. "I think that Jeremy and Susan were in a relationship," he said, and described the rumours from the previous year he had heard, the encounter he had seen on the first day, how he had witnessed Jeremy caught in the act of leaving Susan's room in the night, and the way in which Jeremy's eyes were forever on her.

Sergeant Payne listened without comment or reaction, but Gloria, leaning forward in avid attention, whispered, "Oh, I say!" from time to time.

"The only reason I mention it," continued Leslie, "is because Jeremy's reaction doesn't seem to square with him being her lover. I'm not saying he doesn't seem upset, because in some ways he does. But it's the wrong kind of upset. And then I couldn't help overhearing him say he didn't know anything more about Susan than anyone else. If they were in a relationship, that seems, well, unlikely to say the least. I think he's completely phoney."

"You dark horse, Leslie," said Gloria wagging her finger at him. "Do you know, Sergeant Payne, he's never breathed a word of this, and you can be sure I'll say nothing about it, not a hint. Not even to Valerie. I wouldn't burden her, in any case."

"I think that would be very wise, madam," said Sergeant Payne. "It would be most unfortunate if any nasty rumours went around while we are still searching for the poor lady."

The sound of voices heralded the arrival of two more policemen and one of the coastguard team Leslie recognised from the previous day.

"If there's nothing more, you must excuse me now," said the officer rising. To Leslie he said, "Thank you for that information, sir; you can leave it with me now and, as I just said, it would be best to keep it to yourself for the moment. We know where to find you if we need further information, and of course if anything else relevant should come up, you can let us know. This is the number to call." He gave a card to Leslie, and he went across to join his colleagues, leaving Leslie to wonder whether he could possibly have been taken seriously.

"I thought it was just Bennett who was like a clam," said Gloria, and remonstrated with him, in perfect good humour, for his secrecy. "Now it's my turn to give you some news. They found Susan's bag down on the rocks. It was that big straw bag she used to carry her writing things about in. That policeman we were just talking to came up earlier and asked Val to identify it. Val told me. Apparently, there was nothing much in it, just some tissues and suntan lotion and writing things, but no phone or anything personal. They're still trying to find out who her next of kin is."

Gloria stopped speaking suddenly. She was looking towards the conservatory behind Leslie's back, her eyes bulging. Without thinking, Leslie swivelled round, in time to see Jeremy moving away from the window.

"Oh, I say, did you see that?" said Gloria. "If looks could kill! I see what you mean about him. He didn't like us talking to the police, did he?"

"Had he been there long? Do you think he saw us talking to the sergeant?" Leslie asked.

"I only just noticed him, but I think he must have. Why else the murderous look?"

"But he can't have known what we were saying," said Leslie. "He can't possibly have heard anything."

"Exactly!" exclaimed Gloria. "No one else would have thought anything of seeing us chatting to a policeman, would they? That look he gave us must mean something; the sign of a bad conscience, I'll be bound. I think it's a jolly good thing he did see us; it's given us more evidence of his guilt."

"I'm not sure it counts as evidence," said Leslie, who was quite certain it did not.

"It is to me," said Gloria confidently, and she loaded the empty mugs onto the tray.

As she disappeared back into the house, Leslie wondered if Jeremy's hostile expression was a figment of Gloria's fevered imagination. If not, what did it really mean?

8

The rest of the morning passed without incident and Leslie saw no more of Jeremy or the writing group. The two men took lunch on their balcony and then Leslie went for a stroll, out from the front of the hotel this time, having no desire to venture anywhere near the clifftop. There was a large park opposite which he had only explored once, when they first arrived. Sheltered from the sea breeze, it was a complete suntrap and he had not stayed for long.

Forgetting quite how hot it had been on his previous visit, Leslie wandered there now, and soon found himself in the wonderfully scented rose garden. He went from bush to bush, dipping his nose into the flowers like a bee sampling nectar, but the heat soon defeated him again. An avenue of trees afforded some shade, but it was still too hot to linger and he made his way to the shelter of a square-towered church which backed onto the park. Finding its wooden panelled door unlocked, he went inside and sat down in the welcome coolness.

It was a large, dimly lit church, with a high vaulted ceiling and lots of dark wood, built and furnished in a day when people liked their religion to be a serious business. Resting in a rather uncomfortable pew, Leslie could not rid his mind of the perplexing events of the past few days. Now that he had told his tale to Sergeant Payne, it was no longer his problem, or so he told himself repeatedly as he tried to banish the stubbornly preoccupying thoughts. To distract himself, he peered in the dimness at a leaflet about the church which he had picked up on his way in. It had rather small print, and it was densely packed with information about the history and architecture of the building. It failed to hold his attention and, after struggling with the detailed descriptions of the carved rood screen, the rare sandstone font, and a nineteenth century replacement stained glass window depicting the activities of St Peter, after whom the church was named, he gave it up.

Leslie got to his feet and dutifully viewed the rood screen, font, and window in turn, then wandered across to the bell tower, the neatly stashed bell ropes suggesting it was still in use. A carved oak plaque on the wall listed those lost in the First World War, and another next to it added those who perished some two decades later, the same surnames recurring in both lists. They were headed by a solemn inscription from John's gospel, chapter fifteen. Glancing down he noticed, with disquiet, that he was standing on a slab proclaiming the resting place of some great man of the past, his name and lifespan all but obliterated by the feet of subsequent generations. This was a melancholy place to be sure.

He moved along the aisle and looked into the Lady Chapel, surprised to find it in a completely contrasting, modern style. A contemporary stained glass window, with large geometric panes of yellow and gold, flooded the interior with brightness, and the altar cloth and kneelers in the same colours gave the place a welcome cheerfulness. Leslie was not usually a fan of modern church decoration, but there was no doubt that in his present mood it was preferable to the sombre ambience of the main building.

He sat down on one of the padded chairs just inside the chapel entrance and put his mind to how he was to occupy himself for the whole week ahead once Gloria had gone home. Could Bennett possibly be persuaded to take the bus with him to one of the neighbouring resorts, or go on one of the advertised boat trips, or even simply take a walk around this park? He was not optimistic and, if he hadn't known how deeply offended both Val and Gloria would be, for two pins he would have packed his case and gone home the next day.

A couple of flames flickered from tealights on the votive candle stand, and Leslie gazed at them, half mesmerised by their gentle shimmering. He wasn't much given to prayer these days, but he remembered his desperate pleas when Bennett had been so ill and, seized by the numinous atmosphere, he sent out some belated thanks into the unknown, and added on a petition about his current anxieties for good measure.

The church clock struck the hour dolefully—three o'clock—bringing Leslie back to the present. Feeling simultaneously gullible and restored, he made his way towards the church porch, replacing the uninspiring leaflet on the way and making what he hoped was a generous donation. The visitors' book caught his eye and he glanced into it, finding recent entries from Dee, Deborah, Cassandra, Ann and Carol. It was perfectly obvious that they were the delegates, if for no other reason than that they seemed to have tried outdoing each other in the flamboyance of their praise for the church. Its 'sublime, ethereal coolness' and its 'shelter from thou burning sun with golden beam' were cited, qualities which had also drawn Leslie inside, though he would not have put it quite like that.

Even Lee and Lauren seemed to have taken refuge within; this time, an ambiguous and scurrilous observation about the organ confirmed their identities. There was nothing from Barbara, who had probably accompanied Ann but deigned to leave any comments, or poor Thelma who could barely make it as far as the hotel terrace. Neither was there any sign that Susan or Jeremy had ever been there. Susan: she seemed to have left no trace of herself anywhere. How on earth had she come about her death? And had Jeremy really had a hand in it? Leslie sighed; he could not go ten minutes without being haunted by the tragedy. In sudden need of Bennett's society and a cup of tea, he returned to the hotel.

***

Dinnertime came, and the two men were surprised to find themselves alone, until they discovered that owing to the addition of the afternoon tea into the writing group itinerary, they were skipping dinner. Instead, there was to be a quiet supper and social in the lounge later, replacing the planned games night. No one felt like games at such a time.

Bennett made a comment on the peacefulness resulting from the alteration but Leslie, to his own surprise, rather missed the group, and their absence reinforced his misgivings about the week ahead. However, he supposed more guests would arrive, and that would furnish some interest at mealtimes at least. The dinner was the best they had been served by far. They both opted for the lemon sole with asparagus which, they discovered, had been cooked by Sadie who was more than able to cater for just the two of them.

"She put on a wonderful afternoon tea and has stayed on to do the dinner and supper," said Val as she cleared away their plates. "Lee and Lauren asked for a half day's holiday to recover from what they had the nerve to describe as stress. Cheeky, that's what I call them. Lee has been strutting about like cock-of-the-walk after his bit of a swim in the sea, and how can the tragedy have possibly affected Lauren? Still, I let them go off as Sadie is available, and I knew we'd get on better without them for the rest of the day."

A long evening stretched ahead and nagging in Leslie's mind was a notion that Lantern Cove ought to be searched for clues to the crime, supposing that a crime had been committed. He had no confidence that Sergeant Payne had taken his concerns seriously enough to instigate a search for evidence, and he could hardly blame him when he thought about it, especially with Gloria's bizarre contributions to the conversation. True, the police had found Susan's bag, but it could hardly have been missed. He mentioned his thoughts tentatively to Bennett, unsure as always what response he would get.

When Bennett, looking up from his laptop, said, "Well, don't break your neck on the steps," he took this as approval of the scheme to go and have a look around the cove.

Leslie set off through the hotel gardens and, in the oppressive heat which had now built up, he instinctively made for the shelter of a small clump of trees at the foot of the grounds to snatch a few moments of shade on his walk. There were only half a dozen or so trees, hardly enough to qualify as a copse, but he was within its cover before he noticed someone else already there. The person was propped against the trunk of a tall birch, and appeared to be absorbed in sending a phone message. There was nothing at all strange about this—it was natural for someone strolling outside to take cover from the sun as Leslie himself had done, even more so to see a phone screen out of the sun's glare. Moreover, if the wireless network had gone down in the hotel again, this would be the nearest place to get a signal.

But Leslie saw at once it was Jeremy, the last person he wanted to encounter at that moment. There was something in the man's present manner that, to Leslie's excited imagination, looked furtive and put him even more on his guard. Moreover, he had no intention of searching the cove while Jeremy was on the clifftop, so he turned back quickly. Stepping hastily aside to get out of view, he collided with a tall metal feature which was part of the sculpture trail. This alone made enough noise to draw attention to himself but, catching his toe on the base of the structure, Leslie went crashing to the ground.

"You!" was the exclamation Leslie heard as he fell, and even as he lay, momentarily stunned by the shock of falling, he thought he had never heard so much venom put into a single word. Jeremy recovered himself quickly, and said in a voice now oozing with concern, "Are you all right? Can you get up?" But as he spoke, he stayed at a distance, making no move to help.

Indignation replaced the humiliation which Leslie felt from finding himself in this undignified position. Luckily, he'd fallen away from his injured shoulder, and he was able to struggle, unaided, to his feet. Jeremy launched into an earnest explanation for his own presence among the trees which, he said, was occasioned by the Wi-Fi having failed again and some urgent messages in connection with his business that needed attention. This was not a holiday for him, after all, and work had to continue even though he was away from home. The needlessness of this unsolicited explanation struck Leslie forcibly and caused him to wonder what Jeremy was really doing there if he felt the need to make such a robust account of himself.

"I was about to make tracks back up to the hotel, in any case," Jeremy continued smoothly as Leslie brushed himself down. Leslie turned to walk back with him; even with Jeremy gone he was in no mood now for tackling the steps down to the cove. Jeremy talked on. "We're having a supper and social and, if everyone is in agreement, I think we will have a final silent gathering on the cliff." He waved his hand in the direction they had just come from. "To pay our respects. Closure, you know. You and... er... um, are very welcome to join us."

Mumbling something incoherent, Leslie parted from the odious man as soon as he could and hurried back towards his rooms, only to be intercepted by Gloria emerging from the coach house door.

"Did you find anything? Any clues?" she hissed in a loud whisper. "I came to invite you both to the supper and social, but Bennett told me where you'd gone."

As soon as Leslie had related the mishap that had befallen him, Gloria said, "Oh, I say, you poor thing. But let's go down to the cove now. Jeremy's safely back at the hotel, and what if he did see us in the cove, anyway? There's nothing he can do about it. It's ages until the social starts and if I'm late they'll just think I'm helping Valerie. We'll be back long before the vigil. Your mind won't be at rest until you've been down to Lantern, you know it won't."

It was the truth of Gloria's last sentence that forced Leslie to turn and make his way back towards the cliff, though insisting they walked unobtrusively along the edge of the grounds and past the back of the outbuilding.

"It's funny that you saw Susan and Jeremy down by this barn," said Gloria, indicating the building. "Only, last year, when the writing course was on, Valerie discovered that someone had been in here. It's used for general storage, and she doesn't usually bother to lock it, but when she came down here for something, she found that things had been disturbed. Nothing was missing, and it was just at the time rumours were circulating about Susan and Jeremy, and she wondered if it had been them." Gloria's crimson face flushed even darker as she related this. "She's locked it while they're here this year," she continued. "Valerie's no prude and she knows you can't stop people from carrying on, but she certainly didn't want any of her staff to walk in on anything."

Leslie made a noncommittal reply. He was recalling that first encounter he had had with Jeremy and Susan; presumably, Jeremy had not realised at the time the barn was locked. Susan's refusal then had been very definite. If Jeremy had not had an alibi for the entire afternoon of Susan's death, it might easily be believed he had pursued her to the cove and then murdered her in a fit of frustrated rage at her rejection. But this simply did not fit the facts. If Jeremy was involved in her death, it must have been in some indirect and premeditated fashion, not an impassioned outburst.

Leslie was recalled to the present by Gloria loudly exclaiming about the heat. His anxiety not to be seen by Jeremy was renewed, though there was no logical reason why he should be so concerned about being seen taking a walk to the cove with Gloria. He felt as though he was engaged in some nefarious activity, and the perspiration that trickled down his forehead was only partly explained by the raging heat of the evening. Gloria had produced her brightly coloured oriental fan once more and wafted it about, doing nothing to conceal their presence. To Leslie's fevered mind, she might as well have sent up a flare.

This was the first time Leslie had walked along the clifftop in this direction as far as the steps. It was a meandering piece of coastline. Fortunately, the path was set well back from the edge, but it was very hot and dusty, and Leslie felt as though they would never arrive. However, at last they drew near, and he could see there was a long hedge-lined path to the right, where the public coast path, which had turned inland at the opposite boundary of the hotel, rejoined the cliff. The clifftop track they were walking along was accessible only from the hotel. "Is that where Lee would have come from when he did his heroics?" he asked.

"Oh yes, the path goes up to a cul-de-sac that comes off the main road. I expect he left his motorbike there and ran down the path."

They wrestled with a gate that was stiff with infrequent use and, from the public footpath side, bore stern warning signs: 'No Entry' and 'No through route along coast path'. They took a few more paces to the top of the steps which led down the cliff and found a strip of blue-striped police no entry tape. Leslie experienced an unexpected sense of relief but Gloria, seizing the tape confidently and wafting it up and down, said, "Look, we can easily get under this, it's very loose." And to Leslie's protests she replied that it was surely left over from when the police and coastguard were actively searching the area.

"They'd never remember to come back and remove the tape; not in an out-of-the-way place like this. In any case, who's going to see us now, in the evening? And even if they did, what could they do? They're not going to shoot us on sight, are they?"

Gloria's arguments did nothing at all to assuage Leslie's concerns and when he saw the gradient of the steps, his phobia paralysed him.

Gloria, who was aware of Leslie's fear of heights, pressed on, exuding confidence. "Oh, do let's go down. It's as safe as anything, especially in this dry weather," she said, swooping her majestic frame under the tape. "Let me go in front and you won't be able to see how steep it is. I've done this dozens of times, so I know which the loose and narrow steps are and where you need to hold on. I'll give you a shout when you need to be extra careful."

Far from reassured by these loosely disguised warnings, but unable to oppose the force that was Gloria, Leslie found himself following her down, treading with extreme caution. Gloria talked without ceasing until, a few metres above the beach, the steps curved round towards the shore. Abruptly and without warning she stopped both walking and talking, and Leslie nearly collided with her ample back and very nearly lost his footing. He had no time to protest though as he immediately saw the reason for Gloria's sudden halt. There on the shore, looking up at them from the pebbly sand, was Sergeant Payne.

The policeman's posture was still and his expression inscrutable, and after a short pause that felt like a lifetime to Leslie, he walked to the foot of the steps to meet them. "Good evening, madam, sir," he said.

"Oh, officer, it's my fault," cut in Gloria, with a winsome laugh. "I said to Leslie that I bet the cove was open now, and that the tape had just been forgotten. We really didn't mean any harm."

"No, no, madam," said Payne in even tones. "I assure you we know how to clear up after ourselves down in these parts."

Leslie found his voice. "I'm terribly sorry," he said. "We shouldn't have come down. I do apologise."

"It's all right, sir. I hope this will reassure you that we take the things the public tell us seriously." The policeman's expression softened, and he gave Leslie a smile. "I know you're worried and if it's of any help to you, we had a team down here looking about as soon as we could after the lady was reported missing, and I had them back again after you reported your concerns. And once the tide would let me this evening, I came back to have a last look around. Come and have a see for yourself."

They walked down the final few steps and joined Sergeant Payne on the beach. The officer indicated the rocky cliffside either side of the steps, full of crevices and little caves.

"We've had our torches in all those, and I've been over the spit." He pointed at the jutting rock that separated Steps Bay here from Lantern Cove which was directly below the hotel. "I've searched the big cave in Lantern, and I've gone all the way along the shore beyond, over all the rocks, out on all the spits, and believe me I know this part of the coast very well. We've found nothing connected with the lady, other than her bag which I dare say you've heard all about, and nothing at all to indicate any kind of foul play."

"I'm dreadfully sorry," said Leslie, mortified with contrition.

"Think nothing of it, sir," said the officer brightly. "No hard feelings. I might have done the same myself in your position. Now, shall we make our way back up? I've finished here for the day."

With many stops, they made the steep ascent, and at the top the policeman carefully removed the strip of blue tape declaring the steps open once more. "There now, you were only a few minutes premature, after all," he said.

Declining a ride back to the hotel in Sergeant Payne's police car, they all shook hands and the officer disappeared up the public footpath. Back at the hotel, Gloria hurried off to join the evening social, and Leslie regaled Bennett with the events in minute detail.

9

Breakfast the next day was rather an anticlimax. Leslie had expected at least a farewell speech from Jeremy, with a gushing vote of thanks to Val and her staff, and something reciprocal from the group. But it seemed that if anything like that had been said, it had been said at the social the night before. There did not even appear to be the desire to linger over the final meal together; the course was over, and they all looked keen to get home. Even the lacklustre Lauren seemed more eager than usual to serve and clear away. None of the delegates came over to say goodbye to the two men, other than Gloria who promised to see them later in the morning; she wasn't planning to leave until after lunch.

"Do let's have coffee together this morning," she said eagerly. "Come across at about eleven, why don't you? Val, Sadie and Lauren will have their work cut out making up all the rooms, but we won't be under their feet if we sit out on the terrace, and I can make the coffee. It'll be nice to have five minutes' peace after everything that's happened, and before I go back home."

But when Leslie and Bennett dutifully appeared at eleven o'clock, they found a fresh drama fulminating.

"You won't believe it!" exclaimed Gloria, bursting out onto the terrace to meet them. "Lee and Lauren have upped and gone. They've not even given a day's notice. They walked up to Valerie after breakfast, bold as you like, and told her they were off." She threw up her hands in disbelief at this heinous behaviour. "Let me go and get the coffee and I'll tell you all about it."

She duly returned with a laden tray, and the two men settled back to assimilate the story. According to Gloria, Lee and Lauren had appeared from their rooms as usual in the morning and carried out their breakfast duties without saying a word about their plans. Then as soon as breakfast was over, and even before most of the delegates had departed, they presented themselves to

Val and announced they were off, that very hour. Lee had declared he wasn't being paid enough for the head chef responsibilities he had taken on, and Lauren expressed a grievance about being treated as a thief, when she had simply been about to shut a guest's drawer which had been carelessly left open and could have caused an accident. The last straw, they said, was the lack of support they had received following the recent tragedy, meaning, said Gloria, that they had been expected to get on with their work as usual.

"The cheek, the bare-faced nerve of it," cried Gloria, puce with indignation. "The truth is, they've found what they think is an easier billet somewhere else and they're finding excuses to leave straightaway. Val found out that they moved all their stuff from their rooms yesterday—that's what they really wanted the half day holiday for; not stress at all! Such ingratitude. Val has been more than patient with the pair of them, useless as they both are, and this is how they repay her."

There was a pause while Gloria fortified herself with coffee and a large, white chocolate cookie. Crumbs cascaded down her front like a minor avalanche, and she reached for a napkin from the table, sending two teaspoons to join the crumbs on the floor.

"I dare say Val will be pleased to see the back of them, in the long run," ventured Leslie, stooping awkwardly to retrieve the fallen teaspoons. "But they seem to have gone about it shamefully. Such terrible timing. How is Val going to manage until they can be replaced?"

"The new chef is due to start on Monday, and Valerie is trying desperately to get hold of him to see if there's any possibility of him starting sooner, but she isn't hopeful as he's coming straight from another job. Sadie will stand in when she can, but she can't commit herself from one day to the next at the moment. These cookies are delicious, do have another; I'm going to." She leant forward and matched the action to the word. Leslie looked on in wonder, for the cookie was the size of a saucer and Leslie was still working his way through the first one, while Bennett had abandoned his completely.

"This will need to keep me going until I get home," she said, as if to justify the indulgence. "As soon as we've finished coffee,

I'm going to pop back home, go to my shop and, if my poor assistant is managing OK, I'll pick up some extra clothes and come back for a few days to help out. I've never been a chambermaid or served at table, but I believe it's never too late to learn something new!"

Leslie started to say something about Val no doubt appreciating this, when the lady herself appeared, carrying her own mug of coffee.

With a great sigh she sat down at the table with them. "I'm not joking, I think there is a curse on the place this year. I'm thinking of calling in the bishop to perform an exorcism."

Leslie wondered if Gloria would pounce on this and offer some kind of spiritual cleansing from her own resources. Fortunately, her thoughts seemed to be elsewhere.

"Any luck with the chef?" she asked.

"No, he won't budge. He was very apologetic, but he's committed to working his notice which is, of course, a good sign. There was no point trying to press him further and, to be truthful, I thought I might put him off if I sounded too desperate. If he finds out I've lost three chefs and two maids all in the space of a few months, he might have second thoughts about coming. I know I would."

Val paused to decline the cookie which Gloria was pressing her to have, declaring that she couldn't eat a thing. "I'll have to manage the breakfasts myself, but there are three couples, plus yourselves, booked for evening meal. I'm about to contact them and—"

"I've got it! I've got the answer!" Gloria slapped her hand on the table triumphantly, causing plates to jump and coffee to spill, and they all looked at her in surprise. "Leslie! Leslie can do it!" There was an astonished silence before Gloria continued, "Leslie's a wonderful cook, Val. And he can easily cater for those people; I've been to his dinner parties when he's had loads of guests. And he was in charge of the catering at the choir supper in the village hall; that was for dozens of people."

The idea was so unexpected that for a moment no one had anything to say. Leslie felt quite bewildered. His immediate reaction was absolute refusal as, despite Gloria's claims, his cooking was no more than a hobby. It was one thing to fantasize about the hotel menu, but quite another to turn the dream into dinners on plates for paying guests. And it was impossible to judge from Val's startled expression what she thought of the suggestion. How embarrassing if he were to rashly agree, only to find that she was against the idea, as she surely must be.

In the end, Bennett was the one to break the silence. "It would justify your food handling certificate, Les," he said, adding to the others, "I bought Leslie a place on an advanced cookery course as a Christmas present last year. When he got there, it turned out that he'd been booked on a food safety course by mistake, so he did it anyway."

"I'd gone all the way to Exeter for the course so I thought I might as well," Leslie said, half laughing and glad of something neutral to say. "Actually, it was more interesting than I expected. I did go back the next week for the cookery course."

"There now, I knew he was properly qualified, certificates and all," said Gloria, directing the comment to Val, as though the matter was settled.

"I can't expect a guest to work in the kitchen," replied Val, as though the two men were not there for a moment. "Not that it wouldn't be an absolute answer to prayer, but don't forget the poor man is here to convalesce."

"Oh tosh," cut in Bennett. "Leslie will never get better while he's got nothing to do, and if you've got any compassion for the pair of us, you'll give him an apron and a few saucepans and things to occupy him. He was threatening to make me go to the model railway with him."

Leslie found three pairs of eyes fixed on him; Gloria's filled with confident certainty, Val's with desperate hope, and Bennett's with wry amusement.

"I'm not promising anything," said Leslie cautiously, at last. Over the top of Gloria and Val's delighted outburst, he added, "Perhaps I could look at the kitchen before I make a decision."

He was ushered into the house before he could change his mind, and was handed over to Sadie to show him round the kitchen and, in Gloria's words, "to let him see how easy he will find it to manage."

They were waiting for him on the terrace when he emerged fifteen minutes later.

"I'll have a go under one condition, Val," he said firmly. She looked at him expectantly and he continued. "That you promise, absolutely, to tell me if anything I'm doing isn't to your liking, however small. And that if the whole thing has been a mistake, you tell me straightaway and I'll stop."

It took a short time for Leslie to be convinced these conditions had been taken as seriously as he intended, and then the group broke up: Leslie to the kitchen, Bennett to the coach house, Val to her duties in the hotel, and Gloria to check up on her shop twenty miles away.

***

The weekend passed for Leslie in a whirl of orders, ingredients, pans and, happily, empty plates. To his surprise, the breakfasts were more difficult to manage than the evening meals, but this was because not only did everyone have breakfast, in contrast to the smaller number of diners, but in the morning, there was only Val to help as Sadie was off duty, seeing to her mother. It was as though Val had never set foot in the kitchen before as she rushed round, rifling through drawers and flinging open random cupboard doors, all the while accusing 'that Lee' of moving, hiding or stealing the sought-after items.

Sadie, by contrast, knew every nook, cranny and foible of the kitchen when she helped in the evenings. "You'll want to watch that small oven, Leslie, love, it's very temperamental; blows hot and cold, just like me!"

But it was her irreverent attitude, particularly towards the guests, that was her greatest asset when Leslie was under pressure.

"I wouldn't worry if it does overcook the salmon; it's for that fat old bloke who stuffs his face like there's no tomorrow. Your cooking's wasted on him. You could give him yesterday's leftovers smothered with that—what d'you call it?—Holland sauce, and he'd be none the wiser."

During the heat of battle, as catering felt at times for Leslie, there was rarely time for the conversation to deviate from the urgent business of the kitchen. But when they were clearing up afterwards, Sadie would chat away cheerily about the hotel, which she had been serving in since long before Val took it over. Naturally, the recent events were chewed over and, as Val did not venture into the kitchen unless she had to, Sadie was quite revealing. "Well, I knew Lee and Lauren were looking for a move." Sadie pushed a mug of tea across the work top to Leslie who was meticulously wiping down. "But it wasn't my place to say anything, and anyhow, I knew Val was going to get shot of them as soon as she found replacements so I thought there was no point upsetting her. They might have got their cards from Val before they found something else."

She paused to clatter the last few items into the enormous dishwasher. "But I still felt bad when they left like that," she continued, wiping her hands on her apron. "Mind you, I wasn't sorry to see them go, and that's an understatement. Lee hadn't a clue, not one clue; he actually had to go on his phone to look up how to do the simplest things. Seriously! He'd once done a turn in a pub kitchen where they took dinners out of the freezer and put them in the microwave, and I bet he never did that properly. If he gave Val a reference when she took him on it must have been a fake. And as for Lauren—moan, moan, moan. I can put up with most things but not all that complaining. I don't know what she thought she had to grumble about, either. She'll never find a better boss than Val."

She poured herself a large mug of tea, very strong and, sighing, rested her back against the tall aluminium fridge. Leslie suddenly felt very tired and longed to finish up and get back to the coach house, even though he did like listening to Sadie chattering on.

"Not that Lauren couldn't be a card when she wanted to be. Always sending up the guests and giving them nicknames and imitating them. And then there was that naughty habit of looking at the guests' things. Not that I approved of it, because I didn't, and I told her she'd get into trouble over it. And see how she did. But I must admit she could be very comical, and sometimes I couldn't help laughing."

"I don't think she ever came into our rooms," said Leslie. "She might have had something to say about Bennett's shabby old clothes, but otherwise I think we are awfully boring." Despite himself, it was impossible not to be curious to know what secrets she may have found hidden among the delegates' possessions.

"Oh no, dear," said Sadie. "I mostly did your rooms, and with Mr Bennett keeping to the suite as he does, she wouldn't have dared go poking about."

Leslie sipped his tea and, to his immense gratification, Sadie lowered her voice and said, "You'll never in a million years guess what Jeremy kept in a funny little bag he had."

"I did wonder about that," said Leslie, trying to sound casual. "I saw him with it once or twice."

"I'd like to know where he was going when you saw him with it, given what was inside," whispered Sadie, a mischievous look in her eye. "He must have usually locked it in the room safe, as according to Lauren it was never left lying about, and she would know. But on the evening they arrived—Monday evening wasn't it?—Val made Lauren go round the rooms and restock the hospitality trays. She hadn't done them properly earlier in the day when she was making up the rooms; lazy-itis I expect. She probably thought she'd get away with it, but Val never misses a trick. She sent her back round the rooms while the guests were having their little evening get-together.

"Well, Lauren went in to do Jeremy's tray and there's his little bag, by the bed. He must have forgotten to put it away. Naturally, being Lauren, she couldn't resist a look, and what do you think was in there?"

There was a dramatic pause and Leslie, wide awake now, shook his head silently.

"Handcuffs and a whip-thingy and some other wicked-looking things. Lauren couldn't tell what they were because she was smart enough to look but not touch. Kinky, wasn't he? And you know who he was doing it with, don't you?"

Leslie did know, of course, but said, "Go on."

"It was that Susan in the next room. There was gossip about them last year, you might have heard. Well, Lauren poked about in her room too and found a rucksack under the bed with some kinky-looking rubber clothes in it. That's what they do, isn't it? Dress up in black rubber and masks and tie each other up, and that. So I've heard anyway, not ever having been into that kind of thing myself. What a carry on! You can imagine what Lauren and Lee made of it. They got awfully vulgar, and I had to tell them to pack it in, but I have to say it was a laugh."

Whatever Leslie had speculated was in Jeremy's bag, it certainly wasn't that. He had no time to think it through, as Sadie was in full flow. "I haven't told anyone; it would have got Lauren into terrible trouble if I'd told Val, not that it matters, now the girl's left. But with poor Susan being dead and gone it's all in the past and it somehow wouldn't feel quite right. Mind you, I did tell my dear mother. She's got a wicked sense of humour. She laughed her head off, and I swear it did her more good than all her tablets put together. Every time I see her, she says, 'How's old Spanker getting on?' She forgets that he's gone home."

Back in the coach house, late though it was by then, Leslie furnished Bennett with all the details.

"Well, well!" said Bennett raising a single eyebrow.

"It's the perfect ruse, don't you think?" said Leslie. "Lure Susan down to the cove for a spot of S & M, tie her up as part of the deal, then bash her on the head or strangle her or whatever, then leave the tide to take care of her." He drank an enormous glass of iced water; the kitchen had been stiflingly hot. "Only it's such a shame he's got an alibi. It all fits together so well, except that he can't have done it. Do you suppose he really was here at the hotel with Ann the whole time? What if he gave her a writing exercise to do and left her for— How long would it take to get down to the cove, commit a murder and return? Less than an hour, surely. Since foul play isn't actively suspected, I don't suppose Ann's been quizzed about the details. He could even have spun her some story and persuaded her to keep quiet about his absence. She's so infatuated with Jeremy I could believe she'd cover up for him if he asked her."

"She's certainly besotted with the man," agreed Bennett. "But don't forget that the two sisters were supposed to have had that tutorial, and it was only when they stood Jeremy up in favour of watching the filming that Ann took their place."

"Oh yes, I'd forgotten that."

"And I was on the balcony most of the afternoon; I saw no one except Susan go down through the garden, though anyone could have gone round the road and down the path just as Lee did."

"I do wish Ridgeway were around. I'd feel so much better if I knew he was on the case," Leslie sighed.

"I messaged him last week," said Bennett. "He's still in Canada, but he's been in touch. He says they're a good team down here."

Leslie was not surprised Bennett had not bothered to tell him this, but he was suddenly too overwhelmed with fatigue to complain. "I'm glad the new chef is arriving tomorrow," he said, and he made straight for the bedroom. He was asleep in seconds.

***

Breakfast on Monday was Leslie's swansong in the kitchen, and he cleared up afterwards even more meticulously than ever, lest he should leave a stray crumb or grease spot. It had been agreed that his assistance in the kitchen would not be mentioned to the new chef; it had been a rather irregular arrangement, and Val was desperate that nothing should deter the new incumbent. Leslie, who worried that he had committed countless professional and culinary errors and would be found out, was more than happy to keep quiet about his involvement.

At lunchtime Gloria came over to the coach house, bringing their sandwiches and news that the new chef had arrived. "Valerie is showing him around now," she said seating herself comfortably in a wicker chair next to Leslie on the balcony. "He's a big man; I always think that's a good sign in a cook. And some more good news: the agency has found a housemaid who can start tomorrow. It hasn't been difficult work, but I'm not really cut out for all that bending, so I'm not sorry to hand it over. I'm going to stay on for the week anyway, to give Val a bit of support until it's all settled down. If I'm not needed, I could show you both some of the local attractions and beauty spots; it's such a lovely part of the world, I don't know anywhere prettier, I really don't. In hot weather like this, nothing is nicer than a boat trip along the coast, and the man who runs Gemini Boats is awfully nice and he's a great friend of Valerie."

She launched into a panegyric of the South Devon coastline and its many attractions, and Leslie started to fear that her raptures would keep her on the balcony for half the afternoon. Luckily, before too long, she recollected herself and departed for the house, ostensibly to help Val but more likely attracted, so Leslie thought, by the novelty of the new chef.

"It's a funny thing," Leslie said to Bennett when Gloria had gone, "it was hot and exhausting work in the kitchen, and the responsibility of getting it right was quite terrifying, but I rather enjoyed it. I'm glad it's over, but for all the hard work, I feel less tired now than I have done for weeks. I haven't even thought about my shoulder for days, and I almost feel like my old self. I hate to admit it, but I don't seem to be cut out for sitting about and doing nothing."

"No, you can leave that to me," said Bennett, reclining back in the chair.

Leslie laughed. "It will be strange sitting in the dining room this evening, picturing what is going on in the kitchen. A bit like watching a show when you've been helping backstage at the previous performances, and you know what's going on in the wings. It adds an extra dimension by being aware of how much effort is going into the performance, but it does take away some of the magic when you know exactly how it all works. The theatre's such a good metaphor for life; 'All the world's a stage', and all that."

He looked across at Bennett who had shut his eyes and had his fingertips together. He opened one eye and peered at Leslie. "Funny you should say that," he said enigmatically.

10

The new guests at the hotel were a dull crew, Leslie decided. They were all of retired age, and conversation rarely seemed to digress from the weather or health. This was just bad luck, he decided, for their own village, Dartonleigh, was largely populated by retired people and most of them had far more interesting subjects for conversation. The new chef, however, was a great success, serving them with a delicious seafood salad followed by raspberry pavlova, made even better for Leslie by Bennett saying casually, "Very tasty. Nearly as good as your cooking." Breakfast the following morning was of an equally high standard, and Val appeared in the dining room looking delighted and relieved.

Gloria came to clear away their plates looking even more pleased. "Sadie's coming in to do the rooms with the new maid who's arriving this morning, so I've been given my cards," she laughed, collecting up the plates and bowls, and sending two forks and a butter knife clattering to the floor. "I insist we celebrate our freedom. I've looked up the times of the Gemini Boats and there's a perfect trip just after lunch. We could walk down into Alemouth along the cliff, have a little bite to eat and ride out. What could be more perfect on a lovely day like this?" Without giving them any time to argue, she disappeared back to the kitchen bearing away a precarious pile of crockery.

Punctual to her word, there was a cheerful yoo-hooing beneath their balcony at a quarter to eleven. Leslie was pleased to have something to fill the day, but Bennett firmly declined to join the outing and even Gloria could see there was no point in trying to persuade him. However, as Leslie was putting on his sandals, Bennett surprised them both by declaring his intention to walk as far as the top of the cliff with them.

"That's the ticket!" said Gloria, as if to a recuperating invalid, but Leslie knew that Bennett must have a purpose in the walk and would not be going out for the good of his health. He knew too that he would only get an explanation in Bennett's own good time, if at all, so he made no enquiries.

"I can't believe it's less than a week since the tragedy," Leslie commented. "It feels like a month ago, at least. For the last few days, I haven't been able to think of anything except catering. I wouldn't say it put the incident out of my mind, but it certainly receded for a while. Now it feels like it was another lifetime."

"I know exactly what you mean. We've been so rushed off our feet in the house that it was only this morning Valerie realised we still have Susan's luggage in the office. The police were going to take it away, but it seems to have been forgotten. Not that it's in the way as she travelled very light. And very stylish, too. Just a suitcase, a holdall and a handbag, all matching. Not like me; I can't imagine anyone having to pack up all my stuff."

"What has happened to Susan's car?" asked Bennett. "Was that cleared out too?"

"That's another thing they haven't collected. It's still in the car park. Apparently, there wasn't really anything in there to clear out, either. She was a very tidy person."

"Did the police take any of her things away?" Bennett enquired.

"No, I'm sure they didn't, apart from the straw bag which they found in the cove," said Gloria. She rounded on Bennett with an inquisitive expression. "Is there something in particular they might have taken?" When Bennett did not answer, she said, "Well, I won't press you for an answer, because I'm sure it would be a waste of breath, but I know you've got something in mind. Just so you know, I helped Val pack up Susan's room, and we got everything easily into those few bags I've just mentioned. I'm sure Val would know if the police had taken anything away as she was with them pretty much every time they were in the room, but she's never mentioned it."

"It's of no matter," Bennett replied.

"Oh, but it must be, or you wouldn't have asked. I know you!" Gloria wagged a finger at Bennett roguishly. "I'll see if I can find out from Valerie, just to be sure, but I'll be completely discreet, don't you worry. I won't ask you another thing about it, but I'm so glad you're on to something."

She seemed to be addressing these last remarks to both men, and Leslie quickly said, "I honestly don't know what Bennett's referring to, really I don't. And please don't think we're investigating. There probably isn't anything to investigate at all."

Gloria's expression suggested she did not believe a word of it, but she said nothing more. They had arrived at the clifftop by this time and all three stood looking out across the neon blue ocean, in the direction of Alemouth. The beach and the village could not be seen from there, but the sea was busy with yachts and pleasure boats, and further out fishing boats and a few big commercial vessels moved imperceptibly along the horizon. In Lantern Bay below them, the sea splashed up against the rocks in foamy breakers, completely covering the rust-coloured sand. It was an idyllic scene and impossible to equate with the dreadful events of the previous week.

"I was hoping the tide would be out, and we could have gone down the steps and walked along the beach into Alemouth," said Leslie. "I haven't done that walk yet and, I know it sounds macabre, but I'd still like to see the cove where poor Susan met her end, since it's had such an impact on the holiday. I don't think our effort last week really counts."

Gloria looked down into the cove again. "Well, perhaps…" Her words tailed off. Even her indomitable optimism could not deceive her into suggesting they try it.

Bennett cut in with, "This is where we go our separate ways." He repelled a further attempt by Gloria to continue on to the village with them and he gave a wave of the hand declaring, "The pain of parting is nothing to the joy of meeting again," as he turned back towards the hotel.

After a very pleasant walk, they found a table in the Tea Shop Gloria had eulogised about on their previous visit to the shops; that seemed like a lifetime ago, too. Although Leslie had not had a hint of indigestion since the new chef's arrival, just to be on the safe side, he chose a simple ham sandwich with a mango sorbet for afters. He watched with admiration as Gloria conquered a large brie and cranberry baguette followed by a fresh cream doughnut. As before, she seemed to know everyone in the village: the café owner, the occupants of the adjacent table, and several passers-by in the street. Then, when they reached the harbour, the skipper of *The Gemini* gave her a wink when they approached and, undoubtedly to the annoyance of the other customers, led them to the front of the queue so that they could be the first to choose their seats on the boat.

The Gemini was a small, orange and white catamaran and Leslie thought he had seen it going along the coast when he was on his previous walks down to the village. Disregarding the lad who was poised to assist passengers onto the vessel, Gloria boarded with enviable agility. "This is the best place to sit," she said, and made for one of the seats round the edge on the port side. "On the way out, the skipper—I think he's called Michael—will point out all the interesting things along the coastline. When we turn around at Scour Head, he takes us out to sea for some wildlife spotting. If we sit here, we'll be facing the right way for the commentary for the whole trip."

Gloria was correct, it was the best location in the boat, and it was indeed the perfect excursion for a hot summer's day. Nothing was more welcome than the sea breeze and spray as the little boat powered along the coastline. Above the noise of the engine the skipper's voice could be heard in snatches through the speakers.

"...house where the actor, Robert... It's said he kept the house for his mistress, a local woman known... And before he filmed *The Great...* in 1917 *HMS Bunny...*" – surely Leslie must have misheard that – "...and was wrecked just off... 18 crew were rescued by the local... The memorial is outside the village hall."

Leslie was not in the least worried by the information he missed. He knew he would have forgotten it all by the time he got back to the hotel and tried to recount it to Bennett. They rounded a promontory and Leslie was surprised to see some old and ugly concrete war defences on the beach. He was just thinking that the cliff path above must be set well back at that point as he hadn't seen them on any of his walks, when a shout of excitement went up from some of the passengers who were facing out to sea.

Leslie and Gloria twisted round to see half a dozen sleek shapes leaping from the water and arcing through the air.

"...pod of dolphins... you lucky people... rarely come in this close... I can see at least six."

It was an enchanting sight to watch these beautiful creatures leaping effortlessly from the sea and travelling with such speed. Binoculars were pulled out of bags and people jostled for a place to take a video or photo. Michael, the skipper, was evidently a wildlife expert, and a veritable fount of knowledge about their diet, breeding habits and population, among other things, issued forth in crackling half sentences from the speakers. Gradually the dolphins moved further and further out to sea until eventually they were nothing more than specks.

"What a shame Bennett didn't come," said Leslie to himself, "he'd have enjoyed seeing them."

Both Leslie and Gloria had swivelled round in their seats to watch the show, Gloria's viewing plan having been temporarily thwarted. As they turned stiffly back, Leslie noticed that *The Gemini* was now level with Lantern Cove, below their own hotel. It was certainly a very pretty spot, with its amber sand, red cliffs and mysterious-looking cave. The coastline was particularly rugged here with long knobbly fingers of rock jutting out to sea every few metres.

"Oh, I say, look up there," laughed Gloria, and she took her binoculars from her eyes and passed them to Leslie. "On the clifftop."

Leslie could just make out a figure, but even at this distance he didn't need binoculars to identify it. However, he took the glasses from Gloria and, after a struggle because of the movement of the boat, he found the right spot and adjusted the focus. Laughing, he gave a broad wave of his arm. The figure in the distance did the same. It was Bennett, who had brought his own binoculars to the clifftop and was watching them go by.

"I bet he saw the dolphins after all," said Gloria. "There's not much that man misses, even though he doesn't venture very far."

Leslie was wondering what Bennett was up to; he clearly had some idea in his head and was not standing on the clifftop for any sentimental purposes, much as Leslie would like to kid himself.

Now that the dolphins had disappeared, Michael resumed his usual script, and gave an abbreviated account of the war defences which were no longer visible. He moved on to the present piece of coastline. "Some people believe Lantern Cove is so named... lanterns were lit to guide in pirates... smuggling," the partially audible commentary continued. From what Leslie could piece together as the narrative progressed, the skipper believed that it was highly unlikely the cove was linked with smuggling, since it was impossible to land a boat within the bay. It was more likely to be because the entrance to the cave was lantern-shaped. Leslie, who had been looking at Bennett while listening to this, now glanced back at the cave but they had gone too far beyond it for him to test the theory.

The two men gave each other a final wave as the boat passed behind the spit of rock, leaving Lantern Cove, and Bennett on the clifftop above, out of sight. The steps leading down onto the shore now came into view and Leslie winced when he remembered the embarrassing meeting there, with Sergeant Payne. A minute or two later and they were round a headland and into a very scenic bay that seemed to be completely inaccessible except by boat. The engine stopped abruptly and for a moment there was a heavenly quiet with only the sound of seabirds and the water lapping at the sides of the boat. The lad who had helped the passengers to board now came out of the cabin and stepped nimbly round to the bow where, with a clanking sound, he lowered the anchor.

The skipper appeared and gave the welcome news that the kettle was boiling in the galley, and he took an order for tea and coffee. He appeared a few minutes later, along with the junior, bearing a tray of mugs and a square tin filled with biscuits. By this time the passengers, all holidaymakers, had started up the polite conversations which had not earlier been possible over the noise of the boat's engine.

"Well now," said the skipper, "this is as good a place as any to take a bit of a breather and enjoy as secluded a spot as you could find in these parts."

Leslie dunked his biscuit absently into his tea as he listened to the skipper's exhaustive information about the guillemot colony nesting on the high and rugged cliffs of the bay, and the flock of plovers scurrying along the shoreline. He peered with wonder over the edge of the boat into the sparkling turquoise water in which, they were told, bred a rare species of crab that he did not quite catch the name of. A large and translucent jellyfish wafted by, and deeper below a shoal of small fish darted about. It was a spectacular and magical location; he might have been in paradise, but for the regret that Bennett was not there enjoying it too.

He was brought back to reality with a jolt that nearly cost him his mug of tea. One of the passengers had just asked whereabouts the poor lady was drowned last week. Gloria gave Leslie a very expressive look but to his relief she said nothing. The skipper seized on the subject with great enthusiasm as, he explained, he had been aboard the inshore rescue boat that had been deployed in the initial search.

Having identified the location as Lantern Cove, luckily with no mention of the hotel, he said, "It looks pretty enough but it's a wicked stretch of water. It's not the first time someone's been carried off by a riptide, and it's a devil of a place to search. You can't get a boat anywhere near the shoreline, not even our rib. Every year we get calls from visitors who've been cut off by the tide in one of these little coves and they expect us to pick them up. We tell them they'll have to sit it out on the rocks. I swear I wouldn't like to try getting even a kayak up to the beach anywhere along that stretch, whatever the tide. I expect you saw the concrete slipway back there."

Someone reminded him that the dolphins had appeared just at that moment.

"Ah well, you may not have seen it, then. But they had to put in that slipway to get sea access to the defences there in the war. It's still the only place to pull in along here, but you can only walk in this direction from there when the tide's well out. So, if someone's trapped in Lantern Bay or anywhere along that stretch, it's no use pulling into the slipway as you can't get to them along the shore. There are warning signs, but still, every year we get a call from some party of picnickers or beachcombers who've gone and got themselves cut off."

The passengers were clearly impressed by the skipper's status as a lifeboatman, and he happily regaled them with rescue stories, of which there appeared to be a plentiful supply, until it was time to move on.

While everyone was talking, Gloria leaned close to Leslie and said, as quietly as she could, "I'm glad he didn't mention the hotel when he was talking about the tragedy. Amazingly the press don't seem to have got hold of the link with the hotel. I think it was lucky it happened on the day of the filming; that gave the local reporters plenty to keep them busy."

The rest of the excursion was inevitably rather an anticlimax. The boat powered out to sea at an exhilarating speed to commence the wildlife-watching part of the trip, but naturally there were few creatures to be seen. Half a dozen shag and cormorant stood dutifully to attention on a little rocky outcrop, one cormorant obligingly opening its wings in a characteristic and sinister pose, but this was insignificant compared with the earlier dolphins. Someone thought they saw a gannet, but it turned out to be nothing more than a herring gull when the expert opinion of the skipper was applied to.

Gloria had been, for her, remarkably quiet on the return journey but as soon as they disembarked and were away from the boat, she said, "I've been thinking about it, and it must have been that sailor who did for poor Susan after all, don't you think? He'd have known all about the slipway and the tides and how to work it. But never mind that for now. I don't know about you, but I think an ice cream's called for and I haven't taken you to Spiro's yet. It's quite the best ice cream I've ever tasted." And, recommending one flavour after another, she led Leslie up the shingle beach to the shops.

***

"I bet I can guess what you were up to earlier," said Leslie over dinner that evening.

Bennett looked up from his salmon en croûte with a mildly questioning expression. Leslie had been determined not to ask

Bennett anything about his two visits to the clifftop, anticipating that it would end in frustration, or even a row, if he refused to explain. But now that he thought he knew the reason, he couldn't resist raising the subject. Across the dining table, Bennett was a captive audience. "I think you were looking at the cove and seeing how quickly the tide goes out over a certain period of time, or something like that."

"I was considering the general geography of the place," said Bennett. He helped himself to another spoonful of the vegetables which even Leslie had to agree were very nicely cooked. "It was nothing to do with the tide."

"Then why did you go down to the cliff a second time?" said Leslie, feeling himself becoming irritated.

"I wanted to watch you go by in the boat," replied Bennett and suddenly gave him a look that took Leslie back twenty years.

For a moment, Leslie was utterly disarmed. He knew that Bennett was being truthful; if he didn't want to give the reason, he would simply say nothing, or come out with an enigmatic quotation. He would never say something just to keep the peace.

"You saw the dolphins?" said Leslie at last.

"Wonderful," Bennett affirmed.

Before they could say anything further in praise of those oceanic mammals, they were interrupted by the appearance of the new waitress-housekeeper, Zophia, a lively Eastern European girl, enquiring if the meal 'vas to their likings', which indeed it was.

It was probably the sight of the new waitress that prompted the thought, for it suddenly occurred to Leslie to wonder if there was anything suspicious about Lauren and Lee. They had left so suddenly, and with no notice, less than two days after Susan's demise. They had only been with Val for a few weeks, and she knew nothing about them. Were they really as lazy and incompetent as they appeared? After a moment's reflection, he thought that they probably were and, for all he knew, the normal turnover of staff in the hospitality sector might not make their short tenure particularly unusual. But still, it was a coincidence.

Zophia was still close by, attending to the next table, so Leslie said nothing to Bennett, and his mind raced on. What about the other staff, or Val even? It was a ludicrous thought, but the previous year's tragedy had benefitted the hotel, so perhaps her fear of the press getting hold of the story was just a blind. Even in this fanciful state of mind, Leslie could not construct any scenario that implicated Sadie, but what about the other guests? Leslie dismissed Thelma, but there was Barbara who no one had seen all the afternoon of the tragedy.

As soon as he could speak without being overheard, Leslie tentatively shared these ideas with Bennett. "I know it's utterly absurd, particularly imagining Val doing anything so dreadful," he said as he finished.

Bennett reflected for a few moments before replying. "Whether or not it's absurd to think of Val as a murderer isn't really the issue. More to the point, the facts don't support the theory you put forward. There has, in fact, been no press interest in Susan's case and Val could easily have contacted them herself if journalists had not appeared spontaneously. As for any, or all, of the others being suspects—remember what it was that made you doubtful in the first place. You only suspected foul play because of Susan's strange interactions with Jeremy and the man we call the sailor. Take them out of the equation and there wouldn't have been anything to raise your suspicions. So, on that premise, the only reason to suspect anyone else is if we think they were in league with Jeremy, the sailor or both."

This last part was said without any hint of raillery and, after a brief moment's thought, Leslie accepted the logic of Bennett's argument. It was certainly a relief to Leslie not to mistrust everyone. He then remembered something else that was puzzling him and, since Bennett seemed to be in an unusually candid mood, he asked, "What was that about Susan's luggage? What did you think the police had taken away?"

"Nothing."

"But didn't you suggest the police had removed something?" Leslie asked, realising that this was going to be one of those frustrating conversations after all.

"No, I didn't," said Bennett.

"Well why did you ask Gloria if the police had taken anything away, then?" hissed Leslie, only restrained by the presence of other diners from raising his voice and drumming his fist on the table. "Stop being so bloody annoying. What's missing?"

Zophia chose that moment to return to clear their plates, so the conversation was suspended, but once she was gone Bennett said, "The rucksack. I'd rather like to know what happened to the rucksack that Lauren saw under Susan's bed."

11

The following day, they were deprived of Gloria's company as she had taken herself off to the market town of Torbury. Leslie had very nearly agreed to go with her but fortunately, before he had committed himself, Gloria had launched into a eulogy about its merits as a centre for natural health and alternative living. Her purpose in visiting on this occasion was to see what else she could pick up to further her current interest in crystals and what she described as 'the healing metaphysical'.

Leslie had firmly but politely declined joining her, but this left the day to fill. By mid-morning, when Bennett was engrossed in his work, Leslie decided to find out what the tide was doing and see if he could get down to Lantern Cove at last for a look around. He had no expectation of finding any clues, but he could not rid himself of a strong urge to visit the place where Susan had befallen her fate.

Before he could put the plan into action, Val appeared at the coach house with the news that a lady had arrived at the hotel looking for her husband who was missing. "He was in Alemouth last week apparently, but now he's disappeared. She showed me a picture of him on her phone. I'm pretty sure he came into the bar but what with all the problems we had, I could be mistaken and, if it was him, I couldn't tell you which day it was. Would you mind coming over to the house to look at the photo to see if you recognise him?"

Leslie felt an unpleasant sense of foreboding, and he looked across at Bennett who had risen, evidently intending to join them.

"She's trying to behave casually and play it down, but I can see she's upset," said Val as they made their way from the coach house to the main hotel. "She's called Sandra, by the way." They had reached the terrace at the back of the hotel by now and Val stopped and lowered her voice. "If you ask me, he's gone off with a woman, or she thinks he has, and she's trying to track them down." With that, she put a finger to her lips, and they carried on to the lounge without saying anything more.

The lounge was empty except for the figure sitting at the far corner in the bar area. The lady did not see them for a few seconds and that was long enough for Leslie to think that he had never seen anyone who looked so ravaged with misery. As soon as she was aware of them though, she gave them an unconvincing smile and rose hesitantly to her feet. Val introduced the men and left to fetch some tea and coffee, and they all sat down around the bar table.

Sandra fumbled for her phone and tapped at the screen in an agitated manner. "I had a picture of him a minute ago—my husband, Pete, that is." She continued to scroll through dozens of pictures while she spoke. "He was in Alemouth last week. I spoke to him a few times, but then suddenly I couldn't get hold of him anymore." She struggled to control a quavering voice. "I expect his phone battery's gone flat or something, but I must speak to him as some business has cropped up, quite urgent, and I need to tell him about it. Here it is, I've found the picture. I don't know if you saw him around here?"

Leslie did not need a second look at the picture to recognise Sandra's husband as the sailor. He looked across at Bennett, uncertain what to say to the lady. She had an agitated and evasive manner that made her story about urgent business thoroughly unconvincing; even Val, who could not have any suspicion of the man being involved in Susan's death, had realised the lady was not telling the truth.

To Leslie's relief, Bennett answered, saying, "Yes, we did see him here. It was on Monday evening; he came into the bar. But then Leslie saw him again in the village the following day, Tuesday, in the afternoon, coming out of the shops. We didn't see him again after that."

Sandra, who displayed no surprise that Bennett had answered with such precision, replied, her manner still cagey, "Do you think there is anyone else who might know anything? I mean, was he with anyone? Or did he speak to anyone, or anything like that?"

This did seem to confirm Val's view that she suspected him of philandering.

Again, it was Bennett who answered. "I think he may have spoken briefly to one of the women who was on a writing course at the hotel at the time. Unfortunately, she can't be of any help as there was a tragic accident last week and it's feared she drowned."

Sandra turned chalky white and looked paralysed with shock, but at that moment Val appeared with a tray and the distraction seemed to revive her.

"I've brought some sandwiches with the drinks," said Val, addressing the distressed lady. "You look like you could do with a bite to eat."

Sandra mumbled a thank you and took a sandwich but made no attempt to eat it. "I think I heard about that accident, in the town," said Sandra when Val had gone. "I didn't realise it had anything to do with ... to do with this hotel. Anyway, I'm grateful for your time and for what you've told me."

Leslie got the impression she was now desperate to get away but could not very well leave since Val had brought this lunch. She broke the sandwich into pieces and stared at it miserably.

"Do you know where he was staying?" Leslie asked.

"On his boat; he always stayed on the boat," she replied, adding a little reluctantly, "I couldn't find that either; I looked in all the moorings. Oh, I do hope he's all right."

The last words were almost a pitiful wail.

"If you are really worried, have you thought of trying the police?" said Leslie kindly. "They're very nice down this way."

Almost before he had finished the sentence, she cut in, suddenly defensive. "This isn't a police matter. It's nothing to do with them. If Pete thought I'd gone to the police about him, there'd be hell to pay. I expect he's met up with a mate and they've gone out for a few days fishing and his phone's run out of charge. It's just the sort of thing he'd do. I'm not worried as such, it's just that there's this business cropped up back home and I need to tell him about it."

This was patently a lie, given her earlier exclamation of anxiety, but Leslie could hardly say so. "What's the name of the boat?" he asked. "We could look out for it."

"Well, I don't really know," she said. The two men looked at her in some surprise, and she added hastily, "What I mean is, there's no need. Pete wouldn't like it. That's just how it is."

"Of course," said Leslie, adding diffidently, "could we perhaps take your contact details? We could get in touch, discreetly of course, if we saw your husband, or if we heard anything."

"Well, no, thank you. And I'll thank you not to be asking around on my behalf. If this gets back to Pete there'll be bother," she said, suddenly quite sharp. "I think I'd better be making a move. Do say thank you to the manageress for the tea and everything." She gestured to the table where her dismembered sandwich lay, uneaten, on the plate.

Bennett pulled a card out of his wallet and gave it to her. "Perhaps you will take our details, instead. Then you can contact us if you need to at any time. It may be that we can help."

Leslie reinforced Bennett's words with an assurance that they would assist in any way they could as Sandra stuffed the card into her bag and, without saying another word, hurried away as though the devil were at her heels.

"Well, what do you make of that?" said Leslie when Sandra had gone.

"No Oscars for that performance," replied Bennett.

"She's a very bad liar," agreed Leslie. "What do you think it's about? I can see why Val thinks it's a woman he's gone off with, but even without knowing everything we do about Susan, I wouldn't have thought it was an affair that was bothering her."

"Why do you say that?" asked Bennett.

Leslie picked up his sandwich and munched thoughtfully for a bit. At last he said, "If she thought her husband was having an affair, it would have been different; she'd have been angry and hurt, but that didn't come across at all. The only time she sounded like she was speaking the truth was when she blurted out that she hoped he was all right. It seemed like she was really worried about him. She was frightened."

For a while, the two men ate their sandwiches in silence. Leslie poured them both a second cup of tea and said, "I don't know where this leaves us. I keep trying to convince myself there was no foul play, but it's looking more and more likely to me that the sailor—Pete, as we now know him—is involved in some way, and his wife knows or suspects it. You saw her reaction when you mentioned Susan's death. And why wouldn't she tell us the name of the boat? Or give us her contact details?"

"And what brought her to this little hotel on the top of a cliff, a mile out of the town?" asked Bennett.

"Yes, I hadn't thought of that. It's not an obvious place to make enquiries." Leslie sighed heavily. "I suppose I'll have to go back to the police, but there's precious little to tell them. A woman called Sandra can't find her husband called Pete or his boat which we don't know the name of. The husband is the sailor we reported earlier and now we think the wife is suspicious too. That's about it."

"That's assuming they really are called Sandra and Pete," said Bennett. "Let's hope you can get hold of that Payne chap. It might take some explaining to anyone else."

Bennett returned to his sandwich and Leslie said, "I suppose this puts Jeremy right out of the picture. I know I keep saying I've ruled him out, given that he couldn't possibly have gone down to the cove at any point that afternoon, but I can't stop thinking that he is implicated in some way. There is still something all wrong about him; he just doesn't add up. The possibility that Jeremy and Pete were in it together seems the unlikeliest scenario of all."

There was no chance to say anything further as Val returned to see how they were getting on. "She's gone already, has she? And without eating anything! I don't suppose the bastard, excuse my French, is even worth it. A woman's better off without a man who can't keep his trousers on, that's what I always say." She piled up the tray and made off for the kitchen, reflecting aloud on what she would like to do to men who carry on like that.

"One good thing," said Leslie to Bennett as they walked back to the coach house. "It looks like Gloria has kept her mouth shut. Val's obviously oblivious to our suspicions about the sailor, or about Susan's death. I know Gloria wouldn't say anything on purpose, but she's so garrulous I'm always worried that she might accidentally give the game away."

"Yes," agreed Bennett, "she is rather like the cup that runneth over."

When they got back to their room, Leslie rang the phone number that Sergeant Payne had given him and eventually got through. With some difficulty he told the story and, although it sounded lamer and lamer as he went on, when he'd finished the policeman said, "Well, thank you for taking the trouble to report that, sir. Any new information is always helpful."

With that polite but limited response, Leslie had to be content.

***

Having returned from her shopping expedition during the afternoon, Gloria made a noisy and conspicuous entrance to the dining room as the men were eating their main course, attracting the attention of everyone in the room. Since the writing course had ended, Gloria had resumed her usual arrangements when staying at the hotel and ate privately in Val's own quarters, not in the dining room. However, she had come looking for the two men and she found a spare chair and pulled it up, managing to catch the chair leg around the handbag strap of a lady at the neighbouring table. The gentleman at the table broke off his meal to crouch stiffly down to disentangle it, and some good-natured banter was exchanged, characteristically effusive on Gloria's side.

"I heard all about the visit of the wife of you-know-who this morning," she said, seating herself at last in the liberated chair, and speaking as quietly as her carrying voice would allow. "I knew straightaway who it was when Valerie said you'd recognised him. I was bursting to say something to her but of course I didn't. Can I come over to your suite later and you can tell me all about it? Unless it's all a big secret, then I promise not to ask any questions. Or not too many, anyway." She gave a whinny of laughter and the couple at the adjacent table looked across with indulgent smiles. "But I must come over anyway as I've something to show you. It's quite wonderful, but I'm not going to spoil the surprise." She rose to leave and Leslie caught sight of the lady behind her making a grab for her handbag as Gloria sailed forth from the room.

As good as her word, there was a hello-helloing from outside their door later that evening and Gloria entered bearing a large box. Leslie was struck by a sudden dread it was a gift, and something he may be expected to display at home. He was just deciding that Bennett would have to have it in his library when Gloria said, "You can tell me all about the visit of the sailor's wife in a minute, but first I must show you this. I've wanted one of these for ages."

Leslie sighed with relief.

Gloria placed the box triumphantly onto the coffee table and opened the lid as though she were about to perform a conjuring trick. "Just look! Isn't it absolutely perfect?"

Within was a small copper-coloured dish and a wooden stick in the shape of a pestle. It was indeed a very pleasing object, and Leslie peered at it curiously.

Gloria beamed. "Now what do you think of that? A beauty, don't you think? But I bet you don't know what it is!"

"If I'm not mistaken, it's a singing bowl; a Buddhist sacred instrument," said Bennett, looking surprisingly interested.

"Is there anything you don't know, Bennett?" said Gloria incredulously. "He's quite right; it's a Tibetan copper singing bowl. As I said, I've been after one for ages, but I didn't want to buy online as I believe you must get a feel for the individual bowl, and listen to it, to see if its note lines up with your own chakra, or whatever it's supposed to do. I haven't quite got my head around it yet, but it's early days." She took the bowl out carefully and struck it reverently with the little mallet and an eerie sound resonated into the room. "Oh, I say," she whispered breathlessly once the sound had died away, "what do you think of that?"

"May I?" said Bennett, extending a hand, and he took the instruments. Holding the bowl rather delicately with its base on the palm of his hand, and at a slight angle, he gently and slowly stirred the mallet around the outside of the rim.

A single tuneful note began to sing out from the bowl, exquisitely clear and, quiet as it was, it slowly filled the room. It had a mesmerising effect and for once even Gloria was rendered speechless. After a minute, Bennett held the mallet away and, to their wonder, the bowl continued to sing out the same hypnotising note for a long, long time.

They sat in silence, even after the bowl had finished its magic, then eventually Bennett said, "I haven't seen one of these for years. It's certainly authentic."

Leslie knew that he meant it was not a tourist gewgaw, but Gloria looked as though Bennett had just told her that she had found the Holy Grail. She seized his arm. "You have the gift," she said in an awestruck tone. "You must teach me."

Bennett inclined his head noncommittally but before he could answer, if he was going to, she continued, suddenly bright, "But not now. I'm dying to hear all about the visit of the sailor's wife. That is, if you're not going to keep it all to yourself in that naughty way you sometimes do."

This last sentence was addressed to Bennett and accompanied by the playful wagging of the finger, which never had any effect on him. However, there seemed to be no reason not to tell her what they knew, and the rest of the evening was spent puzzling over the strange events that had befallen them.

"How quickly the week is flying by," said Gloria as she rose to leave. "And you've only got two more days to solve the crime." She carried on, speaking above Leslie's attempt to protest. "I've offered to help in the hotel on Friday so that the new maid, Zophia, can have some time off. So tomorrow you're going into the village and having lunch with me again at my favourite café, then we'll have a last ice cream from Spiro's—mango for me I think, or perhaps the apricots and cream—and then we'll walk along the beach to the cove. I've checked the tide with Val and that will work out perfectly. You will get to see Lantern at last, Leslie, and by the time we've climbed those steps we'll have walked off our lunch in time for a good dinner."

***

The following day there was a forecast of thunderstorms in the afternoon, but Gloria was not to be deterred, asserting cheerfully that the weather forecast was never right, and anyhow they could do with a spot of rain. The two of them set off along the cliff in the most oppressively hot weather Leslie could ever remember. Bennett had once again resolutely declined the outing. On this occasion, Leslie was glad, as going out on a day like this was madness for anyone. There wasn't a breath of air even at the top of the cliff; heat shimmered from the ground ahead of them, and the horizon was hidden behind a milky haze. Gloria, sporting an enormous sunhat with a wide floppy brim, gasped, "Oh my!" and, "Oh goodness!" from time to time, and wafted hot air about with her oriental fan, but seemed otherwise unfazed by the stifling heat.

To Leslie's blessed relief the café was air-conditioned, and they sat for a long time over lunch. Leslie half listened as Gloria talked non-stop about her thriving health food shop, her growing interest in alternative therapies and her aspiration to expand her wellbeing business into what sounded like the whole of the West Country. He looked through the café window at the shops opposite and, thinking of his own village and house, he was glad that he would soon be home. Susan and her fate would have to be left in the steady hands of Sergeant Payne and his colleagues.

Stepping out of the café was like entering a furnace. The ice cream plan at Spiro's was abandoned, for even Gloria had to admit that an ice cream would melt within seconds, and the presence of some troublesome wasps in the street confirmed the decision.

As they plodded slowly towards the sea a breeze started up, but it was strange and unrefreshing because the air blowing on them was so warm. By the time they reached the pebbly beach the wind was lively enough to produce many excited exclamations from Gloria as she fought to keep her voluminous sundress in place. The sea was a little way out, but they walked down to the water's edge and, as they were both wearing beach shoes for the occasion, they paddled out with relief in the welcome chill of the water. They turned to splash their way along towards the hotel.

"Dear me, look at that," said Leslie, for ahead of them was a huge bank of black clouds in the distance. "Do you think we'd better go back over the cliff after all? That looks nasty."

"Oh, that's a long way off yet. We'll be home long before it rains. And if it does catch us, we may as well get wet on the beach as on the clifftop."

"I think we'd be quicker going over the cliff," said Leslie. "Walking on a beach is always slow-going."

"By the time we've turned back, I don't think there'd be much in it," said Gloria cheerfully, and pinned her dress to her knees with a burst of laughter as another fierce, hot gust caught them. "Don't forget how steep and slow the first bit of the cliff walk is. And if we do get a soaking, which I'm sure we won't, it will cool us off a bit."

Leslie reluctantly yielded, but found himself becoming more and more anxious as they went with what seemed interminable slowness along the shore. There was a concrete walkway further up the beach, but Gloria would not take Leslie's hint that they would make quicker progress if they used that, and she insisted that the delightful coolness of paddling along in the shallows would make up for any delay. Leisurely at the best of times, Gloria now seemed almost stationary as she investigated rock pools and crevices, trained her binoculars onto various seabirds, and stopped innumerable times to remove stones from her shoes. And before they were even a third of the way home, she had collected a bagful of shells and pebbles which then slowed her down further. She was heedless of Leslie's warnings about the ominous clouds coming ever closer.

They rounded a promontory in the jagged coastline and found that they were in sight of the ugly war defence structures and the disused slipway they had seen on the boat trip. This was where the concrete walkway led to, and where it ended; there was a notice warning of the danger of getting cut off by the tide beyond that point. Leslie fervently hoped that Gloria would not take it into her head to start exploring. Fortunately, she showed no interest in the buildings, but as they passed behind them, the full slipway was revealed and Leslie gave a loud exclamation. Tied up, and only visible from this angle, was a blue boat.

"Can it be?" said Gloria, who had also seen the vessel. With a surprising turn of speed, she headed towards it.

Leslie followed behind, slipping and stumbling over the stones until he joined the concrete surface. Ignorant as he was about boats, this was certainly the sort of vessel he had imagined when Sandra had suggested Pete may have gone off on a fishing trip. It was about twenty-five or thirty feet long, had a wooden cabin at the front and, as he approached, Leslie could see some fishing paraphernalia stowed neatly in the open deck.

The name of the boat was *Medway Princess* and its position against the slipway meant they could see into the cabin at the front quite easily. It seemed to be deserted, and there was nothing sinister to be seen anywhere; no corpses lying on the deck or blood-stained footprints or bodies slumped across the wheel. There was not so much as a discarded cigarette butt.

"Are you going to go on board and see if it's open?" asked Gloria eagerly. "Goodness knows what's hidden below."

"I don't think so," said Leslie. "I'll phone the police as soon as we can get a signal. If this turns out to be our sailor's boat, I'm sure they'd be annoyed if they found out I'd been clambering about and disturbing things, rubbing off fingerprints and so on." He added this last bit as Gloria was looking disappointed.

"This absolutely seals it, doesn't it?" said Gloria triumphantly. "The sailor, Pete, moored up here, walked along to the cove when the tide was out, waited for Susan in the cave, did the terrible deed—whatever it was—then came back and waited for the tide to dispose of the body. Simple!"

"But has the boat been here all the time? It can't have been. Surely we'd have seen it when we were out on our boat trip the other day," said Leslie, and they were thoughtful for a moment.

"Of course!" exclaimed Gloria. "When we were coming out from Alemouth, the boat was concealed by these awful concrete blocks. It's not until you go past that you'd be able to see it. Don't you remember? That was when those wonderful dolphins appeared. We didn't look at the shore until we were way past here. If we had looked back, we'd have seen it, but we didn't. On the return part of the trip, we were way out at sea."

"I do believe you're right," said Leslie. "But that means we don't know whether or not it was here then, and of course we don't even know that it is the sailor's boat." However, at that moment, peering once again into the cabin, something caught Leslie's eye. On a seat, amid a small, untidy pile comprising sunglasses, tissues, receipts and other items, was a paper bag bearing the name, 'Alemouth Pharmacy'. And from the bag protruded a box of corn plasters.

When Leslie told Gloria what he'd seen, and explained this was what the sailor had been buying in the chemist when he first encountered him, she set about trying to persuade him again to go onto the boat. She seemed likely to attempt it herself, when there was a great crash of thunder and they realised that the fierce bank of clouds was now overhead, and the storm was about to break.

A dramatic series of flashes preceded another almighty thunderclap and they hurried with unprecedented speed along the shore. The sea had become an angry churning monster and they moved inland, though keeping away from the cliff edge where piles of red clay told of past landslides. The wind, hot as a hairdryer, whipped and gusted, and Gloria gave up worrying about her modesty as they battled along, clambering over rocks and slipping over the stones. Leslie always found a thunderstorm without rain rather disconcerting, but this weather was truly sinister, and horrifying thoughts of lightning strikes and even tsunamis consumed him.

Finally, they came within sight of Lantern Cove and that was when the clouds burst. Mighty drops of rain like huge coins of water, fell from the sky and, having sand under their feet at last, they ran as fast as their weary limbs would take them.

"Make for the cave," shouted Gloria, pointing towards the break in the cliff before her words were drowned out by more thunder. After a few more seconds, they were safely under shelter. Rain splashed in at the mouth of the cave and Leslie picked his way towards the back, but it was very dark and, wet through as he was, he suddenly felt icy cold. He moved nearer to the entrance again and settled down on the rocks to sit it out. For a while the thunder and lightning abated, but the rain came down in torrents like a curtain across the front of the cave. The noise, as it crashed onto the sand and shingle, made conversation impossible, but now that he was safely under cover, Leslie felt quite content to sit in silence and behold this wonder.

The rain eventually subsided to the volume of a normal downpour, but this then heralded another fierce outburst of thunder and lightning. During the longest sustained series of flashes, Gloria, who was sitting sideways on to Leslie, glanced towards the back of the cave and Leslie saw, with awful alarm, a sudden and most uncharacteristic look of horror disfigure her face. As the thunder crashed outside, Leslie slowly swivelled round in time for another flash of lightning to illuminate the interior of the cave. There, on the rocks at the back, sat a man.

Leslie's relief was palpable; he had at the least expected a swinging corpse or a dismembered body, but it was still a shock to have been unaware that a stranger was sitting just yards behind them in the dark. Leslie must have gone within feet of him when he went to the back of the cave earlier. The man clearly realised he had been seen and he stood up awkwardly and came forward. As he moved into the light, they both recognised him, to their surprise, as the new hotel chef.

"Oh, I say, you did give me a turn, Jim. What on earth were you doing there?" gasped Gloria.

Between bursts of thunder, Jim managed to explain that he had a few hours off from the kitchen and had come down the steps to have a look at the cove. Not being fond of storms, he'd taken refuge at the back of the cave as soon as it had started, and was there when Leslie and Gloria came in. He had not wanted to startle them, so he'd just sat quietly without quite knowing what to do. By the time this had been explained, and laughed about, the storm had passed over, leaving just a light fall of rain. Jim, still embarrassed and awkward, made a hasty exit claiming he needed to be back at the kitchen.

"What a day," said Gloria when the chef had gone. "First the boat and now this. If that great big man Jim could sit up there without being seen, there's no doubt to me that this is where the sailor concealed himself until he had his chance. This is as good as proof. I'm sure it's all down to the singing bowl."

"The singing bowl?" repeated Leslie, perplexed.

"When Bennett produced that amazing sound from it last night, I knew that he had released a power."

Leslie knew that Bennett could conjure up an equally haunting note from an empty beer bottle, but he did not like to spoil Gloria's illusions. "See how quickly the tide is coming in," he observed, peering from the cave. "Look, we wouldn't be able to go back the way we came. We'd better get going to the steps."

***

"Gene Kelly's back, at last." Bennett whistled a few snatches of *Singing in the Rain*.

"Yes, yes, I get it," said Leslie, "I don't need the clue. You can't believe what a walk we've had." Peeling off his saturated clothing, he recounted the events in detail.

"What do you think about Gloria's theory, that Pete came from his boat along the shore when the tide was out, hid in the cave, murdered Susan, made his way back and left her body to the mercy of the water?" he asked when he had finished. "It seems to work, though of course it lets off Jeremy, who I still can't help thinking is dodgy despite the alibi. Unless, of course, the sailor was an accomplice."

"Why is the boat still there?" asked Bennett.

"We didn't think of that," Leslie replied ruefully. "Oh, but I must ring Sergeant Payne, I nearly forgot. I'm only going to tell him we found the boat; I'm not going to make a fool of myself by suggesting any more theories. He's a nice man but you know what I'm like with policemen—I always end up saying something stupid. Still, we've found the boat, so that's one up to us for a change."

Leslie got through to the officer without too much delay this time. Apart from some difficulty explaining about the corn plasters, he told his tale of finding and identifying the boat, and Sergeant Payne listened in silence.

"Yes, sir, thank you, sir," said Payne stolidly. "We haven't had a chance to remove the boat yet."

"You knew?" said Leslie, crestfallen.

"Well, sir, I did tell you that we'd taken a good look along the coast when you first reported your concerns. But thank you for mentioning it, anyway. We do occasionally miss things." There was a short pause and he added, "Though not usually something as large as a boat."

***

Before they went to sleep that night, Leslie said, "While I was sitting in that cave today, it struck me how desperately sad it is that there is no one here looking for Susan, no family or friends, I mean. Is there no one who cares enough to bother? To be missing but not missed; what could be more tragic? It's as though she never existed. I think that's the saddest thing about the whole business."

"Yes," said Bennett. "And the strangest."

12

They were served breakfast on Friday morning by Gloria, swathed in an enormous floral apron, chattering loudly to everyone and knocking things over. Her good nature was so infectious that no one seemed to mind. Leslie was, at first, surprised to see Gloria back in this role but then remembered that it was Zophia's day off. She brought out toast for Leslie and Bennett, dropping two of the pieces from the toast rack onto the tablecloth.

In what she must have imagined was a whisper, she said, "Luckily, there are only a couple of rooms to make up today and the others are all leaving tomorrow. Valerie said we don't have to bother with them too much." She replaced the errant toast slices into the rack and flicked the crumbs from the cloth onto the floor. "I've got so much stuff to pack up myself it will take me half the day, but I can always leave some of it here if I need to. Anyway, I'm bound to forget to pack something; I always do!"

As the men only needed to allow an hour or so for their packing, Leslie being methodical and Bennett travelling so light, they had a whole day to fill. But as it was the last day of their holiday, and tomorrow Leslie would be back in his beloved cottage, in his beloved village of Dartonleigh, he did not much mind how he spent the day. Pondering on whether to read or to wander down to the village for a final look at the shops, he was astonished when Bennett said, "How about a last look around the grounds? Shall we take a walk outside?"

Leslie was seized with a powerful urge to hurl the book, which he had just picked up, at Bennett's head, for the man was speaking as though this was a commonplace suggestion and not something Leslie had been vainly urging every single day. However, with great restraint Leslie forced a smile, pleased Bennett was willing to prise himself from the room, albeit on his own terms.

"Yes, of course," he said and moved towards the door, lest Bennett should have second thoughts.

The previous day's storm had cleared the air, and the weather was hot but not uncomfortable. They ambled about, seemingly with no purpose, but Leslie silently suspected Bennett had something definite in mind. They lingered in the scented garden while Leslie sniffed appreciatively at various specimens, and they admired the sundial, whose fascinating history Leslie had now forgotten. Bennett pronounced the various metal structures on the sculpture trail to be "grotesque monstrosities, demonstrating no composition, no form and no taste," which seemed a harsh judgement, but was probably true. They walked along the bottom of the garden but did not go beyond the picket fence, as thankfully Bennett was always respectful of Leslie's sensitivities about heights.

They arrived at last at the outhouse which Gloria had called 'the barn'. To Leslie's surprise, Bennett opened the door, stepped inside and, without having to search, switched on the light. As Gloria had said, it was used for storage, and the light illuminated the neat stacks of tables and chairs, the poles and rolled fabric of several marquees, a pyramid of large patio umbrellas, and numerous other items: the equipment, apparently, for outdoor events.

"Is this where you came on Tuesday when you walked down with Gloria and me before we had the boat trip?"

"I did look inside, then," agreed Bennett. "I'd been wondering why, with the comfort of bedrooms available, Susan and Jeremy would choose a rough storehouse for their pleasures last year. But, knowing what we do now about their proclivities, this place is ideal for the use of apparatus. And, you may notice, it can be barred from the inside."

Bennett pointed to the back of the door which revealed an old-fashioned wooden sliding bolt, and then he indicated overhead. "That beam, for example," he said, "would be handy to throw a chain, or strap over. If I'm not mistaken, those indentations there suggest that something just like that has rubbed away at the wood. The marks could have been caused by anything, at any time, of course, though judging by the dust it doesn't look recent."

"Val kept the door locked last week while the group was here," confirmed Leslie. He suddenly saw the funny side of it. "I suppose they've had to be careful this year," he laughed. "You wouldn't want to break the bedside lamp waving your whip around, would you? Not that I know anything about it."

"You're not starting to get ideas, are you?" said Bennett, with mock alarm in his voice.

"No fear, I'm the biggest coward when it comes to pain; you know that," laughed Leslie. "It seems more certain than ever that was what Jeremy was after when I encountered them on the day they arrived."

"Quite possibly, since he had his little bag of tricks with him," said Bennett.

"Rather keen, wasn't he?" said Leslie, and then he stopped laughing. "But Susan wasn't. What was it she said? 'Not this year, definitely not', or words to that effect. And yet that same night, I saw Jeremy creeping out of her bedroom. I do wonder if this has got anything to do with Susan's death."

They switched off the light and stepped outside.

"I'm still convinced that she was murdered," said Leslie. "I don't know who did it, or how, but there are too many things that are all wrong. What do you think happened?"

Bennett shook his head. "I don't know yet," he replied.

***

Their departure the following day was an emotional one, and Leslie was showered with gifts by Val, who claimed he had saved the hotel's reputation. One present was a delightful hamper of local and regional foods which proved particularly problematic as they had accepted a lift home in Gloria's red convertible and, with Gloria's abundance of luggage and their own, there was scarcely room for it. In the end it was placed on Bennett's lap in the back seat, causing him to say dryly, "Encumbered by a food basket, eight letters."

Val looked a little taken aback, and Leslie said hastily, "It's just a crossword clue. He doesn't mean anything by it."

"Oh! I've got it," squealed Gloria joyfully. "Hampered! That's the first cryptic clue I've ever solved!"

Gloria's erratic driving brought about a return of indigestion for Leslie, and several wry comments from Bennett, but they made the short journey home without incident. Leslie felt an enormous surge of relief as Gloria turned off the main road and brought them through the winding lane to the village centre and their cottage. It felt like the longest time that Leslie had been away from the village since they moved there, and he now had a surreal feeling of everything being familiar and unfamiliar at the same time. The cottage felt enormous; indeed, it was a spacious double-fronted house and qualified as a 'cottage' by virtue of its thatched roof, white-washed exterior and quaint appearance rather than its size. But he felt like a prisoner returning home after years of exile, rather than someone who had been on a fortnight's seaside holiday twenty or so miles away. His beloved garden was the only source of pain; it was in an even worse state than he had expected. At first glance not a blade of grass or a flower had survived the combined assault of the heatwave and the boy who had been employed to look after it; he postponed a closer inspection until he had recovered from Gloria's driving.

Leslie's joy at homecoming was magnified throughout the afternoon as he made a tour of the post office, village store and antique shop. In each place he was greeted with a rapturous welcome and earnest enquiry about the holiday and his and Bennett's health. That shared, he then caught up with news about the imminent horticultural show, a suspected scandal involving one of the church wardens, the demise of Vera's cat, and other such affairs that defined the life of the village. He finished up by popping his head into the Daffodil Tea Shop, which was busy as usual with locals, day-trippers and walkers, and he bought two slices of pear tart for their dessert. Feeling thoroughly contented, he added to his store of bliss by cooking what even he admitted was a superb sesame crusted salmon pie, which they ate with an excellent bottle of wine from the hamper, and he had the pleasure of Bennett's evident enjoyment.

***

This zenith of happiness was not sustained for long and, over the following couple of days, Leslie was unable to shake off his worry about the fate of Susan. She had been an off-putting sort of person, rather intimidating in an inexplicable way, but now that she was dead and gone, Leslie felt an illogical sense of responsibility for her. No doubt it was because she seemed to have no one else in the world, certainly no one who had shown enough interest to come enquiring. It was unthinkable that either he or Bennett could go missing for even a day without the whole village mounting a search party, and a sense of vicarious desolation descended on him. He had a great propensity for siding with the underdog and, although no one could possibly have described the living Susan as an underdog, he was now convinced that she had been a victim. This felt strongly like unfinished business; he ought to be doing something, but what could he do?

His garden was another source of severe misery. The flower and vegetable show was to be held on the coming weekend, and although there had never been any question of him entering anything this year since he had been incapacitated by his accident, it was the first time he had not participated, and he felt it much worse than he had expected. He could not forget that he had been last year's proud winner of the 'Plate of Twelve Raspberries', and the 'Roses' Four Blooms' classes, and runner-up in the 'Carrots Long Pointed' section. On two glorious occasions in previous years, he had won 'Best Exhibit in the Show' with his roses, and he was always chasing a third victory.

"It's really galling," he complained to Bennett over lunch on Tuesday. "You haven't seen Brian Masterson's runner beans, have you? They're huge. But when I was in the shop this morning, Vera was in there and she said that he's completely ignored the hosepipe ban. Everyone else is sticking to it. I knew he was a cheat."

"He'll come to no good," said Bennett gravely. "As you sow, so shall you reap. Though perhaps not in his case, if the radish rumour is true." This referred to the gossip that the enormous radishes which had beaten Leslie's exhibits the previous year had been bought in the farm shop at Lower Stretton.

"Exactly," Leslie grumbled moodily, clearing away the plates. "He won't get his comeuppance; at least not before he's won the runner beans on Saturday." The two men were in the kitchen, which was at the front of the house, facing directly into the centre of the village. Looking through the window, Leslie said, with surprise, "Why, there's Ridgeway about to come up our path."

"Oh yes," said Bennett casually, "he got back from Canada yesterday. He said he might call in today."

"I do wish you'd told me," complained Leslie to Bennett's retreating back. "I'd have done a cherry cake; it's his favourite."

"I expect he'll make do with a slice of your Madeira, or the coffee and walnut or the chocolate sponge. We can't have finished all three cakes you've made since we've been home, surely?"

"You'd be surprised how many people drop by," said Leslie defensively, but the detective chief inspector was now entering the house, so Leslie turned his attention to serving cake rather than arguing about it.

As usual, Ridgeway, who was stick thin, stirred three spoonfuls of sugar into a milky coffee and helped himself to a giant wedge of chocolate cake which he ate with evident pleasure. These preliminaries completed, he said, "That was a funny business down at Alemouth. I've been updated on it, but can you give me the details again? As you were on the spot at the time, your version of events would be appreciated."

This was addressed to Leslie, who explained as well as he could everything that had happened in relation to Susan's death, and his suspicions. The chief inspector was easy to talk to and had the knack of asking exactly the right questions to keep the story on track.

"So, her body was actually seen by those three people?" Ridgeway confirmed. "Do you believe them?"

"I wouldn't believe Jeremy if he said the Pope was a Catholic," Leslie replied. "And I'm sure he could manipulate Ann into thinking or saying anything. Although whatever she did see genuinely sent her into a terrible state of hysteria. But I'm certain that Barbara, who was in no doubt of what she saw, was telling the truth. I'm sure she can't stand Jeremy and would never collude with him, and what motive could she have for lying?"

"Barbara is a scientist," added Bennett. "I think she would have made up her own mind about what she saw and not be led astray by any commentary from Jeremy. She plays a good game of chess, too."

"Right," said Ridgeway, "and your friend Gloria's theory about this sailor, Pete, being implicated. What do you make of that?"

"It seems to work," Leslie replied grudgingly. "I hate to admit it, as it lets Jeremy off the hook unless they were in it together. However, it does seem the most likely thing. Finding his boat tied up along the coast, and the wife's suspicious behaviour, all support the idea."

"And what do you think, Bennett?"

"I'd like to know why the boat was left there."

"I've been thinking about that," said Leslie. "Perhaps it had broken down, or he panicked and decided to do a bolt more quickly and inconspicuously by train or something like that." He turned to the chief inspector. "You seem to be taking this very seriously. I couldn't tell from Sergeant Payne if he believed me or thought I was a mad fantasist."

"Payne's a good man," said Ridgeway amiably. "As you know, unfortunately we have not recovered the body but, at the moment, there's nothing to suggest foul play except for your concerns. Sergeant Payne is very diligent and has followed everything up most thoroughly, but we can't deploy our scarce resources without reasonable justification." There was a pause while more coffee and cake were dispensed. "Having, as you know, the highest regard for your judgement, I've used everything at my disposal to let Payne and the other lads investigate. Up to now that's been quite easy because we are still in an active stage. Trying to locate next of kin and such like means we can have a good old poke around, but once that's over it'll get a lot harder. Especially as there are factors that support the theory that Susan collapsed on the beach from a medical condition and was swept away. It will come out in the inquest but keep this to yourselves just now: she was being investigated for heart problems which could cause a sudden collapse, exactly as seems to have happened."

"Are you allowed to tell us anything else you've found out?" asked Leslie. "Have you found any family or friends? No one came to collect her belongings and, as far as we know, not a soul came to Alemouth to find out what had happened to her. It's tragic."

"This too will come out at the inquest but keep it under your hats for the moment. We've found no next of kin details anywhere so far; a few superficial friends and contacts but no one who could give us much more information about her than we know already. Her neighbours know nothing about her; she kept herself to herself. She had very little personal stuff, no clutter, no old photo albums, and no piles of sentimental stuff that might give us a clue. No will, either."

"I think her personality was a bit like that," said Leslie. "Not that I had much to do with her, but she seemed, well, two-dimensional. It's very odd having no family stuff at all, though. I wonder if she split from her family at some point and destroyed everything."

"I don't know," Ridgeway answered. "It probably seems odd to you, but we come across a lot of loners in our profession. It's always hellishly difficult tying up all the loose ends and closing the case."

"The writing course seems to attract loners," Leslie observed. "Actually, Susan had a friend on the writing course last year. I can't remember her name, but apparently they'd been quite close. She must have known something about Susan. Did you manage to trace her?" asked Leslie.

"I'm sure she'll be one of the friends who has been spoken to," said Ridgeway. "Payne doesn't miss much, but I'll double-check."

"And what about Pete, the sailor? Have you found out anything about him? Or can't you say?" added Leslie hastily.

"I probably can't, but I will," laughed Ridgeway. "There's not much to say, actually. We found out who the boat was registered to. And on the grounds that we have found an abandoned boat tied up where it oughtn't to be, we got the local force to make some enquiries at the man's address. There was no one at home and the neighbours said the lady of the house had been away for a couple of weeks. They couldn't say when they'd seen the gentleman last as he came and went a lot normally, being a boatman."

"East coast," put in Bennett. "Grimsby. And the pilot is Peter Shad."

"Dammit, man," said Ridgeway incredulously. "Where did you get that from? Did you hack into the Ship Register?"

"It wasn't that difficult," said Bennett. "I guessed from Sandra's accent that she was from that part of the country. I just did a simple Internet search of the boat's name, and it came up in someone's blog, complete with photos and name of the pilot. It seems that this Peter Shad had taken the blogger out for a day's fishing in the *Medway Princess*. There was a frightful lot of detail about the trip, and everything else for that matter, including that Peter Shad uses his boat for fishing trips, excursions along the coast, as a water taxi—you name it. There was a wry comment in the blog that he doesn't advertise and likes to take cash. They caught a thirteen-pound sea bass, by the way."

"Well," said Ridgeway, "we'll keep sniffing around for a bit longer, but if you get there before us, do let me know."

"When did you find all that out?" Leslie complained peevishly when they had seen Ridgeway out. "You could have told me."

"Only since we got home. You only found the boat on the Thursday remember, and the Wi-Fi at the hotel was shocking."

"I felt a right fool asking Ridgeway when you had all the answers. I don't know why you always have to be so secretive." Leslie stomped off out into the garden.

He began watering, a job he generally found quite reviving, but the state of the garden distressed him, and his mind refused to stop niggling away at Susan's death. It really was none of his business now and the police were taking an active interest, although Ridgeway's final hint suggesting he and Bennett might solve the mystery first, did nothing to help closure. That is, if there was a mystery. For all his concern about Susan and confident assertions that she had been murdered, now that he was at a distance from the scene, his doubts had returned. Gloomily, he rubbed his shoulder which had started aching again from the effort of using the watering can but was suddenly distracted by a familiar yoo-hoo. Turning towards the side gate, he saw Gloria's unmistakable figure approaching.

Ten minutes later they were sitting on the bench under a shady willow with a cup of tea and the remains of the chocolate cake. "I don't think your garden looks bad, at all," said Gloria stoutly, in response to Leslie's grim observations. "You should see mine! And as for the flower show; give someone else a turn to win this year. Next year will come around quick enough and you can walk off with all the prizes again." Although Gloria lived nearer to the neighbouring town of Temple Ducton, she was a frequent visitor to the village and belonged to many of their societies, so she was well acquainted with Leslie's horticultural achievements.

"I came to tell you that I'm going to stay with Gina, my daughter, in the New Forest. I've only been back five minutes and now I'm off again. Her husband is going away, and she doesn't want to be in the house on her own; she's such a baby like that. 'Mummy', she said, 'you simply must come and stay with me, I can't do without you'. Well, what could I say? I couldn't even make the excuse of the shop anymore as my assistant did so well when I was in Alemouth." She sounded a little disappointed and then brightened. "Gina said it must have been my good training. 'Why keep a dog and bark at it yourself, Mummy?' she said. I'm not sure she got the expression quite right, but I couldn't argue with the meaning, and so I'm off to the New Forest at the weekend."

Leslie poured another cup of tea for Gloria and wondered if it was the desire for tea and cake that had induced her to come here in person to tell him of her plans. He had a feeling there was another reason.

"As soon as I knew I was going to Gina's," she continued, "I rang Barbara, the lady from the writing course who lives in Gina's village, and she's invited us all to tea." Leslie heard the 'us all' but was unable to break into Gloria's flow to query it. "She was really keen for us to go because she's terribly worried about Ann, who seems to have gone off her head completely about Jeremy."

"Hold on a minute," interrupted Leslie determinedly. "Who do you mean by 'us'?"

"Well, I was just coming to that," replied Gloria airily. "The thing is, since you've got no flower show or garden to worry about" – Leslie looked around and winced – "why not come and keep me company? It was such fun in Alemouth, wasn't it?" This was a rhetorical question and Gloria continued without a pause. "I happened to mention my little idea to Gina, and she knew just the place. Her friend has a holiday let, a dear little house, right on the sea at Bridesford and she's had a cancellation for next week. It's called Beach Cottage. As soon as she said that I knew it was meant to be. Do say you'll come," she pleaded.

It seemed impossible to Leslie that he should go away so soon, though in truth there was no reason why he shouldn't.

"Barbara is simply desperate for help," she said. "Ann has found out where Jeremy lives and has almost been stalking him."

"How on earth did she discover his address? I'd have thought he was very careful about his personal details."

"She found it out ages ago, apparently. After one of the weekly creative writing classes, she managed to follow him all the way to his home. Barbara is really worried about her, from a mental health point of view, but I'm more concerned about how Jeremy might react if he sees Ann following him around. What if he really is dangerous? After all, he may have committed a murder. I do wish you and Bennett would come and see Barbara with me; you'd know exactly what to do. And you might find out some important clues and get to the bottom of it all. I'm sure I shan't solve it on my own."

Leslie had completely discounted any notion of going to Bridesford, although the thought of Gloria attempting to investigate Susan's death, possibly with the added help of her crystals or other supernatural aids, horrified him.

"I can't drag Bennett away again," he said, alighting on a legitimate obstacle. "It took weeks to persuade him last time. I wouldn't even dare raise the subject."

"Oh, if that's your only objection," said Gloria springing up with surprising agility. "I'm not frightened of Bennett." Before

Leslie could stop her, she had made for the house, calling, "Bennett, Bennett, you and Leslie are to come down to Bridesford."

The patio doors from Bennett's library opened and he peered out into the garden with a look of mild enquiry.

With great enthusiasm, Gloria explained her scheme.

There was a short pause before Bennett said, "When I was home, I was in a better place," and retired indoors, closing the patio doors softly in Gloria's bemused face.

"All you have to do is persuade Bennett, and I know you will," she said brightly and, after a lengthy leave taking, she departed.

The subject of Bridesford did not arise again until the following day. Leslie hinted at the idea a few times but, surprisingly, it was Bennett who raised the matter. Leslie was preparing the dinner, wilting over the heat of the cooker, and Bennett had just come into the kitchen with his paper and had settled himself at the table, as was his custom.

The only thing that Leslie enjoyed more than cooking was chatting to Bennett while he did so, but today he said querulously, "I wish everyone wouldn't keep going on about the horticultural show. When I went over to the shop for this couscous just now, it was the only topic of conversation, with Vera saying, very tactlessly I thought, what a shame about my garden this year. She said why don't I put a cake into the baking section, but I can't face going anywhere near the show. I think I'll hibernate for the day."

Leslie was continuing in this vein when Bennett interrupted saying, "Where's that bloody phone?" He got up in search and, ignoring Leslie's questions, returned to the kitchen with the phone to his ear. "Yes hello, Gloria. Book us into Beach Cottage. Leslie needs to be exiled from the village until this infernal flower show is over."

Leslie could hear Gloria's squeals of delight from the other side of the room.

13

Beach Cottage, a powder-blue wooden chalet, was idyllic. It was spotlessly clean, bright and airy with a large, white covered veranda facing out to sea. Located in the perfect spot, it was only ten minutes' walk from the main tourist promenade, but at the foot of its own private driveway which branched off the road, towards the beach. The chalet was set well back from the sea, even at high tide, and walkers along the shore were far enough away not to intrude. In any case, beyond the cottage the beach was inaccessible beneath the steep cliff for several miles, and this naturally limited the number of people venturing past. To add to the many attractions of the setting, the Isle of Wight with the three squat rocks of The Needles, made an interesting backdrop across the Solent to the east, and provided an object on which to train binoculars in an idle moment.

The main appeal of Beach Cottage for Leslie, however, was the modern kitchen with its quaint round porthole window looking along the shore. The only deficiency was the strange selection of cooking utensils, which Leslie guessed were cast-offs from the owner's own kitchen. This was a little frustrating as the town was celebrated for its food shops, especially fresh fish, but Leslie felt sure that with a little ingenuity, he could indulge his passion to the full, even in the absence of a decent set of knives.

Their visit to Barbara's house was scheduled for the Sunday and, to Leslie's surprise and delight, Bennett agreed to go. Barbara lived only a short drive away, on the south edge of the New Forest and, despite their willingness to take a taxi, Gloria insisted on collecting them. She arrived in time to make a hair-raising tour of some of the beauty spots in the vicinity on the way. It was a very pretty area, but Leslie was relieved when they eventually turned into a narrow lane, crossed a ford and pulled up at their destination which was an elegant red brick house standing in about half an acre of land. At the front was a traditional cottage garden, with hollyhocks, delphiniums, sweet William and a mass of poppies. Leslie winced in recollection of his own garden when he saw how beautifully the borders had been kept, as they made their way to the front door.

Barbara greeted them with surprising warmth and seemed far more relaxed and open on her own territory. "I've been a bit naughty," she said as she led them through to a very tasteful sitting room overlooking the rear of the property. "I told Ann to come an hour later than you so that I have plenty of time to tell you what's been going on, allowing for her to arrive early as she sometimes does. Her timekeeping is very erratic. We'll sneak a quick cup of coffee in now, but I'll leave the food until she arrives, if you don't mind."

She returned shortly with a tray containing a cafetiere which gave off a most promising aroma, and four elegant china mugs. "If you can bear with me, I'll start at the beginning," she said, once the coffee was poured. "I don't know if you are aware, but I'm a pharmacist, and I worked for a long time at St Michael's, the big regional hospital. That was where I met Ann. She had an admin role in the department and I saw her most days, but I didn't have any reason to get to know her in a personal way. To be honest, she was what my mother would have called a fusspot, and I thought her rather silly. Then about three years ago, my husband was made redundant so I decided to take early retirement; we'd both had good jobs and could afford it. I didn't keep in touch with many people from work, and certainly not Ann." Barbara stopped to marshal her thoughts. "Retirement started splendidly; David and I visited Asia, we 'did Europe', we went to New York. I expect you can guess what's coming. Almost exactly a year to the day of our retirement he collapsed and that was it. It was a massive heart attack."

"How dreadful for you," said Leslie, going cold. This could have been their story if Bennett had not been luckier.

"I can't describe it," she continued, "I was completely poleaxed and, for the first time in my life, I went to pieces. We'd never had any children and I suppose we'd become everything to each other without realising it. Anyway, the point of this is that one day, when I was at my lowest, I happened to bump into Ann—she only lives a couple of miles away—and she took me under her wing. She was extremely kind, and I think I owe her my sanity. Now it seems to be my turn to save hers.

"She's been going to these so-called creative writing classes for quite a long time, and she always had a crush on Jeremy. I took no notice; I found it rather embarrassing and used to change the subject when she went on about him. But at last year's residential course, there was that first dreadful accident, and apparently Jeremy was very kind to her, or at least he paid her some attention, and since then she's become totally infatuated. It's become an obsession."

There was a pause while Barbara topped up the cafetiere, and then their mugs. Leslie waited patiently; Bennett was his usual mute self, and even Gloria sat in rapt attention, silent except for her beads which swung like a pendulum and rhythmically tapped her coffee mug every time her bosom heaved.

"One day, months ago and before the recent residential course, she followed Jeremy after the class right back to his house, so now she knows where he lives. Fortunately, it's in Brighton, a good two-hour drive from here, and she still works full-time in the hospital pharmacy, so her opportunities for stalking him are limited. But I do know she's been to Brighton at weekends—I don't know how often—and hung around hoping that she will 'accidentally' bump into him. She has seen him, only a couple of times I think, though she never plucked up the courage to approach him, thank God. Interestingly, she's also seen Susan in Brighton, though not with Jeremy. She already had suspicions that he was in a relationship with her, but when she saw Susan there, she nearly went out of her mind with jealousy. In the end I suggested she went for some counselling, but she got very upset and she doesn't talk to me about it now."

Barbara got up, walked over to the French windows and looked out into the garden. "About six months ago or so, when Jeremy started to recruit delegates for this year's residential course, it seems that he drew Ann aside and told her how much it would mean to him if she joined again, so much so that he would give her a special price. It was all just salesmanship of course. While I was there this year, I heard that he'd said similar things to the others, so this was obviously just a manipulative device. In Ann's case it was both irresponsible and cruel, as she allowed herself to imagine he had feelings for her, and therefore not for Susan. I was horrified. I'd been along to one of the regular weekly classes with her and I could see what kind of a charlatan he was; it wouldn't be too strong to call him an absolute creep. I'd no idea how he would react if she did something dreadful like pour out her heart to him, but I was certain that his rejection would hurt her tremendously. I had nightmares that she might throw herself over the cliff, having witnessed that other woman's fall the previous year. That's what made me sign up for it, and I'm glad I went after what happened, though the course itself was an utter penance."

There was another pause, and this time Gloria said, "And you told me that Ann has been in a bad way since the course."

"It's been dreadful. Now that Susan is gone, she thinks she's in with a chance, I know she does, but she won't let me mention the subject. I feel rather guilty talking about her behind her back, but I don't know what to do, and I know that you all saw what she was like with Jeremy at the hotel, so you know some of it already."

"I think it's very good of you to be so concerned about her," said Gloria, "and I'm sure we'll help if we can."

She looked confidently across to Leslie and Bennett as though they were about to produce an answer, but all Leslie could say was that he thought it was most unwise for her to go hanging around in Brighton.

Bennett spoke for the first time. "Leslie, you must invite Barbara and Ann over for one of your dinners." When Barbara looked in astonishment, he continued, "Leslie's cooking has a remarkable efficacy."

Barbara's confused expression suggested that she thought Bennett was unexpectedly belittling the problem.

As Leslie was struggling to compose an explanation, Gloria cut in triumphantly. "Of course! Bennett isn't joking you know, and he's quite right. He always is. One of Leslie's dinners is the answer! Ann will relax and talk, if not to you, to one of us, and I'm certain she'll start to see reason. Believe me, you wouldn't want to miss a chance of one of Leslie's meals, in any case."

Thinking of the unfamiliar kitchen and the inadequate kitchen utensils, Leslie felt unsure about providing even an ordinary meal, let alone one that was supposed to have miraculous powers, but he felt obliged to make an enthusiastic invitation. Barbara looked very doubtful but politely accepted, providing that Ann was willing, and as it was near Ann's arrival time she cleared the evidence of the coffee away and took them out to look at the garden.

Ann eventually appeared, rather late on this occasion, and seemed thrilled to see them. Over tea she was eager to talk, alluding frequently to the tragedy which was obviously still troubling her. She made very little reference to Jeremy, but Leslie guessed that she was bursting to talk about him as, on the odd occasion he was alluded to, she bit her lip and glanced nervously at Barbara. It was agreed that they should all come to dinner at Beach Cottage on Tuesday evening, and they took their leave in cheerful anticipation.

However, Leslie's mind had started to become possessed with an idea that preoccupied him and even distracted him from Gloria's extraordinary driving.

"Do you think it could have been Ann?" he asked Bennett as soon as they were through the front door of their holiday home. "Who did it, I mean—who murdered Susan."

Bennett poured them both a restorative brandy. He handed a glass to Leslie and, with an enquiring look, he seated himself in a comfortable chair.

"I think it fits," said Leslie, struggling to contain his excitement. "She's got an obvious motive: obsessional jealousy of Susan. We know from Barbara how fixated she is with Jeremy, and she did make some very negative remarks about Susan. I know this is going to sound far-fetched, but she works in a pharmacy, doesn't she? Even if she's just in an admin role, she might have got hold of some drug, a strong sedative perhaps that has a delayed action. She'd only to get it into Susan's coffee at lunchtime. I wish I could remember if she was at Susan's table that day. Her hysteria at seeing the body could be accounted for by guilt; by realising what she had really done. What do you think?"

Bennett swilled the brandy round his glass. "Sedatives don't work to order like that, their effect is too variable. To calculate a dose that would allow someone to walk down to the beach and then succumb to its effects would be impossible. In any case, if Susan hadn't conveniently gone down to the cove and her body been conveniently washed away, a postmortem would have detected a sedative. That would make it a very risky method."

"Perhaps Susan went to the cove every afternoon last year, so Ann counted on her doing it again this year."

"But don't you remember that the afternoon schedule with tutorials was new this year?" said Bennett. "And, in any case, what about the sailor, Pete? Is he now ruled out? And Jeremy? As we discussed before, it was only Susan's strange interactions with Jeremy and Pete that made the death suspicious. Or were they all in league?"

"Oh, bother you, Bennett," said Leslie irritably. "You always have to demolish anything I suggest. I don't know about the sailor; he does seem to have been involved but it's preposterous to imagine Ann as his accomplice. As for Jeremy, I've nearly given up thinking that he did it, and there's not an atom of doubt that he's Ann's distant idol, not her partner in crime. I'd swear to that."

Leslie paced restlessly about the room. "I'm sure I wouldn't be half so bothered about this if Susan hadn't been so alone in the world. And it's impossible to make any progress, to even guess what her relationship with the sailor was, for example, without knowing something more about her." He picked up a pen from the table and searched about for a piece of paper. "What do we know?" he asked and, muttering to himself, he made a list. "Divorced, financial advisor, ill and so presumably had a doctor, relationship with Jeremy. That's it, I think. Oh yes, and that friend last year."

"There's Cambridge and rowing, too."

Leslie added this to the list and sighed. "The divorce can't help us; we don't even have an approximate date."

"That's assuming she is divorced," said Bennett. "We only have her word for it."

"True, though I can't imagine why she would lie about such a thing. Anyway, that's police work, as is anything connected to being a financial advisor. I suppose she must have belonged to a regulatory body, but that doesn't get us anywhere. Actually, I suppose we only have her word on that, too."

"There is a Susan Gunner listed as financial advisor, with an address in Lewes. The entry is listed as inactive, or whatever the term was."

"OK, clever clogs" said Leslie, tetchily. "So, it sounds like she had really been a financial advisor but it's still not much help. Not even the address; the police will have sniffed around there, and Ridgeway said that her neighbours know nothing. Likewise, her GP: the police will surely have made enquiries. Her time at Cambridge is police work, too. Jeremy, we know, isn't going to divulge anything about her. That friend she had last year must be the best hope of finding out something about Susan, but I can't even remember her name. I suppose Jeremy has all the contact details, but I can't imagine on what pretext we could obtain them, and anyway, Susan said she'd moved away." Leslie sighed again heavily.

"She's called Jean Rook," said Bennett, and he took his phone from his pocket and opened up a screen. "Her address before she moved was 2 Flaxman Terrace, Station Road, Pilsham. That's about a mile inland from Boscombe."

"Did Ridgeway tell you that?" demanded Leslie, feeling peeved at further unshared knowledge.

"No, it was far easier than that. I happened to flick through the visitors' book at the hotel and I discovered that she'd signed it last year giving her full address. I took a photo."

"But that's not too far from here," said Leslie, thoughtfully, his annoyance suspended. "I'm sure Gloria would be happy to drive me there. The new people in her house are sure to have a forwarding address and we might be able to persuade them to tell us."

***

And so, the following day, Gloria and Leslie found themselves in Pilsham, in quest of information about Jean Rook. Number two Flaxman Terrace proved to be elusive. Despite having established before they set out that it was located above a row of shops, the access up to the flats was difficult to find. Eventually they discovered a small archway between a charity shop and an Indian takeaway which led through to the back of the buildings, and they picked their way along a path strewn with litter and discarded items, including a doorless fridge and a disembowelled sofa.

"Oh, I say," said Gloria, stepping gingerly over some scattered empty bottles as they reached the end of the block. "This must be the way up," and they climbed a flight of concrete steps to the row of flats above.

There were only three flats along this section of the balcony, which was surprisingly tidy compared with the area below. Flat number one even had a large tub of geraniums outside, in which, Leslie noticed with a smile, sat a garden gnome. They walked past it to number two and Leslie knocked tentatively at the door. Although they had acknowledged the possibility that the new residents would be out at work, it was disappointing to get no reply, and Gloria knocked the second time, loudly enough to waken the dead. After she had made a third assault on the door, Leslie suggested they try the neighbours, and started off before she could knock a fourth time.

The flat beyond was boarded up so they walked back to the first one which looked much more promising. Stepping quickly ahead of Gloria, Leslie gave a polite ring at the doorbell. This produced a jangling rendition of *There's no place like home* and Leslie, smiling indulgently at the tune and the gnome, was pleased to hear footsteps approaching from behind the door. It was with some surprise, therefore, that the elderly man who swung the door open greeted them with a hostile scowl and an angry, "What the hell is it?"

Apart from uttering a faint, "I say!" Gloria seemed to have been struck dumb by this salutation, so Leslie falteringly explained that they were trying to find the previous resident of the neighbouring flat, but the current occupants didn't seem to be in.

"That's no reason to hammer their bleedin' door down, is it?" he demanded in an unmistakably East London accent.

As the man spoke, Leslie could see the figure of a stout elderly lady down the dark hallway, but she came no further forward.

"I'm sorry, we weren't sure if they could hear us," he replied weakly.

"I should think they could hear you from the end of Boscombe bleedin' pier," he said. "Anyway, they're out next door and they won't know nothin' about anythin', anyway. It's rented out to some of them Eastern Europeans and they're the second or third lot what's been in there. Different people in and out all the time."

"I don't suppose you know how we could contact the lady, Jean Rook, do you?" continued Leslie bravely.

"I don't suppose I do," replied the man, and with that he shut the door with a firmness that just fell short of a slam.

"Well," said Gloria, as they made their way back to the car, "what about that! We didn't get much change from him. But I'm not letting that put us off the scent. I vote we try again tomorrow."

Although Leslie had no wish to encounter the ill-tempered neighbour again, he felt a renewed urgency to get to the bottom of Susan's death, and it did not take much persuading for him to agree. However, he pointed out that the following day was when Barbara and Ann were coming for dinner, so they decided to make the return visit the day after that.

"I'm probably being superstitious," Leslie said to Bennett as they relaxed on the veranda after dinner that evening. "Being with Gloria is enough to make anyone fanciful. But when we were at that flat today, although it should have felt like a complete fool's errand, for the first time I felt we were getting somewhere." He laughed sheepishly; one never knew how Bennett would view these things.

"What was it that made you say that?"

Leslie thought for a moment and then stood up and walked across to the veranda railing. He leant on it and looked out towards the sea. A man was exercising two lively spaniels on the pebbly beach and further away a boy and his parents were throwing stones into the sea.

"Funnily enough, it was the old lady hovering down the hallway behind that horrible, aggressive husband," he said at last. "There was something about her, but it's probably only because I felt sorry for her. You know what I'm like."

Bennett did not answer; he was leaning back in the chair with his eyes shut and the tips of his fingers together.

"You do think there's something fishy about Susan's death, don't you?" said Leslie. Even after all these years he found Bennett as impossible to fathom as his crossword clues.

Bennett opened one eye. "Positively piscine," he said.

14

The following morning relieved Leslie's mind of all thoughts of murder and misery as he went in quest of the ingredients for the evening meal. It was lovely weather, with bright sunshine tempered by a breeze from the sea, and he set out early knowing that the town would quickly become crowded with visitors. He had resolved to keep the meal very simple, given the lack of adequate cooking equipment, and he began with some fresh, juicy scallops, invitingly perched on their shells at the fishmongers. Browsing the neighbouring grocery store for a piece of root ginger and spring onions with which to dress the shellfish, he found that his imagination was irresistibly piqued. Admitting that he would never be content with a meal limited by the existing kitchen utensils, he called in at the hardware store for a set of sharp knives and a decent pan, and then abandoned himself to his culinary fantasies.

The only setback to the outing was a disappointment over a milk jug. Passing an antique shop, Leslie spotted a small Delft-style jug, with a pretty blue and white pattern and a satisfying squat shape. Sadly, on closer examination the handle had been glued back on and there was an ugly crack down one side. Although one or two pieces in Leslie's collection were not perfect, this one certainly would not do. Sighing, he continued with his shopping and after a very agreeable couple of hours, he was so over-laden beneath the weight of everything he had purchased to conjure up the meal of his dreams, he had to catch a taxi for the half mile back to Beach Cottage.

The day passed blissfully with Leslie surrounded by bowls, pans, knives and ingredients, and Bennett working at the other side of the small table, pinching a strawberry here and a pod of fresh peas there, when he could get away with it.

***

"Oh my! What a simply delicious smell!" exclaimed Gloria, who had been dropped off by her daughter more than fifteen minutes early, and only just missed Bennett dripping his way from the shower into the bedroom. She joined Leslie who was putting a tray of salmon into the oven, and the tiny kitchen suddenly seemed to be filled with Gloria and her pleasant but rather overpowering scent. Leslie was generally at his most good-tempered and sociable while cooking but, after having to squeeze past Gloria's ample posterior for the third time, he dispatched her to the veranda to finish laying the table. The distant sound of clattering cutlery and astonished exclamations told that Gloria was accomplishing the task with her usual level of dexterity, but fortunately, before she could do any irreversible damage, a taxi pulled up at the door and a knock heralded the arrival of Barbara and Ann.

It was one of those occasions that everyone would remember for a lifetime. Everything conspired together to create an atmosphere of perfection: the glowing sun, the refreshing breeze, the quiet sea, the easy camaraderie of the friends. The ladies were shown to the veranda where they nibbled some salted almonds and Bennett served them an aperitif of prosecco with elderflower, while Leslie added the finishing touches in the kitchen, calling out an instruction every now and then to Bennett.

The meal was a masterpiece. The exclamations that greeted the scallops, served on the shell with ginger and spring onion, were surpassed when he produced a perfect salmon with lemon and watercress sauce, accompanied by tiny new potatoes and perfectly cooked green beans and peas, dotted with butter and mint leaves. The only potential impediments to perfection were the outdated and mismatching serving tureens, but somehow even they added to the charm of the occasion. Bennett poured out generous glasses of chilled Chablis and they had a long pause before Leslie produced what Gloria declared to be the 'pièce de résistance': strawberries in a reduction of muscovado sugar served with homemade shortbread fans and thick cream.

Long experience had taught Leslie that if he served dainty portions and allowed his guests to linger over the meal, there was almost no limit to the number of courses that could be served.

Consequently, when he brought out a tray with a ripe, round camembert and some oat biscuits, although there were some token protests, everyone filled their plate again, and accepted a glass of Muscat from Bennett.

They had dawdled contentedly over each of the courses, and it was nearly a quarter to nine by the time Leslie was handing round espresso martini in mismatching glasses, and persuading everyone that they could manage a mint chocolate to round off the meal. They sat in companionable silence as the sun, which was on its lazy descent towards the horizon, transformed the sky from pale gold to coral and then to vivid cerise. The colour was reflected into the sea which had now turned an astonishing shade of pink and was so still that there was barely a ripple to be seen. Across the water, the chalky stacks of The Needles and the adjacent cliffs were illuminated by a peachy glow.

Ann was the first to break the silence with a little gasp of wonder. "I've never seen anything so beautiful," she sighed. "The sea looks like a piece of pink satin."

It had put Leslie in mind of raspberry coulis, though he did not say so for fear of breaking the mood.

"And look," Ann went on, "the colour is reflecting on us. Barbara, your hair is quite pink, and it looks lovely." Ann was right—the whole veranda was tinted with a most delightful colour.

"You can see why they talk about looking at the world through rose-tinted glasses," said Barbara, uncharacteristically mellow.

"Yes, just look at us!" exclaimed Gloria, taking in the spectacle. "It's as though we have stage lights on us."

"I can complete the effect." Leslie put down his glass and, stepping towards the house, he flicked a switch. A proscenium arch of fairy lights came on, twinkling along the front edge of the wooden roof that overhung the veranda, and down the two supporting posts. "The veranda makes a perfect stage, don't you think?" He glanced at Bennett who had, the previous evening, denounced the lights as 'twee'. But Bennett had pushed his glasses onto his head and was staring thoughtfully into space.

"Rather apt," said Gloria, reaching across for another chocolate mint, "after the drama that brought us all together."

"I hate to disturb the magic moment," Barbara said, business-like again, "but Bennett and I have a game of chess to play and, unless we're going to stay here all night, we'd better get started."

Leslie wondered if Barbara's interruption was really to avoid getting Ann started on a discussion of 'the drama', a topic they had managed to avoid throughout the meal.

Bennett and Barbara made their way into the living room, but before they had even set up the game, the others were forced inside as the lights had attracted a cloud of insects.

"Come and talk to me in the kitchen," said Leslie to Ann and Gloria, "then we won't disturb the game. So long as you promise not to help me clear up. I have my own way of doing things and I'll get cross with you if you interfere."

"What nonsense," Gloria replied, closing the kitchen door behind her and taking a seat at the little table. "Leslie never gets cross with anyone. But actually"—and here she dropped her voice to a conspiratorial whisper—"I do happen to have my crystals with me..."

Ann gave a giggle of excitement, no doubt fuelled by the heady mixture of alcohol she had consumed, then shot a guilty glance towards the door. Relieved to see it firmly shut, she whispered, "Oh yes, do let's have a go with them. I was fascinated last time and I didn't think I'd get another chance."

Leslie hastily cleared a space on the table, piling plates, bowls and cups high on the work surface, and Gloria produced her capacious bag from beneath the table. After some rummaging, she brought out the silk pouch containing her stones and a square piece of velvet which she carefully unfolded onto the table.

"I've been practicing on my daughter, Gina," she said encouragingly, "so I hope we get some better results. Though I'm still far from expert, of course. First, we must cleanse our hands from impurities." Gloria produced the little bottle and squirted some liquid into Ann's, then her own, hands. "Now sit quietly and empty your mind of all doubts or negative thoughts. We've found it helps to think of a positive picture; a flower or an animal, perhaps."

"I'll think of that wonderful sunset," said Ann, breathlessly.

Leslie stopped the noisy job of loading dishes into the bowl, and quietly wiped down the cooker whilst Ann sat in her reverie.

"Are we ready?" hissed Gloria, and when Ann nodded emphatically, she held forth the bag. "Move your fingers round in the bag until you find the stones that speak to you. You can take two or even three if they feel right."

Leslie glanced round to see Ann, eyes closed, fishing about in the silk bag, with an expression of rapt wonderment on her face.

"Here, this one. And… this," said Ann, producing her chosen nuggets. "I hope I've got it right. It isn't that easy to be sure."

"Practice makes perfect," said Gloria cheerfully. "Gina was just the same as you at first, but she says it gets easier the more you do it. Now let me see. Ah, you've picked the citrine and the pyrite."

Ann peered with credulous expectation at Gloria's face, which had now taken on a sagacious expression.

"That crystal combination is about a special place. Probably the first place you just thought of when I said it. You don't have to say where it is, though…"

But before Gloria had finished the sentence Ann had murmured, tremulously, "Brighton."

"Have another go," said Gloria. "We've found that you need more than one turn to make sense of the interpretation."

The process with the crystals was repeated and the second time, after scrutinising the stones, Gloria declared them to be a rose quartz and an amethyst, signifying 'a special person'.

Leslie, who was continuing to clear up as inconspicuously as possible, looked over to the table and saw Ann blush a deeper shade than the evening's sunset, and mouth silently but unmistakably the name Jeremy.

Wincing with embarrassment, Leslie hastily turned back to his washing up, hoping that the kitchen labours would account for his involuntary grimace if anyone had noticed it.

Without any signs of discomfiture, Gloria said confidentially, "You seem to be getting a message. You don't have to say what it is; these things can be very private, so don't feel you have to disclose anything."

"Oh, but I must tell someone," Ann burst out. "I think I'll go mad if I don't. Barbara's very good, but she doesn't understand, and she tells me off if I even mention him."

Gloria settled herself comfortably at the table and poured Ann a liberal glass of wine from the bottle she had brought through from the veranda. Leslie put the kettle on, feeling that further coffee would be needed, and Ann, unaware Barbara had already told them something of her story, poured out her heart.

Since she first attended the writing group, Ann explained, she had realised that there was something special about Jeremy, and she spent several tedious minutes in a paean of his praise. It was on the first residential course, she explained, that she had felt there could be something special between them, especially his kindness after she had witnessed the woman plunge to her death over the cliff edge. There was gossip that there was something going on between Jeremy and that awful woman Susan, and she had not at first believed it. She was sorry to speak ill of the dead, but Susan was such an iceberg, and Jeremy so warm and kind, she could not believe it to be true.

As they already knew from Barbara, when the weekly sessions had started back again, Ann had decided to find out where Jeremy lived. She explained that as he never responded to her dropped hints, she decided to follow him home one evening. It was with only the smallest trace of embarrassment that she described all the details, including how she chose the moment when she had bought a new car to reduce the chance of Jeremy recognising it. Leslie, listening from the sink, suspected Ann had bought a new car with the sole object of following the man.

Gloria sat with admirable attentiveness, uttering the occasional encouraging, "Yes, of course," and, "My, how clever you are!" when Ann disclosed that it had taken three attempts to follow Jeremy all the way to his home in Brighton.

"Does he have a nice place?" asked Gloria, quite naturally. "Close to the sea?"

"It's a funny thing." Ann sounded troubled. "But it wasn't at all what I was expecting. It was rather a run-down street. Very run-down, in fact."

"He must be one of those Bohemian types," Gloria said, accepting coffee from Leslie.

"Oh, that must be it!" Ann sounded relieved at the explanation. "Of course, I couldn't hang about on the pavement. I just glanced from the top of the street to see which door he went in and drove past it later."

"Which street is it?" asked Gloria with bold directness. "I know Brighton quite well. A cousin of mine used to live there."

"It's 7c Neville Terrace," whispered Ann, and she spoke with a mixture of pride and secrecy, as if she were disclosing the private address of a celebrity that she alone had discovered.

Affecting to wipe the worktop, Leslie reached across for a pencil Bennett had discarded there earlier, and casually jotted this useful snippet of information in the margin of the dessert recipe.

"It's a basement;" she went on, adding quite seriously, "these Bohemian types always live in basements or attics, don't they?"

Gloria nodded encouragingly and Ann continued. "I went quite a few times—often, really—but I only saw Jeremy twice. I can't get there except at the weekends, and I wondered if he only stays in Brighton during the week and he has a proper place—his main home—where he goes at weekends."

There was a pause while Ann, ignoring the coffee, finished her glass of wine. Leslie wondered if her confession was over, but there was more to come.

"I'll tell you who else I saw, though." There was a note of outrage in Ann's voice. "It was that Susan. I saw her twice, too, actually. She wasn't with Jeremy, of course, so I expect it was a coincidence that she was in the area. A lot of people go to Brighton after all, don't they? I did just happen to see where she went, and it wasn't to Jeremy's place. Both times she went to the same place in Lion Square. I think it's a hotel. It's called The Caligula. I didn't go and look at it straightaway when she'd gone in, of course; I waited until the next time I went to Brighton, when she was nowhere to be seen."

"How shrewd," said Gloria, topping up Ann's glass. "What a detective you are!"

Leslie casually took up the pencil and recipe again and added this name and address into the opposite margin, and wondered how much longer he could spin out the washing up.

"Was she on her own, or did she have that friend, Jean Rook, with her?" asked Gloria.

"Oh, I never saw Jean after the residential course," said Ann. "She was a nice woman. I wonder what became of her. At first I thought it was odd that Susan had lost touch with her as they seemed such close friends. But actually, I think Susan's one of those people who would never really become attached to anyone, and could drop someone at a moment's notice if it suited her."

Gloria had been unashamedly topping up Ann's glass and Leslie had lost track of how much alcohol she must have consumed throughout the evening. He was glad to see that the wine bottle was now empty as Ann had clearly drunk more than enough.

She looked up and said defiantly, "Do you know something? I'm glad she's dead. When I saw her body floating there—before the reality hit me and I relived that poor woman falling over the cliff last year—for a split second I thought, 'Good, I'm glad you're gone. I can have him now'. I know there wasn't really anything between them, but you never really know, do you? She'd dropped him, I think, but I couldn't stand the way he kept looking at her. I don't think anyone else noticed, but I did. All the time; he couldn't take his eyes off her, and I hated her. Oh, how I hated her. Now, isn't that a terrible thing to say?"

Ann's tone had become positively venomous, but she resumed her maudlin state with this last sentence and she looked and sounded as though she was going to weep. Gloria pushed the coffee cup closer, and shakily Ann picked it up and took a few gulps.

"Why don't you tell us what happened that last afternoon?" said Gloria earnestly. "You were with Jeremy for a tutorial, weren't you?"

Ann responded unquestioningly and, with many quite open prompts, Gloria managed to ascertain that Ann had been with Jeremy all afternoon, and he had not been alone until only a few minutes before it was time to go into dinner. If she was telling the truth, as she seemed to be, it gave Jeremy an absolute alibi, and there was little more to be learned from her account.

When Gloria had squeezed out the last drop of information, she said brightly, "I say! Is that the time? I'd better see how those two boffins are getting on with their game. Gina will be here to pick us all up in five minutes." To Leslie she added, "Gina is taking everyone home; it's hardly out of our way."

It transpired that the chess game was already over, with Bennett the victor once again, and the two opponents were enjoying a peaceful liqueur. A punctual tooting outside the door soon broke up the party and they made a noisy, and in Ann's case unsteady, exit.

Leslie felt dog-tired but insisted on telling Bennett everything he had learnt from the evening, between stifled yawns, lest he should forget some small but important detail. "Gloria was astonishing," he said, as they retired for the night. "The way she used those pebbles to get Ann talking was audacious. Ann simply told her everything. I put it down to Gloria's bare-faced cheek."

"And I put it down to that splendid meal," said Bennett, and he flicked off the light.

In the darkness, Leslie lay thinking, and after a moment he said, "I take back what I said about Ann earlier; she can't possibly be a killer." He was picturing the poor lady, pathetic and credulous at the kitchen table. Then he remembered her bitter and spiteful outbursts and added, "Well, I don't think so, anyway."

15

Leslie and Gloria had decided to revisit Jean Rook's old house at five-thirty on Wednesday, in the hope of finding the new occupants at home at that time. The traffic was busy and by the time they had found somewhere to park, some of the shops on the parade were pulling down their shutters, though the food takeaways were just starting to get busy. They mounted the stone steps, and as they reached the top Leslie found himself tiptoeing to avoid arousing the occupants of flat number one. He outstripped Gloria to the door of number two and knocked cautiously. To his relief there was the immediate sound of footsteps, and the door was opened by a young woman with a plump baby on her hip.

Leslie explained the reason for their visit, while Gloria cooed at the delighted infant, which wriggled and kicked and gurgled. The woman, when her attention could be drawn away from her treasure, was all regrets. As the neighbour had told Leslie and Gloria, she had only recently moved in and could tell them nothing about any previous tenants. Would they like the landlord's details as he must know who he bought the property from? She went away and returned a few moments later with a neatly torn strip of letter-headed paper, bearing the name of the estate agent.

After a final joyous exchange with the baby, the door was closed, and as they moved away Gloria said, "We'll have the devil of a job getting any information from an estate agent. They'll never give us the owner's details, will they?"

"I suppose they might pass a query on for us," said Leslie, doubtfully. At this moment they were drawing level with flat number one and before Leslie could say any more the door opened a few inches.

Instead of the angry challenge Leslie expected, they heard a quiet, "Psst," and the lady of the house poked her head cautiously out. "Just step inside a minute, will you?" she whispered, her

London accent apparent even in these few quiet words. As soon as they crossed the threshold, she shut the door. "He's at his brother's and I'm not expecting him back until gone seven, but I won't invite you no further in if you don't mind. He wouldn't like it. But I'm right glad you came back, and especially now when he ain't in."

"Well, thank you so much," said Leslie. He introduced himself and Gloria, and they ascertained that the obliging lady was Marge.

Marge leaned heavily on a stick, and her legs looked painfully swollen. Leslie felt guilty about keeping her standing there, but she seemed keen to talk to them. She began by apologising for her husband's behaviour, explaining that the police had already called enquiring about Jean, and Ron, Marge's husband, didn't believe in getting involved with the police, especially not about 'that stuck-up cow'.

"Not that she were stuck-up," Marge qualified. "She was one of them folks what likes to try and do a bit better for themselves, but Ron didn't hold with that. Not that she had much chance for most of her life, poor dear."

From the explanation that followed, Leslie and Gloria learned that Jean Rook had been married to a parsimonious control freak who had prohibited the lady from any pleasures in life. She was allowed only to visit the local lending library, as the books were free to borrow, but even so she hid some of the books she borrowed, 'poetry and the like', in her wardrobe for fear that he would not approve.

"He was very hard on her, but that's the way with a lot of men," sighed Marge, resigned.

Jean would sneak into Marge's for a cup of tea when both husbands were out, and they had some lovely chats together.

"I was her only friend. That is until her husband died and that Susan come along."

Marge fell into a reverie for a moment and Leslie was worried that either time, or Marge's stamina, would run out just as they were getting to some useful information.

"Do tell us what happened," prompted Gloria.

"Well, he just dropped dead, sudden like. It was a seizure and not a thing they could do for him. When they went through his papers, you'll never guess what! He was absolutely loaded. There was hundreds of thousands of pounds in his bank account. Gawd knows where it all come from, but they said it was all in order and nothing funny about it. He was just a miser all his life and couldn't spend it."

Marge went on to explain that Jean had seen an advert in the library about the creative writing course, had signed up and become great friends with Susan. "I was happy for her at first, of course," she said. "Happy to see her being able to do all them things she'd wanted to do, and making some new friends, and going on that writing holiday. She still came in here and I loved hearing her talking about it all, being as it's years since I've got down them stairs. But then I started to get worried. It was like that Susan started to take her over. It was 'Susan this,' and 'Susan that' all the time. And she weren't quite the same old Jean."

There was a pause while Marge, leaning against the wall by now, caught her breath. "Well, then came the blow. She came in here and told me she was moving. It was all Susan's idea; Susan helped her find a place, Susan did all the arranging of it. It all happened so quickly. I asked her was she really sure, and at first she said she was, though she kept putting off giving me the new address. But when the day came, and I peeked out the door to say goodbye, she looked about, made sure that Susan wasn't watching, and she slipped a paper into my hand with her new address on. Then she gave me a great big hug and whispered, 'Oh, Marge, I hope I'm doing the right thing. But I'm not going too far; I'll come back and see you'."

Marge wiped away a fat tear which had rolled down her cheek. "Now look at me, I'm being stupid. But I'm that worried. She's writ me a couple of letters, but I dunno, they didn't say much. It's not the same when they're done on the computer; she'd gone and bought one of them for that writing class she did. And she still hasn't given me her phone number. I do miss her as I don't see no one now except him." She nodded in the direction of the rooms behind her, and then dabbed at her eyes again with her apron.

"Do you have her address to hand?" asked Leslie, fearing again that the poor lady would need to go and sit down before they achieved their object.

"Yes, dear," she said, and reached into the large front pocket of her apron. "When I heard you next door, I knew what you'd come for. Can you write it down? I don't want to part with it 'cos she wrote me a lovely little poem on the other side, and I often looks at it."

Before Leslie could reach in his pocket for a pen, Gloria had pulled out her phone and taken a photograph of the paper while Marge's eyes bulged in wonder.

"Did you give the police the address?" asked Leslie.

"Oh no," Marge replied. "Ron don't know I've got it. I don't know if I done right or wrong."

"I'm sure that was the right thing to do," said Gloria reassuringly. "It doesn't do to get into trouble with the old man, and the police will be able to find out the address from the new owner of her flat."

"I was that worried when the police came asking, but they said it wasn't any trouble with her, but she might be able to help them with some information. I guessed it was that awful accident when that woman went over the cliff. She'd told me all about it; a terrible thing. It was a long time ago, last year, but is it because the inquest or some such is only just coming up now?"

"Yes, it was just some information wanted to do with that," said Gloria, shamelessly.

"Well, if you do happen to speak to her, you will remember me to her, won't you? And tell her how I misses her." Another bulging tear escaped down her cheek before she could check it with her apron.

Both Leslie and Gloria reassured her that of course they would, but Leslie came away in a mood of extreme melancholy.

"What hateful lives some people do have," he said when they got back to the car, thinking of both Jean Rook and Marge.

"I know," agreed Gloria dolefully. "When I think of my dear husband; he treated me like a queen, and Gina like a princess. We wanted for nothing. You forget they aren't all like that."

"And to give us Jean's new address without even finding out who we were! We could have been anyone. No wonder people get conned."

"Well, thank goodness she did," said Gloria, resolutely. "Did you see? It's in Hove. I vote we go and see if we can find her. I can't go tomorrow—Gina's booked a spa day for the two of us—so let's make it Friday."

***

Gloria talked without ceasing the entire way home, apparently unaware of Leslie's deepening gloom, and her driving was just as eccentric as usual. By the time they got back to Beach Cottage, rather than rejoicing in the success of the mission, Leslie felt oppressed by all the misfortunes they had encountered in the last few weeks.

Making supper in the tiny kitchen, he related the details of the visit, while Bennett sat silently gazing at the ceiling with his glasses pushed up on his head.

"I can't make sense of any of it," Leslie said, cutting thin slices of brown bread and spreading them generously with butter, a concession to the holiday as it was normally avoided since Bennett's heart attack. "Susan befriended Jean Rook, to the extent that she orchestrated her house move and then, just months later, she'd lost touch with her. How unlikely is that? And has it got anything to do with Susan's death?"

He brought out a tub of fresh flaky crab meat from the fridge, with some watercress and a lemon, and set about assembling a plate of sandwiches. "On the way home, while Gloria was rattling on, I remembered it was Susan and Jean who were with Ann when they witnessed the cliff fall of that poor woman, on the residential course last year. Do you think that has anything to do with it?"

Bennett had finished staring at the ceiling and was selecting a bottle of wine, but he said nothing.

Leslie continued. "What if there had been an incident on the cliff last year, and it wasn't what it seemed? Perhaps one of the three pushed the woman over and the other two—" He paused his narrative while he passed the plate of sandwiches across to Bennett and waited while Bennett filled their glasses. "I can't even invent a plausible scenario that would begin to make sense of it.

If either Susan or Ann had a hold over the other one, why would they both come back on the course this year? Perhaps Jean Rook will shed some light on it if we do manage to find her in Hove."

The first rays of an evening sunset were casting in through the round window, filling the kitchen with a strange amber glow. Leslie moved across to the window and was surprised to see that a bank of clouds had appeared, and the sun was glaring through in a great fan of bronze rays. It was rather wonderful to witness, though unlike the previous evening's uplifting spectacle, it exacerbated his already grim mood. He called Bennett over and they stood in silence for a while viewing the ominous sky.

"Many clouds consulting for foul weather," observed Bennett at last, moving back to the table.

"Yes, the weather's changing, and the forecast is awful for Friday when I've agreed to go to Hove with Gloria. It's a two-hour drive along the coast and, by the time Gloria has finished looking out to sea and pointing out all the attractions, we'll be lucky if we get there alive. If we do, we'll probably get soaked to the skin or struck by lightning." Leslie took up his glass of wine and swirled it round. "I don't suppose I can persuade you to come along?"

"Despite that tempting invitation, I think I'll decline." Bennett took a crab sandwich from the plate and munched it thoughtfully. "But you will be careful, won't you?"

"Careful of what?" said Leslie, surprised. Then he added peevishly, "Or are you going to keep that a secret?" Leslie did not expect his question to be answered but, on this occasion, Bennett did reply.

"I don't know exactly; just be careful. I've always agreed with you that there was something fishy about the case." He paused and drank some wine. "But now something tells me that the fish stinks."

***

As predicted, Thursday was a day of heavy showers. Leslie was rather glad as it gave him an excuse to potter about indoors and use up the leftovers from the previous days' cooking, exclaiming from time to time at the dramatic and ever-changing sky above the sea.

By Friday, Leslie's mood had recovered, despite another dismal weather forecast and the thought of an entire day with Gloria. She made her noisy arrival soon after breakfast and they set off in her little red car with the top down, even with a heavy, threatening sky, which she dismissed as 'only a bit of a cloud'. The drive up through the New Forest was very pleasant and Gloria even managed to obey the speed limit for most of the time, in deference to the local wildlife. Once they joined the motorway, Leslie gripped the seat and screwed his eyes shut as Gloria careered along the outside lane, chattering incessantly. He heard snatches of information about the South Coast, with which Gloria was well acquainted, but most of her words were lost into the wind tunnel. Leslie was thankful that as soon as she could, she left the motorway to join the coast road. His relief was short-lived, however, for as they passed through the seaside towns of Littlehampton, Worthing and Shoreham-by-Sea, they left behind a trail of irate road-users as Gloria slowed to a crawl to point out interesting features; shot forward to cross amber traffic lights; braked hard when pedestrians were noticed at the last minute and, on one horrifying occasion, executed a sudden U-turn to show Leslie the charming house a cousin had once lived in, which she had forgotten to point out.

By the time they arrived in Hove by this torturous route, it was nearly lunchtime, and Leslie felt wretched. Despite his eagerness to get on with the task in hand, he offered little resistance when Gloria said that she knew a lovely little café on the seafront. Having revived themselves with tea and toasted sandwiches, they set off for Jean's house. They went on foot, despite the darkening clouds, because the widespread parking restrictions made it impossible to get the car much closer and, in any case, Leslie would have sooner had a soaking than get back in the car again with Gloria so soon.

They reached Jean's road in about fifteen minutes and, turning in, found it to be a long street of bungalows, much like half a dozen others that they had passed on the way. There was not a soul about, and the quietness under the looming sky felt rather creepy after the bustle of the seafront. Leslie could not shake off the qualms he had been feeling since Bennett's uncharacteristic warning for him to be careful.

"They're all very neat and tidy, aren't they?" said Gloria brightly. "This is just the sort of place I could imagine Jean choosing to live, from what I remember of her."

They found her bungalow halfway down and, to their disappointment, there was no reply when they rang the bell. Gloria persisted for much longer than was justified given that there was no car on the drive or other signs of occupation.

"I don't know if Jean had a car," said Gloria, explaining her perseverance. "She came on the course with Susan, and from what that neighbour, Marge, said about her life, I shouldn't think she'd ever been allowed to learn to drive. Bother this big wooden gate; I can't see if she's in the back garden." She crossed the neat square of lawn and pressed her face to the front window. "And she's got nets and Roman blinds. It's impossible to see inside."

"Perhaps we should come back later," said Leslie, conscious that they were probably being watched through any number of the net-curtained and blind-drawn windows opposite. "Let's carry on to Brighton and come back on the way home."

They had already agreed they would include a visit to Brighton in their plan for the day. Since it was so close, it was impossible to resist taking a discreet look at the two addresses Ann had disclosed to them: Jeremy's basement flat and the venue Susan had been seen visiting. They had no clear notion of what they hoped to achieve by this, but since it was hardly out of their way, it seemed like a good idea, and Gloria certainly had no intention of coming into the area without visiting the famous town. When canvassed about the idea, Bennett had yet again urged Leslie to be careful so, as they approached, Leslie felt as though he was advancing on Gallipoli, rather than having a day out at the seaside.

After a short but heart-stopping journey, they found a parking bay on the front just beyond the pier. "How convenient," said Gloria. "Fish and chips on the pier before we begin—that will set us up—and then let's take the little electric railway along to the marina and walk from there. If we've got time afterwards, we can visit the pavilion."

Leslie sighed inwardly. He had barely digested the toasted sandwich which he had eaten but an hour ago and which he had thought was lunch, and he was impatient to get the business of snooping over with. However, he knew that Gloria was impossible to oppose when she was determined, so he surrendered himself to the frivolities on her itinerary.

The fish and chips were particularly good and the effect of eating them on the windswept pier, with scudding clouds above and lashing waves beneath, was invigorating. Leslie's mood recovered itself and when, returning, they passed the entrance to Madame Rosetta's: Clairvoyant, Tarot, Palmistry, and Gloria announced they absolutely must have a go, Leslie did not even attempt to dissuade her. Before he passed through the beaded curtain Leslie cast a brief look at Madame Rosetta's credentials displayed on the boarding outside, which listed an astonishing range of celebrities and royal personages whose fortunes she claimed to have told. A brief calculation suggested that Madame must be nearly a centenarian if this was true, but he was not really surprised to be greeted by a black-haired, hoarse-voiced woman not much his senior.

Having introduced herself, and before even taking them into the little inner booth where she carried out her craft, she said, with a wry smile, "I know you'll be expecting me to say cross my palm with silver, but nowadays you need to cross this little gadget with your payment card, my dears." She produced a card reader and Gloria completed the pragmatic process.

The inner sanctum was everything that would be expected: crystals dangled from above, the tapestried walls were hung with strange symbolic images, and tarot cards, figurines and other mysterious objects were all in evidence. The centrepiece of the room was a table covered in a tasselled cloth and bearing a huge glass ball displayed on a splendidly ornate golden stand.

They sat around the table, and Madame Rosetta took Gloria's left hand and examined it, back and front, in detail. Leslie marvelled at the lady's skills in eliciting snippets of information from Gloria and piecing them together into a surprisingly accurate sketch of selected aspects of Gloria's character and circumstances.

He was, however, unable to explain her confident and correct assertions that Gloria was widowed and had only one daughter, as he had detected no prior clues, but no doubt her intuition was based on decades of practice.

"Oh, I say, how clever you are," said Gloria, with complete satisfaction. "It's truly wonderful."

"Do you want the ball now, my dear?" Madame released Gloria's hand and gestured towards the centre of the table. "It's included in the price."

"Oh yes, most definitely."

Madame Rosetta drew the crystal ball towards her bejewelled chest and, after some moments in silent meditation, she peered intently into its interior. Gloria leant forward eagerly and even Leslie found himself pulling his chair, which he had withdrawn to a polite distance, towards the table.

Without removing her gaze, Madame Rosetta said in a hoarse whisper, "Your visit to Brighton today…"

There was a long pause broken eventually by Gloria saying urgently, "Yes, our visit—what about it?"

"It has a purpose."

Another long pause followed until Gloria said, "Yes, yes, it does have a purpose."

Madame Rosetta hovered her hands above the crystal ball, then looked abruptly into Gloria's face. "I believe you will succeed in your purpose," she hissed. "Though not perhaps in the way you expect."

Seeing Gloria's rapt expression, Leslie could not help admiring Madam Rosetta's art. She was very convincing.

"But," she sat back and looked round at Leslie, then again at Gloria, "you must be careful. Be careful." She repeated the last words with emphasis and then pushed the crystal ball away, which seemed to indicate the session was over.

"Oh, I say, how incredible," said Gloria again. "Are you sure you won't have a go, Leslie?"

Before Leslie could construct a polite response, Madame Rosetta gave a derisive snort. "It would be no good. He's not a believer. I always know."

It is never pleasant to feel slighted, even by a seaside psychic, and Madame Rosetta's sudden warning to be careful was also disturbing, even though Leslie told himself she had picked up a subtle response from Gloria or himself. However, he had no leisure to dwell on these ambiguous feelings as they made their way out of the shop and off the pier, for Gloria was now galvanised to get on with the day's mission. They even managed to pass the doughnut, ice cream and candyfloss stalls, and the aquarium, with no more than a wistful glance and a "what a shame we don't have time—perhaps later."

In no time Leslie found himself on board the little electric train, riding along parallel to the beach with Gloria proclaiming landmarks as they passed them, such as a kiosk that had once been run by a friend's uncle and, in a loud whisper, the location of the nudist beach. They alighted at the marina station and made their way across the road, around a grand Regency-style crescent before zigzagging through the backstreets. Gloria led the way at a stately pace, confident in her knowledge of the area and Leslie followed on, unquestioning at first. They had expected to reach the address which Ann had disclosed for Jeremy's basement flat in about ten minutes, but that time elapsed and then another ten minutes.

"Isn't that the school, again?" Leslie asked. "I think we passed it a little while ago, in the opposite direction."

"I say, I do think you're right," said Gloria with a peel of laughter. "I knew these streets so well when my cousin Louie lived here, but that must have been twenty years ago, and it doesn't look quite the same now." She delved into her bag and, after much feeling about, produced her phone and tapped in Neville Terrace. After consulting it they turned and retraced their steps. In a few minutes they found themselves approaching Jeremy's street, and Leslie's anxiety increased, feeling that they had no business being there.

They had prepared a story in case they should actually come face to face with Jeremy, but Leslie was more concerned that they might be unknowingly seen by him from his basement as they walked past, and not have the chance to explain themselves.

It was not a road a day-tripper would walk along without a reason. Would he suspect that they were on to him and, if so, what would be the consequences? Without knowing what Jeremy's involvement was, if anything, it was impossible to conjecture. To make matters worse, Gloria seemed to have conspired to make herself as conspicuous as possible, dressed, as she was, in the multi-coloured 'circus tent' sundress topped by a canary yellow jacket and matching wide-brimmed hat. In contrast, Leslie had bought a dark green baseball cap in Bridesford, a garment he would never otherwise consider wearing, just to make himself less recognisable. Alongside Gloria, the effort was wasted; their chances of being noticed were maximised to the full.

"Do you think it might be wise if I go on alone from here?" said Leslie cautiously, and then felt rather foolish. He was in Brighton, after all, not Soviet Leningrad. "If Jeremy is looking out from his flat, he's much less likely to recognise me on my own than both of us together, and especially if I pull this awful cap down over my face."

"You think of everything!" said Gloria cheerfully. "I'll go across to that little park and wait for you there. I'm ready for a sit down."

The streets they had walked through so far had varied considerably in style and type, from those lined with grand old hotels to bland modern apartments, but they had all looked tidy and well kept. In just a few paces though, Leslie stepped into the rundown area which had so disquieted Ann. The properties had once been stylish three-storeyed townhouses fronting the pavement, but it seemed that all of them had been converted into multiple dwellings and, even at first glance, the broken gates, accumulated rubbish and peeling paint told of neglect. Perhaps they were mostly student lodgings, but surely these days even students expected better than this.

Jeremy's basement flat was near the top of Neville Terrace, only a few houses down and on the right as Leslie turned in. He walked past as slowly as he reasonably could, but it was still impossible to do more than catch a quick glimpse through the rusting railings. Even so, Leslie could see that Jeremy had risen above his neighbours, for the area at the foot of the metal staircase was clean and tidy and the front door was either new or recently painted. Once past, Leslie hurried on to the bottom of the road, grimacing as he passed properties whose windows had cracked glass, grubby curtains or blinds hanging askew, and dodging the carcasses of bicycle frames which hung from railings.

As he reached the end of the road, Leslie felt the first spots of rain on his face and he hurriedly turned right, and then right again, up the street which passed the backs of the Neville Terrace properties. The back gardens and yards were all as unkempt as would be expected, but when he got to Jeremy's, there was nothing to see as it was hidden by high wooden fencing with a rear gate. By this time, a steady drizzle was falling and when he arrived at the park, he found Gloria sheltering under a tree, finishing an ice cream cone.

"Perfect timing," she said, wiping her fingers on a large handkerchief. "With a bit of luck, we'll find the place in Lion Square and be back in the car before this rain gets any heavier. You can tell me all about Jeremy's flat as we go along."

Gloria seemed incapable of rushing, so they trundled steadily on, and Leslie recounted the little he had to tell about what he had seen, at which point the heavens opened, overcoming even Gloria's inveterate optimism.

"Look, that shop has an awning," she said, making for its cover with a rare turn of speed. "I've got an umbrella in my bag. Ah, it's a curio shop; I do so love them. Shall we take cover inside?"

Tempted as he was to prowl around the shop, especially as he had just spotted a very promising Toby jug in the window, he persuaded Gloria that they should carry on, and come back that way after their mission was accomplished. While Gloria wrestled with the mechanism of the umbrella, Leslie looked more closely at the jug. It seemed to be in particularly good condition and bore the legend: Toby or not Toby... A present from Paignton. It was grotesque, to be sure, but that was no deterrent, for Leslie had several vulgar specimens in his collection. He had just pictured the perfect spot for it in his cabinet when an exclamation from Gloria indicated the umbrella was securely aloft. Refusing Gloria's offer to squeeze beneath it with her, Leslie pulled his hood over the baseball cap and they broke cover.

After only a few minutes they turned into Lion Square, at which point an unexpected gust of wind turned the umbrella inside out and drew from Gloria an equally unexpected expletive. They were only metres away from their destination which conveniently had a porch, so with a final burst of energy they ran for shelter.

To their surprise the door opened immediately and a large man, evidently in the role of a bouncer, said tersely, "You members? Got your cards?"

Before Leslie could explain that they were taking shelter, another blast of wind blew in a great cataract of rain and the man moved quickly aside saying, "Better step in."

It was all rather confusing as they entered. The reception area was small, darkly painted and dimly lit, and Leslie nearly fell over a man who was crouched on the floor to his left, apparently fixing an internal door.

"Get that door shut, Kev," said the woman behind the reception desk directly in front of them, addressing the crouching repair man.

"Can't. 'S off its hinges."

"You'll be off your hinges in a minute if you don't get it shut." Then, looking at Leslie and Gloria the receptionist said, "Uh huh?"

She was probably about forty, Leslie thought, and very striking in appearance with heavily lined eyes, purple lips, a shaven head, and a skin-tight scarlet PVC top which zipped up as far as her tattooed décolletage. The top of the zip was adorned with a padlock and a key hung next to it on a chain. On the wall behind her was displayed the bust of an emperor, presumably the club's namesake, Caligula, and an array of mock Roman artefacts, mostly shackles and scourges.

Leslie had no story planned for this scenario as he'd had no intention of going inside the venue, even before he realised its business. He was hastily forming some words to politely extricate them from this embarrassing situation when Gloria began.

"We weren't expecting to come in," she said earnestly, and the receptionist raised an eyebrow. "But the wind blew my umbrella inside out. Do you serve tea?"

She broke off, for at that moment there was a noise from beyond the unhinged door. Both Leslie and Gloria turned to see a further door at the end of the short corridor swing open revealing an exotically attired couple.

"Oh!" exclaimed Gloria. "Fancy dress!"

Before she could say anything more, Leslie made a polite apology for troubling them and ushered Gloria out onto the street, hoping that she did not hear the howls of laughter as the door closed behind them. They made straight for a café opposite.

"Oh my!" repeated Gloria, turning puce when Leslie explained the nature of the establishment. "I say!" Her eyes opened so wide that Leslie thought they would pop out. "But that's where Ann saw Susan going in," she added in astonishment. "Oh, I say! A dominatrix! Well! I can just see her as that, can't you?"

Leslie had never told Gloria about the contents of Susan's rucksack and Jeremy's bag, so it was no wonder that Gloria was surprised and, as there was no reason why Jeremy's inclinations in this direction would have occurred to her, Leslie did not mention it.

The rain had abated, so as soon as they had finished their coffees, they splashed their way back to the antique shop, only to find it had closed. Leslie was preparing to be consumed with disappointment about the jug when Gloria's phone buzzed and, after the customary fumbling in the depths of her bag, she read the message and announced, "It's from Val. They've just pulled a body from the sea."

16

Back at the car, Gloria phoned Val, who reported that there had been a lot of coastguard activity since lunchtime but all anyone knew was that a body had been recovered along the stretch between the hotel and the village. She would let Gloria know as soon as she heard anything further, and she sent her love to Leslie and Bennett.

It was in sober mood that they drove back towards Jean Rook's house in Hove, for neither of them was in any doubt that poor Susan had at last been found. They agreed it was not their place to say anything about the body to Jean, if they should find her in.

"And to think that I was only laughing about her half an hour ago," sighed Gloria. "At least they may now get some clues about her death."

Leslie was not so optimistic; he did not care to imagine what state a corpse would be in after this time at sea.

"I'm going to drive down Jean's road," said Gloria as they got nearer. "Let's take a chance and pull up on the yellow lines outside. If she's not in, it would be annoying to have done that long walk again for nothing, especially with all these puddles. If she's in and feels like talking, we can ask to park on her driveway."

"But look," said Leslie as they approached, "that's Jean's bungalow there, isn't it? And there's a blue car on the drive."

"I say, what luck," said Gloria. "Excellent, let me pull in."

Without warning she applied the brakes, no doubt to the annoyance of a car behind which was forced to squeeze round the outside of her. The car passed, and Gloria had started to reverse into a residents' bay on the opposite side of the road, when the door of Jean's bungalow opened, and a tall grey-haired lady appeared.

They were about three bungalows away from Jean's, and Gloria, neck craned over her shoulder as she reversed towards the curb, was not aware of her until Leslie said, "Look, is that Jean? I think she's going to get into her car."

Gloria spun round and, with the car half skewed across the road, she leapt out, waving and shouting frantically, "Hello there, yoo-hoo, hello, Jean!"

The lady seemed to glance across for a moment but then, to their dismay, she got straight into the car. Pulling quickly off the drive, she accelerated down the road, away from them.

"Surely she heard me," said Gloria, getting back into the driving seat as quickly as she was able. "Let's go after her. You never know…" She edged the car out of its awkward position, but by the time they reached the bottom of the road, Jean's blue car was nowhere to be seen. "I can't understand her driving off like that. She must have heard me. But perhaps she was in a hurry and thought I was some holidaymaker wanting directions. I don't suppose she would recognise me; it was over a year ago and I wasn't even on the writing course last year. She would only have seen me in passing at the hotel."

"So near, yet so far," groaned Leslie. "And we're going back to Dartonleigh tomorrow so there's no chance to come back and try again."

There was nothing to be done but to continue their journey home. Gloria talked incessantly and, with the car roof now up, was fully audible, but Leslie only heard half of what she said, preoccupied as he was with his own gloomy thoughts.

***

The first piece of news for Bennett was about the finding of the body, and Bennett listened in grim silence. They were sitting on the veranda of Beach Cottage, watching the waves lashing on the shore and the clouds racing across the dark sky. Then Leslie told of the frustrating near miss with Jean Rook, and Bennett sat patiently while everything was related in minute detail, as was Leslie's wont. After these two pieces of stop-press news, Leslie reverted to a methodical account of the day, starting with the hair-raising journey, the fortune-teller and train ride, a description of

Jeremy's flat, the only tidy dwelling in a row of near-slums, and even the elusive Toby jug. Bennett sat impassively throughout, his only activity being to top up their glasses.

However, when it came to the account of the visit to the Caligula Club in Lion Square, Bennett put his drink down and started laughing. If amused, Bennett normally rationed himself to raising a single eyebrow, but occasionally, very occasionally, he could go into convulsions, and this was one of those occasions. By the time Leslie described their hasty exit, he was dabbing his eyes.

"Stop," he said, holding his sides. "I can't believe you didn't realise what it was before you went there."

"I know," said Leslie, who was also laughing by now. "The name didn't register until I went in. It should have done, of course, especially knowing Susan's tastes. You obviously knew, you sod."

Leslie went through to the kitchen and assembled a cold supper from the week's leftovers which he brought out to the veranda. They ate in thoughtful silence for a while then Leslie said, "I'm not sure how much further today's trip has taken us in understanding what befell poor Susan. That was a strange business with Jean Rook, though. From what I'd heard of her, I'd expected a timid, diffident woman, not someone who would speed away from us as she did. It was as though she was scared of something. I do wish we'd managed to speak to her." Leslie took the last slice of salmon quiche onto his plate and added a couple of cherry tomatoes. "But, having said all that, she might simply not have seen us, and perhaps she was just rushing off, late for an appointment. Once you get suspicious, it's so easy to sensationalise the smallest thing. I was thinking about it in the car on the way back and it is actually possible to give an innocuous explanation to just about everything in this drama. There's nothing sinister about Susan and Jeremy keeping their relationship secret and if, from Jeremy's perspective, it was simply—how shall I put it?—'carnal gratification', he may well be able to put a brave face on now she's gone. Susan's health condition causing her to collapse into the sea is substantiated by her medical history. Even her splitting up with Jean may not be especially strange; perhaps Jean got on her nerves, and they had a row. Ann's comment that Susan was a glacier—or was it an iceberg?—and could easily drop someone, certainly rings true." There was a pause while Leslie ate, and Bennett topped up their glasses.

Leslie went on. "Then there's the sailor. Susan was probably an old flame, and they had some unfinished business. It doesn't have to involve murder. Val certainly thought that the wife suspected he was chasing after a woman. There," he said, putting down his plate with an air of finality, "I've accounted for everything." He started to stack the tray.

Bennett passed across his plate and cutlery. "What strikes me," he said, "is how many things need accounting for. By the way, how do you account for the rucksack?"

Before Leslie had a chance to reply, they were interrupted by the buzzing of Leslie's phone. It was Gloria calling and, after listening for some time he said, "OK, let me know when you hear anything else," and he rang off. "Gloria has had an update from Val, about the body that was recovered," he said to Bennett. "It can't be Susan. It's a man."

Bennett responded by pushing his glasses onto the top of his head and staring at the ceiling.

Leslie continued. "Val says that the police have been at the hotel and, from what they've been asking, she thinks it's the sailor, Pete Shad, although they haven't said so." Leslie paused uneasily. "Perhaps we should go back to Alemouth instead of going home tomorrow. We need only stay a couple of days and I wouldn't expect Val to put us up." He spoke diffidently for, although it was impossible to predict what Bennett would think about almost anything, he thought that Bennett would want to go home at the earliest opportunity.

"No, I don't think we should go back to Alemouth," Bennett said. "I believe that the key to this is to be found in Brighton. How about we go on there?"

***

There was much to do; accommodation to be booked and the journey planned in addition to packing up. Leslie began by phoning Gloria as they had all arranged to travel back to Dartonleigh the next day and she would be expecting to pick them up. She immediately insisted on changing her plans and driving them to Brighton, despite Leslie desperately trying to put her off.

"The journey will be impossible without a car," she said. "I think you'd have to get a train into London and back out again. I don't need to go home tomorrow; I'll take you there and then stop on here with Gina another night. You're not going to persuade me otherwise."

That decided, Bennett was put in charge of arranging the accommodation, which Leslie allowed with some misgivings, while he packed up and cleaned. Bennett had retired to bed long before Leslie had the house in the pristine condition that satisfied his high standards.

Despite his late night Leslie slept badly, and by the time they had endured nearly two hours of Gloria's traffic contraventions, he wished he had never agreed to go to Brighton at all. At the outskirts of the town, they slowed down sufficiently for speech to be possible in the open-topped car.

From the back seat Bennett said, "This journey has taken me back to my childhood."

"Oh really? You used to come to Brighton then, did you, Bennett?" Gloria asked.

"I've never been here before in all my life," he replied. "No, I was thinking of the last time I went on the dodgem cars."

Gloria threw her head back with a peal of laughter. "You're such a tease," she said. "But surely you've been to Brighton before?"

"No, I have spent my life avoiding the place, but I suppose it had to happen eventually. And if we continue visiting the coastal resorts at this rate, we should be at Great Yarmouth by Michaelmas."

They turned down a street which Gloria failed to notice was a no entry until it was too late, and she came nose to nose with an oncoming car. Obligingly, she mounted the pavement to allow the legitimate vehicle to pass.

"It's one way!" the woman driver shouted angrily through her open window as she squeezed by.

"It's all right, madam," called out Bennett, "we're only going one way!"

This sent Gloria into further paroxysms of mirth. Her good humour was undaunted when, close to their destination, they became trapped in another minor labyrinth of one-way streets, and repeatedly passed the road that Leslie and Bennett were staying in without being able to access it.

"It's just like Hampton Court maze," said Gloria cheerfully. "You can see the middle but can't get to it. And once you've got to the middle you can't get away from it."

Leslie, whose endurance had now been tested to the limit, said, "I think you'd better pull in here, Gloria. It's only just over there, so we can easily walk."

They extricated themselves from Gloria and her car with many thanks on their side and good wishes on hers, and at last she went toot-tooting off down the road.

"We could hardly have announced our arrival more conspicuously if we'd been Billy Smart's Circus," said Bennett wryly, as they struggled along the road with their luggage, with Leslie fearing for his shoulder as he dragged a wheeled suitcase noisily along the bumpy pavement.

"Yes—I've only just realised how close we are to Jeremy's flat," Leslie replied anxiously. "We came at it from the other direction yesterday. But surely this can't be the road we're staying in; this can't be the house. Is this a joke?"

They were standing in front of a slum dwelling, in Leslie's eyes, every bit as bad as the properties in Jeremy's road. The houses in this street were more modest, only two storeys high and with no basements. They would have been smart enough in their day but now they were in a dismal state, and the door which they were proposing to enter could not have been wiped down, let alone painted, for decades. The adjoining house to the right was shored up with scaffolding and the pavement was obstructed by the scaffolding supports and an untidy heap of builders' debris, though there was not a workman in sight.

Leslie was seized with sudden fury. What was Bennett thinking of, booking such a place to stay in? And he was angry with himself for committing any practical task to Bennett, however basic; he should have known that no good would come of it. They would have to find somewhere else, but for the moment there was nothing for it but to go inside, and Bennett was already punching a code into a metal box on the wall, which opened stiffly to disgorge a thick mat of spider's web and the front door key.

"Let's see how bad it is inside," Leslie said through gritted teeth and, poking his head through the door, he was met by a powerful smell of damp. "Dear God, what a hovel. Whatever possessed you?"

Bennett went past him into the hall, making no reply.

"And look, here." Leslie, stepping back out onto the pavement for his case, pointed at some tools propped up against the wall of the adjacent house. "A sledgehammer—very handy for anyone who wants to break in and murder us in our bed."

Putting down the luggage, Bennett came out and heaved the sledgehammer into the hall, leaning it against the wall. "Every home should have one," he said and carried their two cases up the uncarpeted stairs.

Leslie lugged in the remaining bags and shut the front door. He peered into a dreary sitting room and then went into the kitchen which looked as though it was fitted out in the nineteen fifties. The cooker must have been obsolete years ago, but there was an electric kettle, a microwave oven and a modern-looking fridge. Gingerly he pulled back a grimy net curtain to reveal the back garden which was waist high in weeds and vegetation.

Going upstairs, he found Bennett in the back bedroom looking out of the window. As he joined him, Leslie realised that they were overlooking Neville Terrace, and the front of Jeremy's flat could easily be seen, albeit at a distance. "Oh!" he exclaimed, slightly contrite. "And I thought you were just being stupid."

"Probably that as well," said Bennett ruefully.

"Surely we can't stop here, though. It's disgusting. We haven't stayed anywhere like this since we ended up in that hostel in Greece by mistake. That was your fault too, if I recall rightly. Do you remember?"

"We survived that."

"No thanks to you. And we were twenty years younger, then." Leslie turned back the covers on the bed and cautiously ran his hand inside. "Still, these sheets are clean, and the bed doesn't feel damp. But look at those curtains. And you haven't seen the kitchen."

On further examination downstairs, however, the kitchen surfaces were not actually filthy, if one overlooked the line of black mould where the worktop met the tiles, and everywhere else where there was a join. The microwave oven was useable and, when Leslie steeled himself and opened the fridge, he decided that, once wiped over, it would be acceptable for wrapped items. "I suppose people live in much worse than this as their normal," he said stoically, "but God alone knows what I'll cook. My normal repertoire doesn't involve much microwaving. Thank goodness I bought that new pan and knives in Bridesford. And to think I nearly sent them home with Gloria. At least I'll have something I can use, which won't give us food poisoning. That's if the cooker doesn't blow up."

Over a makeshift lunch out of the food they had brought with them, Leslie asked, "Do we have a plan? I'd like to go to Hove again to try to speak to Jean Rook but, other than that, I'm not sure what we've come here for."

"Let's wait and see. I've a feeling that things are coming to a head," said Bennett enigmatically.

Leslie, who knew that he would get no more out of Bennett, felt restless, and after doing as much cleaning as he could with the available equipment, declared that he would have to go to the shops if they were to eat for the next few days. Once again Bennett urged caution, this time reminding Leslie that they were now on Jeremy's doorstep, and even adding that things might be dangerous.

"Do you really think it's that serious?" said Leslie. Such words of warning were most out of character.

"There have been several deaths already," said Bennett. "We don't want any more."

"Several? Susan and, we presume, the sailor, have died. That's two. Who else?"

"That's what I'm trying to figure out," said Bennett and, infuriatingly, leaned back on a kitchen chair and shut his eyes.

Leslie stomped off towards the shops hurt, as he always was, when Bennett would not let him in on his thinking. He set off in a round-about way to avoid passing too close to Jeremy's flat and made for the little parade of shops where he had sheltered in the rain while Gloria was getting out her umbrella. He remembered there was a small supermarket there and, of course, he was still hoping to obtain the Toby jug. That, at least, would be some compensation for the dreadful accommodation.

It was a nerve-wracking walk and at every step Leslie expected to come face to face with Jeremy.

But it was not Jeremy who Leslie saw. As he approached the row of shops, about fifty metres ahead, the figure of a tall woman with grey hair emerged from a side street and turned up the pavement in front of him. Despite having seen Jean Rook only once, he had no doubt that it was her. He had no intention of alarming the lady again by calling out to her, and she was far enough away that even Gloria would have had to bellow to be heard, so he quickened his pace in pursuit. He passed the Toby jug with a pang of regret; it would have to wait, as would his shopping. Jean was a brisk walker and Leslie was nearly trotting to make any gain. Fortunately, she suddenly stopped and darted into a doorway. Puffing and panting, Leslie kept his eyes glued to the spot she had disappeared from and as he got nearer, he could see that it was within another short parade of shops.

Fear of encountering Jeremy was still very real, so rather than hanging about on the pavement, Leslie pushed open the shop door and, still breathing heavily, stepped inside without pausing, though he had no plan for how he would introduce himself to the lady. His first thought, as he looked around, was that he had made a mistake and gone through the wrong doorway, for it was immediately and embarrassingly obvious that this was a sex shop.

But there, to his unutterable surprise, was Jean Rook with her back to him and taking something from the shelf. Leslie's second thought was that this was certainly not the place for him to introduce himself, so he sidled down one of the aisles and stooped as if looking at the lower shelves, to avoid being seen.

Though not prudish about such things, it was disconcerting to find himself unexpectedly surrounded by so much explicit erotica and his astonishment at seeing Jean Rook there was extreme. He supposed that Susan must have introduced her to this world, but it was still unbelievable. There was a mirror in the aisle and, glancing into it, Leslie saw Jean take her goods into a cubicle and pull across the curtain. This was the chance he needed, but as he was about to escape, he noticed that the curtain was caught on Jean's bag on the floor and had not fully closed. Jean was standing sideways on, holding what looked like some sort of headgear in black. He turned round furtively, to replace an item he had unconsciously taken hold of, when a movement in the cubicle caught his eye. With fascinated horror, he saw Jean put her hand to her head and pull away her hair. Standing there, holding a bondage hood in one hand and a grey wig in the other, was Susan. Susan, who had last been seen floating out to sea, whose killer he had tormented his mind about, and whose unmourned death he had taken on himself to grieve for.

Susan pulled on the hood and, noticing the open curtain, she reached round to close it. By chance, the item still in Leslie's hand was a fetish mask which he rammed onto his face, desperate not to be recognised if she saw him. As soon as the curtain was shut, Leslie restored the mask to the display and began his hasty exit.

"Oi," said a voice. Horrified, Leslie quickened his steps and the voice said, "Where d'you think you're going?"

Leslie turned and, to his relief, it was the woman behind the counter at the far end of the shop. He looked at her but did not dare speak.

"You gotta buy that gimp mask. If you try it, you buy it. Says so on all the shelves, see."

As speedily as he could, and in complete silence but for his pounding heart, Leslie made the purchase, all the while expecting Susan to emerge from the cubicle. He escaped before she appeared, though as he hurried away, he could not decide if it had been through luck or because she had recognised him and equally wanted to avoid a meeting. He made haste, without even breaking stride beside the antique shop with the Toby jug, and he was back at the dismal house in no time.

Despite the seriousness of the circumstances, Bennett's perverse sense of humour was tickled for the second time in as many days by Leslie's account, and by the time Leslie produced the mask, he was doubled up with laughter.

"You won't believe how much I had to pay for this," Leslie said, holding it up to his face. They were upstairs in the bedroom where Bennett had been keeping watch. Leslie caught sight of himself in the dressing table mirror. "Dear God, Darth Vader visits Brighton."

"Take it off," begged Bennett, wiping his eyes. "I'm afraid it does nothing for me."

Leslie hurled the offending object onto the bed and sat down. "I don't know if she saw me. She had a hood on at the time so I couldn't tell."

"We'd better work on the assumption that she did, and that the balloon's gone up."

"You don't seem surprised that Jean Rook was Susan. Don't tell me you knew all along and let me go through that terrible shock? But what does it mean? And if the balloon has gone up, as you say, what's going to happen? I can't understand any of it."

"I'm still piecing it together," said Bennett, "but we should know more soon. It's been an eventful day. Before we left Bridesford this morning, I had a message from Sandra, you know, the wife of Pete, the sailor. You remember that I gave her my card when we saw her at the hotel? She contacted me to say she'd just identified her husband's body and could she speak to us. I gave her this address and, while you were out, I had a message to say she's on the way."

"Oh, the poor woman," said Leslie, his sympathy for her overcoming his vexation that Bennett had said nothing of her earlier communication until now. "I don't know what I can give her to eat. I never managed to get to the shops. There's enough milk for a cup of tea if you'll have yours black."

Ignoring these prandial considerations, Bennett continued. "And look at this photograph." His laptop was balanced on the window ledge, and he opened a picture onto the screen. Rather grainy, it looked like a cutting from an old newspaper or magazine, and it showed two rows of track-suited young women posed in front of a boathouse. The caption beneath gave the date and proclaimed it to be Cambridge University Rowing Club with the names of the women pictured, and their respective colleges.

Leslie leant forward, adjusted the screen and, after peering at it for a moment exclaimed, "Oh, it's Susan, standing in the back line! She said she rowed for Cambridge. She's much younger there of course. Where did you get this?"

"From my old colleague, Giles. He rowed for the men's team. Much longer ago than this, of course, but he went into coaching at Cambridge after that and I asked him to see if he could find a picture, and someone who knew Susan. I'd found her name easily enough on the lists of past crews, so I knew the year, but I couldn't find any photos online. The women's sport wasn't very prominent back then."

"But what's the point?" asked Leslie.

"Look at it again," said Bennett. And when, after a minute or two, Leslie shook his head, he said, "Look at the names—at the order of them."

"Oh," said Leslie. "Susan is second from the left, but the name makes her third from the left. Surely it's just an error."

"This email just arrived," said Bennett, opening it on the screen.

Puzzled, Leslie read it.

Bennett,
Giles asked me to confirm that the names on the photograph are correctly assigned, which they are, and to give you any personal information I can about the two girls whose names you were querying, Susan Gunner and Jennifer Baker. I remember them quite well, though I don't think I can tell you anything useful as it was a long time ago and I have no recent information.

I remember most of the girls I coached, especially if they were good enough for the crew, but these two stay in my mind because they were both rather odd. Forgive me if either is related to you, I don't know why you are enquiring, but I will be honest. With hindsight, Susan probably had something like Asperger's, though nothing was diagnosed as far as I know—back then no one was in a hurry to put labels on people. She was intense, quiet and completely obsessed with rowing; if you know anything about competitive rowers, you'll realise that to stand out as obsessional is impressive! She was befriended by Jennifer, though it was clearly an unequal relationship as Jennifer was always dominant, if not domineering. She is much harder to describe. She was undoubtedly reliable, hardworking, ambitious and talented. With hindsight, though, I never really warmed to her as I always felt that, below the surface, there was something rather calculating, cold and self-interested about her, though I can't now remember quite why I thought that. It was widely believed that the two girls were in a relationship, but I don't know if that was true. I remember they went off travelling together immediately after they went down, but I have never seen or heard anything about either of them again.

These are, of course, my personal views, and Giles assures me that you are to be trusted with them, though I hardly think I have betrayed much in terms of confidentiality. If I think of anything else I'll let you know, and once again please forgive my opinions if either of the women has some close connection with you.

John Barque

There was a pause while Leslie digested the content of the email. "Does this mean," he said at length, "that the person currently masquerading as Jean Rook, who we have known as Susan, is really called Jennifer Baker?"

"It would seem so."

"What has happened to the real Jean Rook and Susan Gunner?"

"That's what I'd like to know," said Bennett. "Ah, look. Here comes the polyonymous lady now. And it seems she's been on a shopping spree."

The person who they had been calling Susan, and was still disguised as Jean, had turned the corner into Neville Terrace and was approaching Jeremy's flat. She was laden with two bulging carrier bags which, though they had no distinguishing marks, were of the same design as the one on the bed with the mask beside it.

"Do you suppose Jeremy is at home?" said Leslie, his mind boggling at the content of the bags.

"He is," said Bennett. "I didn't get a chance to tell you that you only just missed him this morning when you went out."

"Is he an accomplice?" Leslie asked, although he was now more confused than ever about what it was Jeremy might be complicit in.

"In a way," said Bennett. "But also possibly the next victim."

Before Leslie could question him on this alarming assertion the doorbell rang.

Bennett moved to a front bedroom and peered down into the street. "It's Sandra," he confirmed.

"I hope you know what you're doing," Leslie said over his shoulder to Bennett, as he led the way downstairs. "She might be part of the plot and has come to murder us both."

17

It was immediately obvious that the woman standing on the doorstep had no murderous intent. She was in the same forlorn condition that Leslie remembered when they last met her, but this time she made no effort to disguise her misery. As Leslie ushered her into the kitchen, always the most natural place for him to talk, she showed no signs of noticing the general squalor and seemed oblivious to everything except her grief. Leslie put the kettle on and set about assembling some cheese and crackers onto a plate.

"I don't know if I've done right by coming here," she said to Bennett, who was sitting opposite her at the kitchen table. "I didn't know what else to do. I had the feeling you knew something about it all when I saw you at that hotel and I had no one else to go to. But whatever anyone says, Pete never killed her. Or if he did it would have been an accident. I don't know what happened, but I do know he wouldn't have murdered a woman, not even Susan."

"He won't be accused of that," said Bennett. "No one murdered her. She's still alive."

"Oh God, then she has done him in," wailed Sandra. "I knew it. I warned him, but he wouldn't listen and now he's gone." She felt in her pockets and brought out a handful of tissues and held them to her face.

Leslie could make no sense of what the poor lady was saying, but his impatience for information was subordinate to his feelings of sympathy.

"We were so sorry to hear about your husband," he said, as he put mugs and plates on the table, and he was aware of how ineffectual the words sounded.

"But that's just it," Sandra cried, "he wasn't." She sobbed silently into her tissues but made no attempt to explain what she meant.

When he could wait no longer, Leslie asked, "I'm sorry, what do you mean? He wasn't what?"

"He wasn't really my husband," Sandra said, between sobs. "He was hers."

"Hers?" exclaimed Leslie, incredulously. "You don't mean he was Susan's husband?"

Sandra nodded miserably. "Yes. He was still married to that evil bitch."

Leslie was more bewildered than ever. If this was true, it meant that Susan was also Mrs Shad, adding yet another identity to her ever-growing list.

"He wasn't a bad man; he didn't deserve this," Sandra protested. "When he never rang me for days, I knew something terrible had happened. He always rang home, whatever. I thought straightaway that she'd done him in, but when I got down to Alemouth I heard that she was dead, and I thought that maybe he had done her in and was lying low somewhere. It would have been an accident—he only wanted money, he wouldn't have murdered her, as I said. That's why I couldn't say anything about it then or go to the police. Only now you're saying she isn't dead at all, and he is, so I was right all along."

She pulled her mug of coffee towards her and stared into it desolately. "He hadn't seen her for years, not since they split up," she went on. "Then last summer he got some work down on the south coast at the marina in Chichester. Money was tight for us, work was drying up, and he had a mate who was working down there. And there she was one day, bringing in a fancy cruiser. Oh God, I wish he'd never laid eyes on her."

"Perhaps you could start from the beginning," prompted Leslie.

For a time, Sandra was unable to marshal her thoughts, but slowly, and with many digressions, they pieced the story together.

Sandra had been with Pete, she told them, for about ten years, living together in her native seaside town of Grimsby. He was originally from the Essex coast and had never known any other life than boats and the sea. He did some fishing and tourist work in the season, and a bit of water taxi work.

"And there's usually someone wanting help in the boatyards. It's not regular work, but we had enough to get by," she said. "When he met me, all he wanted was a peaceful life. He'd had enough trouble in the past."

Trouble for Pete had started soon after he left school, she said, and he had drifted into black market work. "Only cigarettes, wine; that kind of stuff. From Europe mostly," said Sandra. "No hard drugs or anything like that, maybe a bit of cannabis, but nothing big."

This illicit activity brought him into contact with Susan, who was also involved in the same line of business. They joined forces and got married quite quickly. "She never loved him, I'm certain sure of that. She used him. He had the boat and was brilliant with it; he could pull it up just about anywhere. And when they couldn't bring the boat right in, if that was too risky, he'd sit out at sea and make out he was fishing, and she would go over the side and swim in underwater, carrying whatever they were smuggling to the shore. But she was after the big time, and got them into carrying expensive stuff: hard drugs, currency, people even. Susan was the mastermind, and Pete told me she did it for the kick as much as the money."

It was not long before Pete got cold feet, according to Sandra. It seemed that Pete was a man who was fearless in his boat, and had no great moral scruples, but there was a limit to the risks he was prepared to take, with regard to the law. He tried to get Susan to pull back from serious crime and, finally, he put his foot down over the most risky jobs. At first, she put a lot of pressure on him to carry on, but then suddenly her attitude changed, and she backed off. That made Pete suspicious because it was so out of character.

"She wasn't one to back down," said Sandra, "and he thought she was scheming up something. You can see how he didn't trust her even then. So, when she said they ought to take out life insurance policies, you can just imagine what he thought. He kept making excuses to put it off, and when she went quiet about that as well, he wondered if she'd gone ahead with the insurance policy and forged his signature somehow. When she was out, he searched the flat they were living in for the paperwork. He never did find any insurance papers, but when he slid out a drawer, there, hidden on the shelf beneath, he found a passport."

Susan reached into her bag and, opening a large envelope, took out some papers and passed one to Bennett. "That's a copy of the page with the name and photo," she said.

Bennett took it, and looking over his shoulder Leslie could see a slightly blurred but recognisable passport photograph page showing the woman they were all calling Susan, when she was much younger, but with the name of Jennifer Baker.

"It was a terrible shock to Pete to find that the woman he'd married had another name, and he didn't know what to make of it. He was scared of her by now, so he never asked her about it. He just put the passport back in exactly the same place, and the next time she was out of the way he took it and secretly photocopied it."

"Did he copy all the pages," asked Bennett, "the ones with visa stamps on?"

"He did," said Sandra. "Here." She passed the papers to him looking rather puzzled, but Bennett offered no explanation.

"May I keep these?" he asked, "or are they the only ones you have?"

"The original copies are still at home," said Sandra. "Those are copies of copies, which is why they're a bit fuzzy. You can keep them if you think they'll be of use."

She passed Bennett the envelope, looking questioningly at him and, still with no explanation, Bennett took it and folded the papers back in.

Sandra went back to her story. "In the end, Pete decided that Susan had this other identity as a backup in case the police ever caught up with her and that she would use it, if she needed to, to cut and run. He never let on about any of his suspicions, but knew he had to leave her and get out while he could."

There was a pause while Sandra drank a little of her coffee and while she gathered her thoughts for the next part of the story.

"There'd been another problem between Pete and Susan, as well," she said. "He didn't know at first, but Susan was into all that bondage stuff, you know what I mean? Pete couldn't stand anything like that but, in the end, he was able to use it as his reason for leaving her. She didn't make much fuss about him going and he thought she was glad to see the back of him because he'd stopped being useful to her. But then he found out she'd really done the dirty on him. They discussed how to split their money, but the day before he was due to move out she vanished, and he discovered she'd taken nearly everything out of all their joint accounts. They were renting a furnished flat so the only property they had was the boat, which was his anyway, but she'd gone off with every penny they'd ever made. There was nothing he could do; it was all made illegally, and they'd paid no tax on it. The money was split across lots of different accounts in different banks and he could think of no way of tracing her that didn't mean he'd get found out. She was very clever."

Leslie poured more coffee and pushed the cheese and crackers towards Sandra, but she shook her head.

"Pete got a job in a boatyard along the coast near Grimsby. I was working behind the bar in a pub there, and that's how we met. Eventually he moved in with me and for a while we had enough work to make ends meet. But I never earned much, and his work was always touch and go so we never had any to put by for a rainy day. The boat was getting old and needed a lot of work, and money was getting tighter and tighter, and although he never saw hide nor hair of Susan, he never forgot how she did him out of all that money. Last year things were really bad. He wouldn't be persuaded to get rid of the boat, no matter that it was draining us of money every month, and we got into debt. An old mate of his offered him work down at Chichester, in the marina, so last summer he went down there to do the season. He used to ring me every morning, but one afternoon he called to say he'd seen Susan, with a bloke, bringing a flash cruiser into the marina. Even though he hadn't seen her for so long he knew her straightaway, seeing her there on the deck of a boat. It was an awful shock to him, and he kept out of the way so she wouldn't see him. Oh, why did he ever see her?"

There was a long pause while she buried her face in her hands, overcome by a fresh wave of grief. When she was able to continue, she said, "When Susan and this bloke of hers were leaving, Pete stepped outside the office where he'd been hiding and watched them go. That was when the coincidence happened. A woman working at the marina pointed to them, quite out of the blue, and told Pete that she knew the man. His name was Jeremy, 'a right arsehole' was what she called him. He ran writing seminars at her library, and she'd signed up, but she only stuck it for two of the lessons because the man was a complete phoney. She claimed he knew less than her about writing and that the course was full of old spinsters all drooling over him."

Sandra went on to tell them that having seen Susan, Pete started to become obsessed with the money she owed him and fixated on getting it back. "It was like a madness with him," she said. "It was seeing her with that big expensive boat, and us so hard-up. No matter how much I warned him, he couldn't leave it alone. He found out her home address and her email quite easily; they had her contact details on the database at the marina. I'm surprised she'd given them the right information but I suppose she didn't expect anyone to be looking for her there and, besides, I think she was that sure of herself. Anyway, Pete emailed her, telling her he wanted the money she owed him. It wasn't what you would call a threatening message, but he did point out he knew her address and that he knew stuff about her. I told him how stupid that was, how it could be used against him, but he wouldn't listen.

"She didn't reply at first, but Pete sent her a load more messages and eventually he got an answer more or less telling him to go to hell. She made out she didn't know what he was talking about and that if he carried on contacting her she would get her lawyers onto him for harrassment. It was all a bluff, of course, and Pete knew it. So then he told her he knew about Jennifer Baker—that's the name on that passport."

"That touched a nerve because she told him then that she wanted to see his copy of the passport. And Pete was to bring it to her; she wouldn't have what she called a 'sensitive document' put in the post or uploaded in a message.

"I knew it was some kind of a trick, a scam, but he wouldn't listen. Susan seemed to have the power to convince him, and they arranged to meet at a little bay about five miles along the coast from Alemouth. It was a place they used to pull the boat up when they were working the Devon coast together.

"He thought he'd come up with a plan to outsmart her. He'd got enough information from the woman at the marina to find Jeremy's website and he'd seen that Jeremy did a summer course at a hotel in Alemouth. When he looked again, he found that there was a course in Alemouth that very week, so he reckoned that's where Susan would be.

"So he went down there and he was right, she was there. He thought he'd been clever because Susan had told him to meet her in the bay on Wednesday evening, but he turned up in the hotel on the Monday, two days before she was expecting him, and took her by surprise. He rang me, so pleased with himself. He showed her the passport copies and she agreed to give him the money he thought he was owed. He wouldn't tell me how much, but it must have been a lot because he said all our problems were over. She said she couldn't get the money together until Wednesday, so he was going to meet her again then, just along the coast from Alemouth, at the spot where they found his boat.

"The last time I heard from him was on the Tuesday evening. He'd had a few beers on the boat, and he was going to get an early night. He was laughing about the money we were going to have and how he could get the boat done up properly. But for all his laughing and cocksure words, I could hear he was nervous.

"I was still pleading with him not to go through with it and come home. I told him it was a trap. We had an awful row and the last thing I ever said to him was that he was a stupid bastard. And I hung up on him. And now he's gone for ever."

Her words finished in a wail of grief, and she dropped her head on her forearms on the table and sobbed inconsolably. Leslie, almost moved to tears himself, could not restrain the thought that Pete had not deserved this woman. There was nothing to be said or done and they all sat united for the moment in sorrow.

"What will you do now?" asked Leslie when Sandra was drying her eyes.

"I'm going back to Alemouth tonight," she said. "I have to register the death and all that stuff. I've got a van which I've been sleeping in. I suppose I have to tell all this to the police, though I can't face it. But if Susan is still alive, as you say she is, I want her caught."

"I think we can help with regards to the police," said Bennett. "We happen to know the detective chief inspector. With your permission, we can tell him your story and he can then arrange for someone to speak to you."

Sandra gratefully agreed to this and gave Bennett her details. When Leslie offered to walk back with her to her van, which she had left in a car park near the town, she accepted that too, having, she said, got terribly lost on the way there.

It was only when they were walking back, by a route which bypassed Jeremy's flat, that Sandra asked what Leslie and Bennett's involvement was in the case. Leslie made a vague response that they were staying at the hotel when the incident occurred and were friends with the hotel owner and the detective chief inspector. It was a totally inadequate answer, but Sandra accepted it without, Leslie thought, even listening. He saw her safely into her van and insisted she took the package of cheese and crackers which he had brought along. With further thanks and promises to keep in touch, they parted.

Leslie had managed to successfully navigate to the car park through the backstreets, but as he returned, he lost his way and eventually emerged into the main street. He was about to double back but, afraid of losing his way again and anxious to get back to their lodgings as quickly as possible, he decided it would be safe enough to carry on down the main road for at least a little way. He checked the time and was surprised to see it was only twenty to five. It felt as though days had passed since lunchtime. Despite the dreadful circumstances, the Toby jug had not been forgotten and the antique shop was almost in sight. It would only take a minute to pop into the shop, if it was still open, and from there he could return by the route that gave Jeremy's road a wide berth. He hurried along, vigilant for any signs of danger in the persons of Jeremy or the disguised Susan; it was impossible to think of her by any other name.

Leslie realised he was approaching the sex shop, and he was suddenly seized with panic, though surely after filling those two bulging bags, Susan would not be back. Nonetheless, he now wished he had gone a different way and was regretting his decision. He hurried by without incident, passed the two takeaways next door and was just coming level with a currency exchange shop when a woman stepped quickly from its door. Leslie was rushing so fast he nearly collided with her and, to his horror, he found himself face to face with Susan, in the persona of Jean Rook. There was no escape. For a brief moment they were staring directly at each other, both betraying recognition though neither spoke, then Susan turned and walked smartly away without looking back.

Leslie was utterly paralysed, his heart pounding and his mind a mass of confused thoughts. His overwhelming feeling was dreadful guilt that he had done something terrible and irreversible by this encounter, though he could not begin to think what the outcome would be. As soon as he could move himself, he stepped back into the shop doorway to phone Bennett, his hands shaking so badly he could hardly function, and then to his dismay he got the answerphone message.

Susan was disappearing out of sight, so he did not wait to leave a message but followed in her wake, keeping close to the line of buildings, though she never once looked back. His mind began to clear and the best plan he could think of was to let her get ahead and back to Jeremy's flat, assuming that was where she was going. There was no reason that Susan should suspect he knew where Jeremy lived, and if he kept well behind, she would, he hoped, go straight there as quickly as she could. Leslie would make his way slowly to the top of their road and keep watch, as unobtrusively as possible, contacting Bennett as soon as he could. Bennett could then phone the police, though it was impossible to think how this situation and its urgency could be explained.

The entrance to the park which Gloria had previously waited in would make a good place to position himself; he should be able to see the back gate from there and he could alert Bennett to keep watch on the front. If Susan and Jeremy made an escape from the flat from either the front or the back they would be seen. It was a scheme full of risks but Leslie could not bear to think of them getting away now; he knew he would feel responsible if there was a disaster at this point caused by his stupidity in bumping into Susan. Bennett's incomprehensible suggestion that Jeremy was potentially the next victim went through his mind but, even if that were true, there was nothing more he could do until help arrived.

He felt increasingly nervous as he approached his destination but was relieved that the pavement was narrow and shaded and lined by overgrown gardens with hedges and shrubs spilling out onto the pathway which offered at least some cover. When he was about twenty yards from the turning into Neville Terrace, with the park entrance just across the road, he brought up his phone, which was still in his hand, to ring Bennett.

There was a quick step behind him and a voice said, "You can give that phone to me. And don't speak a word."

At the same time, he felt the painful jab of a knife tip between his shoulder blades. For one desperate moment Leslie tried to hope that he was being mugged for his phone, but it was in vain, for he knew the voice was Susan's. Without looking round, Leslie obediently passed his phone over his shoulder.

Susan snatched it from him and said, "Say nothing at all and start walking normally. If you try anything, I'll put this knife between your ribs and straight into your heart. Believe me, I know what I'm doing. Now walk."

Moving like an automaton, Leslie managed to put one foot in front of the other, never doubting for a moment the veracity of Susan's threats. She walked closely beside him, with the knife now pressed painfully into his chest. There was no one in sight so, even if Leslie had had the courage to shout for help, it would be to no avail. They turned into Neville Terrace and Leslie nearly betrayed his knowledge by slowing down as they reached Jeremy's flat, but he realised in time that it might be wise to feign ignorance and so he did not break stride until Susan said, "Down here."

Halfway down the metal staircase she shoved him roughly and he grabbed the handrail as he fell. The jolt on his arm caused an excruciating pain in his recently injured shoulder, and he lost his grip, falling down the last few steps and landing painfully on his hands and knees. He struggled to his feet and, by then, Susan had the basement front door open and the knife in his flesh again.

"What's all this about?" gasped Leslie, as they went through the door. "There must be some mistake." His shoulder was extremely painful, and he was surprised that he had sufficient command over himself to speak.

"Too right there's been a mistake," replied Susan coldly. "And you made it when you followed me to Brighton. Get on the floor on your front with your arms above your head."

"No, really," protested Leslie, "it's all a misunderstanding. Just let me go and there'll be no more said about it."

"Get down or I'll kick you down," said Susan savagely and jabbed the knife in the direction of his throat. Leslie noticed, for the first time, that she was wearing thin latex gloves; she clearly planned to leave no prints anywhere.

He dropped to the floor and lifted his arms, though his right arm stuck out at a painful and awkward angle.

The front door had opened directly into a living room, but Leslie could make out very little from his position on the floor, and as soon as Susan kicked the door shut there was hardly any light. He heard the sounds of a cupboard door opening and the rattling of metal, then she grabbed his wrists roughly and tried to drag them together behind his back to handcuff him. It was horribly painful and he made an involuntary shout. Susan responded by kicking him in the ribs, on the side of the damaged shoulder, not hard enough to break a bone but enough that he was silenced in a wave of pain and nausea.

She snapped the handcuffs onto one wrist and then, giving up the attempt to get Leslie's right arm behind his back, ordered him to roll over, and she finished applying the handcuffs with his arms in front of him.

"Now get up," she said. "Quickly, moron."

The thought of the knife or of another kicking enabled Leslie to manage what felt like an impossible task and he struggled clumsily to his knees, then his feet. Even with the agony of his shoulder and in the terror of the situation he wondered in what kind of a house handcuffs were conveniently to be had. Now that he was standing up and his eyes adjusted to the dimness, the explanation was clear. A large dresser displayed not china or ornaments, but an array of shackles, manacles, chains and fetters, and on the floor, large vase-like containers held, not dried flowers, but whips and switches. He had no time to take in more than an impression, for Susan was goading him on into a back room.

"Quickly, through there," she said, prodding his back with the tip of the knife. "This has played right into my hands. Everything does, you know, even when halfwits like you try to interfere."

Nothing could have prepared Leslie for what he saw. On a bed, naked except for stockings and suspenders, grotesquely bound and gagged and with a face contused with near suffocation, lay Jeremy. The obscene cruelty and humiliation were more than Leslie could bear and he nearly passed out but, staggering against the doorframe, a fresh spasm in his shoulder brought him to his senses.

"Touch the straps," Susan ordered Leslie, pointing the knife at Jeremy's bound body. "All of them, especially where there are buckles and knots."

She had such a look of insane exaltation that Leslie thought for a moment he was being made an unwilling participant in her sex games, but then she said, "I want your prints all over them. This is so much better than I planned. I got his own prints on them, but a twosome is so much more convincing. Go on, do it."

Leslie found himself physically unable to approach until Susan grabbed the noose-like strap round Jeremy's neck, already half throttling him into slow asphyxiation, and tightened it.

Jeremy's face went a deeper shade and, through the gag, barely coherent, he begged, "Do it, do it."

Leslie approached, and with feelings of shame and disgust that defied description, he did as he was ordered as quickly as possible without looking at either Jeremy or Susan. Susan then said, "Now, put your wrists by his hands. I want his prints on your cuffs."

Leslie's arms felt so leaden that he could barely lift them but, as Susan was still gripping the noose, he did as he was told and it was all over in moments. Susan ordered Leslie back into the living room, selected a long chain from the cabinet with her gloved hands and got Leslie's fingerprints on that too. She had backed him up to the wall and, holding the knife to his neck with one hand, with the other she looped the chain through his wrists and then round his neck. It was a low-ceilinged room, and he was standing beneath a beam which, he now noticed, had a series of metal hooks and rings hanging from it. Susan was tall enough to reach the ring above his head easily and Leslie realised she was going to thread the chain which was attached to his wrists and round his neck through it.

"Shame I've no time to strip you," she said, "but I have to be away."

She glanced up momentarily, ready to pass the chain through the loop and, certain that this would be his last and only chance, Leslie took it. He kicked out as hard as he could and she fell back, overturning a vase of flagellates. She had tightened her grip on the chain, however, and Leslie was pulled towards her, falling heavily on his shoulder and half throttled by the tightened chain. She sprung up, grabbed the knife which had fallen from her grasp and started towards Leslie who was flat on his back, still choking and paralysed with pain and fear.

Possessed by blind rage, and presumably with no thought for her carefully constructed plan, Susan advanced on Leslie's supine body with the knife held high above her head in both hands. Tangled in the chain and stunned, there was nothing Leslie could do to save himself and a mass of confused thoughts rushed into his mind in a single second: of Bennett and of his home that he would never see again, of the tragic events of the past few weeks, and finally that the mad hatred in Susan's face towering over him now would be the last thing he ever saw.

There was a thundering crash from the front door and the sound of splintering wood. All motion was arrested by the shock of this interruption and from his prostrate position Leslie saw the front door disintegrating before his eyes. Through the cavity that had opened up, Bennett appeared, wielding a sledgehammer.

In the moment that Susan was distracted by this astonishing intrusion, Leslie mustered the power to roll out of the way and scramble awkwardly to his feet, snatching up a cat-o'-nine-tails between his two shackled hands. He spun his whole body round and, by sheer luck, caught Susan across the face as she turned round towards him. She screamed, dropped the knife and, in a moment, Bennett had kicked it out of reach, grabbed another whip, applied it hard to her legs and brought her to the floor. There was a sickening crack as her head caught the corner of the dresser and, for a moment, she was motionless on the floor.

"Handcuffs," gasped Leslie, nodding to the cabinet, and Bennett, understanding, seized a set and wrestled the dazed Susan into them with her hands behind her back, applying a second set to her ankles

"Mind if I borrow your necklace?" Bennett said to Leslie, unwinding the chain and passing it through Susan's wrist shackles, behind her back.

"Now let's see if bondage is as much fun when it's for real," he said to the lady who was quickly recovering her senses and attempting to stand, while giving vent to some choice expletives. Bennett assisted the cursing woman to her feet and immediately passed the chain up through one of the rings on the ceiling. He wrenched it up high, until Susan was stooping forwards with the chain short enough for discomfort and restraint, but no further. Two great red wheals disfigured her face and her mouth was bleeding from the whip Leslie had wielded, but she was able to scream insults and obscenities at the two men and writhe about in her uncomfortable and undignified posture.

Leslie had staggered back and was leaning against the wall for support.

"You're hurt," said Bennett, approaching him.

"It's only my shoulder, but it's OK," said Leslie quickly. "Go and help Jeremy, he's through there." He indicated the back room. "He's suffocating."

Bennett moved quickly to the door, uttered an uncharacteristic oath, quickly retrieved Susan's knife from the living room floor and carefully cut the leather noose around Jeremy's neck.

Then to Leslie's consternation, and Jeremy's too, by his expression, Bennett took out his phone and started to take photographs. "For evidence," he said, seeing their reactions. Under his breath, he mused, "Shame, though; some people would pay good money for pictures like these."

He took a series of forensic pictures of Jeremy's bonds, and Leslie's too. Once satisfied, he quickly released Jeremy from all but the foot straps which he left safely fastened to the bed and, opening a cupboard, found a black silk sheet which he used to cover the man's indignity. He returned to Susan and, ignoring her tirade of abuse, added a chain to the cuffs around her ankles and attached it to a mysterious piece of apparatus which was fixed firmly to the wall. He then emptied her pockets, and relieved her of Leslie's phone and a bunch of keys. Finally, possibly from mischief, he took a photograph of her, too. "I don't want her giving us the slip while we wait for the police to arrive," he said, checking all the restraints. "I phoned Ridgeway when you left with Sandra, to update him on everything we'd found out, and he was getting onto his counterpart in this area. They won't be expecting this, though. I didn't know it was coming to a head quite like this when I spoke to him."

Bennett then went through the set of keys and found the one needed to free Leslie's hands. Lastly, he wheeled a tall freestanding mirror, probably another item of gratification, across the room to cover up the jagged opening in the front door.

"Just in case anyone is inquisitive," he explained, "though the neighbours may be used to strange noises from this flat. Now, while we wait for the police, let's have a chat with Jeremy."

"You don't think we should ring 999?"

"You fancy explaining this to the response unit, do you?" said Bennett looking round at the bizarre scene.

"Not really," conceded Leslie. "I bet we would end up in custody and Susan be released."

They returned to the back room and, for a long time, Jeremy, utterly broken, talked.

18

"I couldn't believe it when you appeared through that door," said Leslie. "How did you know?"

Jeremy's basement flat had a very small kitchen, modern, fastidiously clean and, thankfully, devoid of any fetishist accoutrements. There the two men waited after Jeremy had finished telling his tale.

"I was keeping watch from the window," said Bennett. "I'd just finished talking to Ridgeway when you came round the corner."

"So that's why you didn't pick up my call," interrupted Leslie.

"Yes, and before I could ring you back, I saw you appear with Susan and go headfirst down the stairs. That sledgehammer came in handy; I said that every home should have one."

"That was quite a story Jeremy's just told us," said Leslie, shaking his head at the astonishing narrative they had heard.

For the first few minutes, Jeremy had done no more than mutter, repeatedly, "I can't understand it," and, "I can't believe it." He'd shown no signs of embarrassment at the humiliating situation he had been found in, but perhaps that was because he seemed hardly aware of the presence of his liberators.

They'd sat in silence, except for the faintly muffled sounds of Susan in the background. The room that Jeremy was in had evidently been soundproofed, for reasons upon which Leslie did not care to dwell.

At last, Jeremy had started talking. "She's the only woman I've ever wanted," he said, simply.

Leslie had already managed to rally some sympathy for this man who he otherwise found completely repellent, and at this, he felt genuinely sorry for him.

"I could have had any number of women," Jeremy added absently. "There's never any shortage of them flocking round me."

Leslie's sympathy took a nosedive.

"When did you meet Susan?" Bennett asked.

"A couple of years ago," Jeremy replied. "In the autumn. It was at a club in London. We hit it off straightaway."

Leslie and Bennett had exchanged glances at this pun, but it was obviously unintended.

Jeremy continued. "I can't understand what's gone wrong; everything was going so well. She always played it cool, but I knew how she really felt. She came to all my classes, and she followed me round from one venue to another. She even rented a flat down here to be near me."

Apparently oblivious to Susan's duplicity, Jeremy went on to describe the story that she had fed him. Although Leslie's mind was still in a whirl and he couldn't piece together everything he had heard in the last hours and days, it was perfectly obvious that Susan had given Jeremy a completely fictitious history of her life.

She had told him she was married to a man who refused to divorce her, despite them having lived separate lives for years. She claimed that she had been in business with this husband and, unbeknown to her, he had carried out fraudulent dealings; had set it up to look as though she was the guilty party and was now blackmailing her. Despite seeking legal redress—so she said— there was nothing she could do. She had nearly run out of options. All she could do now, she told him, was to escape by going abroad and changing her identity. This meant leaving Jeremy, which he had clearly been distraught about.

"I suppose he had no reason to disbelieve her," said Leslie doubtfully when they were talking it through in the kitchenette.

Bennett raised a sceptical eyebrow.

"You're right," said Leslie, agreeing with Bennett's tacit judgement, for the story which Jeremy had related to them certainly stretched the limits of credibility.

"Then the lucky accident happened," Jeremy had said. "There was a lady in one of my groups who Susan had befriended. Jean was her name. Her husband had died and she was very depressed. Susan did a lot with her to try to take her out of herself. Well, one day they went out in Susan's boat and, while they were far out at sea, Jean suddenly took leave of her senses. Shouting that she couldn't go on any longer, she flung herself over the side of the boat. A very dreadful thing to do, and very upsetting for Susan who'd done so much for her.

"But amazingly Susan saw it as fate, because by the time she got back to land, she'd seen a way of freeing herself from her husband's threats. She realised that she could fake her own death and take on Jean's identity; Jean had no one else in the world, you see, no one who would miss her. And the big thing was, this meant that Susan didn't have to go away; we could be together. See why I thought she was crazy about me—to plan such a thing."

Jeremy described the plot with naïve awe and with no acknowledgement that he had been complicit in a terrible crime. It was a complex and minutely planned scheme. Having disposed of Jean Rook, Susan temporarily assumed a double identity, continuing the normal life of Susan Gunner but also spending time in Hove, disguised as Jean Rook. Jeremy saw it as miraculous, or so he said, that the accident had occurred the very week that Jean had moved to Hove, so neighbours would not recognise the switch.

With meticulous care Susan set up the drama that was played out at the hotel. In the first couple of days of the course, she dropped hints about having a heart condition. On Wednesday, after lunch, she put on a wetsuit under her clothes and, taking her straw bag, went down to the cove. At her direction, Jeremy had set up afternoon tutorials all week, to make sure that he had an alibi on the day of the drama, if foul play or deception were suspected.

Susan stayed down at the cove until dinnertime when Jeremy was sure everyone was gathered in the dining room, so that there was no chance of any delegates or staff being on the cliff. He messaged her to give the all-clear. When she received Jeremy's signal, she drifted out into the waves. She was wearing a long-sleeved top and loose summer trousers which hid the wetsuit and, face down, the snorkelling mask which she had carried down in the bag could not be seen, especially as she floated further out to sea.

Jeremy's next job was to go down to the cliff, taking someone with him to act as a witness—it didn't matter who. Jeremy then had to send the witness back to the house while he supposedly kept watch. A system of communication had been devised between Jeremy and Susan, via Susan's phone, a waterproof one, of course, which was set to vibrate. A certain number of rings indicated that the coast was clear for her to swim round the spit of rocks where she was quickly out of sight, and into Steps Bay.

She then escaped up the steps and along the path to a car which she had parked ready the previous evening. This car, not the one which was left in the hotel car park, had been concealed round the back of St Peter's Church before she arrived on the course, but she moved it to the cul-de-sac near the path on Tuesday evening, after the quiz.

Lantern Cove was cut off at high tide so there was no danger of anyone appearing there, but there was a slim possibility of meeting someone on the steps or on the path to the car. As with everything, Susan planned for this. When she got round the other side of the spit, she took off her wet clothes, rolled them up and hid them in a carrier bag which she'd carried with her in a pocket. Although Steps Bay was not the most obvious place for swimming, if anyone saw her in wetsuit and goggles, they would be unlikely to associate her with the description of the missing holidaymaker from the hotel.

She then resumed the role of Jean Rook, and Jeremy was expecting to resume their passionate, if ferocious, affair. As he finished his narrative, he resumed his opening mantra: "I can't understand it. I can't believe it."

***

"Susan must be quite a manipulator," Leslie said to Bennett as they waited afterwards. "It's easy to believe that Jean was naïve enough to be taken in, but can Jeremy really be that credulous?"

"It suits Jeremy to believe it," said Bennett, "otherwise he has to admit to being an accomplice."

"True. He seems to be so infatuated that he'd have put his head into the proverbial gas oven if she'd told him to."

"And with pleasure, if she'd been standing over him with a cane in her hand," said Bennett wryly.

"Don't!" exclaimed Leslie, who still hadn't recovered from the sight of Jeremy in the bondage room. Banishing the nightmarish image from his mind, he said, "I can see how the deception was carried out now, but there's so much I still don't understand. Pete, to start with."

But before he could go any further, there was the sound of feet descending the stairs outside and the place was suddenly filled with uniformed and plain-clothes police. They took in the scene with raised eyebrows and inaudible exclamations but, to Leslie's relief, they had obviously been briefed by Ridgeway. The two men were escorted to a police car outside and preliminary statements were taken. Leslie refused to go to the hospital; his wounds from falling down the stairs were superficial, and he knew that his shoulder, though painful, was not broken or dislocated again. They were eventually allowed to go, receiving the welcome news that Ridgeway had, somehow, arranged for a car to take them all the way home to Dartonleigh.

They walked slowly back to the rented house to gather their things together. Presently, the police car pulled up outside and a young policeman jumped out and loaded their cases, which had never even been unpacked, into the car. Leslie, his arm now in a makeshift sling, looked on gratefully.

"I can still say that I've never actually stayed in Brighton," said Bennett with satisfaction, as they pulled away.

"I'm not sorry to be seeing the back of that place," said Leslie. "But you know, I'll always regret missing out on that Toby jug."

19

From his second favourite chair in the sitting room, Leslie sat talking to Gloria. His favourite seat looked directly into the garden, a view he currently preferred to avoid. He was, however, so overwhelmingly relieved to be home that if he was not actually confronted with the parched lawn, straggling flowerbeds and empty vegetable patch, he was content.

They had returned the previous day and now Gloria was visiting, ostensibly to bring flowers, a basket of fruit and a box of herbal remedies to promote Leslie's recovery, but really to hear, first-hand, the finale of the great drama. Leslie was still one-armed, so Bennett was on catering duties, something else Leslie needed to ignore if his peace of mind was to be complete.

After Gloria's involvement in the events of the past month, Leslie felt he owed it to her to share the details of the final episode and, despite her capricious and eccentric manner, he trusted her to be discreet.

"Let me get this right," said Gloria, "Susan was really called Jennifer Baker?"

"So it seems."

"Well, I shall never be able to call her anything other than Susan," she declared.

Leslie had just explained that the two young women, Susan Gunner and Jennifer Baker, having met in the university rowing club, had set off to travel through South America, judging by the visa stamps on the passport. At some point on the trip, the real Susan Gunner had disappeared, and Jennifer returned to England posing as Susan.

"The police are now investigating what happened to the real Susan," Leslie explained, "and why Jennifer took on her identity."

"I expect they'll find it was money," Gloria replied. "I bet the real Susan was worth bumping off. But, I say, what a risk-taker she must be. I'd never dare to try to use someone else's passport, even if they looked identical to me."

Leslie smiled to himself; unless Gloria had a twin sister, it was inconceivable that she could have a doppelgänger.

"Superficially the two women were similar enough," said Bennett, who had joined them, "and in those days, remember, there were no biometrics. A quick glance at the photo was all that used to happen. But you're right, she was a risk-taker, and still is."

There was a pause for refreshment. Bennett poured coffee from the cafetiere, and, sighing, Leslie leant forward awkwardly to blot the puddle which Bennett had dripped onto the table. A light fruitcake had been kindly sent across by Annie from The Daffodil Tea Shop, and Bennett had succeeded in reducing it to a pile of crumbs which was nearly impossible to eat. Gloria, undeterred, scooped up cake and sultanas in her fingers, and squeaked with delight when the pieces bounced from her bosom and into her lap.

They drank their coffee and, giving a potted version of Sandra's story, Leslie continued. "Susan, who was really Jennifer, met and married Pete."

"Do just call her Susan," pleaded Gloria. "I shall get terribly confused otherwise."

That agreed, Leslie went on to explain about the couple's smuggling business and how Susan ran off with all the money, leaving Pete fuming and harbouring vengeful thoughts. "Bennett, will you take over the story from here? I'm still not entirely clear about it myself."

Bennett put down his mug and pensively brushed his lap, sending a light shower of cake crumbs to the floor. He pushed his glasses onto the top of his head and, after a short pause, addressed the middle distance. "Some time after she'd split up with Pete, Susan met Jeremy through the S & M world," he began.

"Oh, who'd have thought it?" interrupted Gloria, her eyes bulging. "Susan I can credit, but Jeremy!"

"She'd become a personal finance advisor, as she told you. I suspect that she made her money by preying on vulnerable customers and fleecing them of their hard-earned savings.

The attraction of Jeremy was not his blond hair and suntan, or even his partiality for flagellation, but rather his clientele which included some rich, lonely and gullible women. She followed him from writing group to writing group, not in besotted devotion, but in search of her next unsuspecting client. Susan found exactly what she was looking for in Jean Rook, and initially her motive in befriending her must simply have been to become her financial advisor. But then everyone's luck changed for the worse when Pete came back on the scene."

"My crystals were right, after all," interrupted Gloria in triumph. "Pete was a bad omen."

Ignoring this interjection, beyond raising a quizzical eyebrow, Bennett recounted how Pete had seen Susan quite unexpectedly, and how he had contacted her, demanding the money he believed he was owed. "At first," Bennett explained, "Susan sent him away with a flea in his ear. But Pete was persistent, and Susan decided she must put a stop to it. Ignoring him, alone, was not an option as he'd revealed he knew where she lived. Nor moving house—if he'd found her once, he could find her again, and she wasn't a woman who'd want to look over her shoulder forever. So Susan formulated her nefarious plan."

There was a short pause while Bennett drank some coffee and marshalled his thoughts.

"In fact," he continued, "piecing it together, I think that there were two plans. The original scheme which Susan set in motion when it was obvious that she had to get Pete off her back. She carried that out. But then Pete revealed that he knew about her identity as Jennifer Baker and Susan had to get rid of him, too."

"Oh, I say! I'm even more baffled than before!" exclaimed Gloria.

Leslie caught a quick look of amusement in Bennett's eye and suspected that Bennett, who was perfectly capable of giving a coherent account, was enjoying himself rather at poor Gloria's expense.

"Come on, Bennett," he chided. "Let's have the story properly. All the details in order, please."

Bennett finished his coffee in a leisurely manner and then continued. "As I said just now, Susan had no intention of spending her life running or hiding from Pete. A complete vanishing act was called for, and what better than to fake her own death? This would draw a solid line under her past, with no nasty loose ends that a determined avenger like Pete could follow up and trace her by. And adopting a real person's identity would avoid the difficulties of having to conjure up, out of thin air, all the documents and accounts that everyone needs. Remember, Susan already knew the advantages of taking on a ready-made identity; she'd done it before, when she became Susan Gunner in the first place. She would step straight out of one skin and into another. And if Pete continued sending emails, they would go unanswered. If he was foolish enough to pursue her in person, and even turn up at her door, he would hear that she was missing presumed dead."

"How devious and cold-blooded," said Gloria. "Do you think Susan thought Pete would be taken in by that?"

"Who knows?" Bennett replied. "But, even if he thought it was a scam, what could he do about it? There wasn't really any way he could go to the police and make enquiries or raise his suspicions without incriminating himself."

Gloria looked puzzled so Leslie cut in. "Pete could hardly go to the police and say, 'I think this woman has faked her death to get away from me because I was blackmailing her, and I was blackmailing her to get back the money we got from smuggling.'"

"Of course!" Gloria gasped. "Do go on, it's quite thrilling!"

Bennett resumed the narrative. "So, Susan put in motion her plan, taking poor Jean Rook out for a boat ride and pushing the unsuspecting woman over the side, way out at sea."

"Oh, what a wicked, wicked thing to do," Gloria said.

"She enjoyed cruelty," Leslie replied, thinking of his ordeal at Susan's hand.

"Susan then commenced a double life as Jean in Hove and Susan in Lewes," Bennett continued, "for a temporary period. And it was probably around that time that Pete made his fatal error. Trying to pile on the pressure, he revealed that he knew

Susan was really Jennifer Baker, and that he had a photocopy of the passport."

"Why was that such a big mistake?" Gloria asked.

"Once Susan realised that Pete knew about her previous change of identity," Bennett explained, "it must have been obvious to her that he would be highly suspicious of her disappearance at sea. And he now had something he could go to the police with, which did not incriminate himself."

Again, Gloria was looking confused.

Leslie explained. "Pete could say to the police, 'This lady, who is my estranged wife, has been living under a false persona for twenty years' – or however long. 'I never said anything before as it didn't seem to matter. But this disappearance, without the recovery of a body, looks a bit dodgy, don't you think?'"

"Susan's whole plan," said Bennett, "relied on the police having no serious grounds for suspicion. Obviously, they would make enquiries and look for any suspicious circumstances when she vanished at sea. But Susan believed that she had set up the scenario and covered her tracks sufficiently for superficial enquiries. She certainly could not risk a full-blown investigation. The trail would lead to Jean Rook, and if the police were not convinced that Jean was the genuine article they would uncover the truth in no time."

"Pete had to go," said Leslie, "before he started sowing the seeds of doubt."

"Susan arranged to meet him five miles away from Alemouth and, in the meantime, she bought a ticket to Venezuela, where she planned to flee after she had completed her killing spree," Bennett explained.

"She had it all worked out," said Gloria, shaking her head in disbelief at such malignant cunning.

"But Pete startled her by turning up at the hotel, and he pulled his boat up, not along the coast where they had agreed, but within a short walk of Lantern Cove. Although all this must have been disconcerting for Susan, she used it to her advantage. She told him she couldn't get the money earlier than Wednesday. Then she played him at his own game and on the Tuesday night she ran along the shore at night and murdered him."

"We don't know how she got on the boat," added Leslie. "We didn't see any signs of a break-in, did we? So my guess is that Susan tricked Pete into letting her on board. Perhaps she said she'd got hold of the money early, after all. He seemed to be easily duped by her and if she was holding a big wodge of bank notes, he wouldn't have been able to resist it."

"The poor greedy, stupid man," said Gloria, shaking her head with regret.

"Can't you just imagine Susan suggesting they have a drink for old times' sake and then, when his back was turned, giving him a bash over the head or whatever it was she did?" Leslie added.

"Very likely," agreed Bennett. "Having murdered or incapacitated the man, we presume she took the boat out and pushed him over the side. Remember, at one time she knew that boat as well as he did. Something must have gone wrong for his body to have washed up so soon and so close to Alemouth. Perhaps she couldn't risk going out too far at that time of night, and she must also have had to work quickly; the tide, that night, would have been coming well in by the time she returned along the shore to the hotel."

"I actually heard her come back, around three in the morning," put in Leslie. "I was out on the balcony; I had cramp. I heard something rustling in the garden, which at the time I assumed was some nocturnal animal, and I also heard a door clicking. It must have been Susan going back into her room, but obviously I had no idea of that at the time."

"If I'd heard a door at that time in the morning, I'd have thought it was Susan and Jeremy up to their old hanky-panky again," said Gloria mischievously.

"I must admit that did cross my mind," Leslie conceded.

"It would certainly have taken prophecy on a biblical scale to have divined the truth at that point," said Bennett. "I noticed at the time that Leslie only heard one room door being opened and shut. If it had been one of them visiting the other's rooms, both doors would have been heard. I thought it a bit odd, but at the time nothing untoward had happened. It was only much later when we heard that Pete was dead that it meant anything."

"It didn't register with me, at all," Leslie said.

"When Susan looked below par on Wednesday morning it was genuine," added Bennett. "She'd been up half the night, murdering her husband."

The cafetiere was empty and, since Bennett showed no signs of bestirring himself, Leslie picked it up and started for the kitchen. Recalling another detail that he thought would interest Gloria, he paused in the doorway. "That row Jeremy made about the security light: Jeremy told us that it was Susan who insisted he go to Val and get the light disabled on the Tuesday morning. Obviously, she told him it was to keep their liaisons a secret, but she really needed to be sure that she could creep out undetected on the Tuesday night to go to Pete's boat."

Gloria followed Leslie out with the empty plates and mugs. The tray was replenished, Leslie replacing the crumbled fruit cake with a Victoria sponge, also supplied by Annie. Back in the living room, they sat with their fresh drinks and cake.

"I'm probably being very dense," said Gloria, licking jam from her fingers, thoughtfully, "but why didn't Susan just murder Pete in the first place? It would have been so much less complicated!"

"Less complicated, perhaps," replied Bennett, "but with so many more risks. Unlike Jean, Pete was bound to have people who would miss him and make enquiries if he disappeared. And there was the possibility Pete had told someone all about Susan and his recent interactions with her. In the event of his mysterious disappearance or death, Susan would be the chief suspect. Murdering Pete was a last resort, a change of plan.

"Even then the lady kept her head," Bennett continued. "She made plans to escape to a country which has no extradition treaty with the UK, and she probably hoped to hide herself for a while in South America where she'd been before. When she saw the two of you outside Jean's bungalow in Hove, she brought forward the travel arrangements and, when she was caught, she was only hours from leaving the country."

Gloria stirred sugar into her coffee thoughtfully. "Do tell me about poor Jeremy," she said. "He's another one who wasn't what he seemed."

Bennett related the yarn that Susan had spun Jeremy, of a malicious husband she was trying to escape. "At some point, Susan had brought Jeremy into her plot, convincing him that Jean had thrown herself overboard, and declaring it an act of fate. He knew nothing about the existence of Pete Shad, or Susan's real motives for changing her identity."

"What a foolish, dishonest man," said Gloria. "Even if he didn't realise that Susan had actually murdered Jean, anyone would know that concealing a death and stealing someone's identity was wrong."

"He was blinded by vanity," said Leslie. "And completely infatuated with Susan."

"And she made sure that she did everything to keep it that way," added Bennett, "especially by satisfying his desires. It's obvious that she had no genuine feelings for him, but she did have the same proclivities."

"Oh, I say," gasped Gloria, flushing deeply.

"Yes, it certainly all goes on," Bennett sighed. He drank some of his coffee and continued. "But of course, Susan hadn't finished her slaughter; Jeremy had to go, too. I believe Susan would have got rid of him in any case, as she would never be safe so long as he knew any of her secrets, but he was also proving to be unreliable. On the writing course he couldn't disguise his infatuation with her; he couldn't stop pestering her for his pleasures, and after the death had been staged, I suspect he couldn't resist contacting her even though there was an agreement that he wouldn't. He would make a serious mistake sooner or later, so she carefully planned a little accident for him." Bennett gave a very selective summary of the escapade in the basement flat, omitting all the humiliating details, not to mention anything that might have sounded heroic.

"Well!" said Gloria, and gave them a look that indicated she knew that she was not being told all the gruesome facts.

Leslie said, "We found out from the chief inspector that Susan's meticulous planning included having used Jeremy's computer in the preceding days on search sites that would help to reinforce the impression he died accidentally at his own hand, whenever the time came. Keep it to yourself, though," he added as an afterthought, "I'm not sure I should have mentioned it!"

Gloria was effusive in her assurances of secrecy, then turned her attention to her cake for a while and they fell into thoughtful silence again.

Eventually, Leslie said, "Do you suppose that Susan got the idea from the accident the previous year—that poor soul who fell over the cliff?"

"Very likely," said Bennett. "It introduced the useful fact that a body might never be found along that stretch of water."

"But that was a very different sort of incident," Gloria observed. "Surely Susan took a heck of a risk; there was so much that could go wrong."

"She left very little to chance," said Bennett. "She studied the tides and worked out when she would need to be in the bay. Then, the month before, at the equivalent tide, they did a practice run. Jeremy arranged to come down to the hotel to see your cousin on some pretext."

"Of course!" exclaimed Gloria. "Val was rather surprised about that, but she didn't suspect anything."

"Why would she?" said Bennett. "While he was there, with some excuse, Jeremy went down to the cliff; perhaps he said he needed to make a phone call and had no signal. Susan was ready and waiting in the cove and, when Jeremy messaged her that the coast was clear, they did a trial run."

"And Jeremy told us that Susan chose the Wednesday of the writing course to carry out the scam so that they had Thursday to fall back on in the unlikely event there were unforeseen problems," said Leslie.

"She thought of everything," Gloria sighed.

"Nearly everything," said Leslie. "Jeremy said he was frantic when that young chef, Lee, went rushing off to the rescue on his motorbike. He thought that Lee was going to come face to face with Susan on the footpath or in the street, and he wouldn't have been taken in by the disguise for a minute. Jeremy did his best to delay him."

"Oh yes," said Gloria. "I remember, at the time, wishing that he would shut up and just let the boy get on." Gloria finished her coffee, uttering occasional sighs and exclamations as she assimilated all that she had heard. "You seem to have explained it all, but there's just one thing I'd like to know: what was it in Susan's luggage that you thought was missing?" she asked.

"It was a rucksack," Bennett replied. "Susan had a rucksack under her bed, and it wasn't there when you cleared the room." Leslie went on to explain to the mystified Gloria that the prying Lauren had found Susan's hidden S & M apparatus in the bag.

"In fact," said Bennett, "the black rubberwear Lauren saw in the rucksack was Susan's wetsuit, not S & M accessories."

"Oh, of course," said Leslie. "She wouldn't have wanted that found."

"The missing rucksack was the key for me," said Bennett. "When I knew it hadn't been found in her possessions, it confirmed my conviction that the thing was a scam."

"I can't quite see why it was so important," said Gloria as she dabbed up cake crumbs from her plate.

"Rucksacks don't just vanish. If Susan had really died a natural death in the cove," said Bennett, "the rucksack would have been in her room. Or, if she had hidden it from the prying Lauren, it would surely have been locked in the boot of her car. I dare say that one could concoct other explanations for its absence but, realistically, where else would it have been? I concluded that its absence meant something was decidedly dodgy."

"I suppose she moved it secretly into the car hidden behind the church when she realised Lauren was given to snooping about, and then sneaked the wetsuit back into the hotel to carry out the death charade," Leslie said.

"Yes," said Bennett. "If there hadn't been an issue with Lauren snooping about, I expect the rucksack would have been found in Susan's room, empty or with a few innocent items in it. She made a mistake in not bringing it back to the room."

"I suppose it never occurred to her that it would be missed," said Leslie.

"Ah," sighed Gloria with great satisfaction, "little did she know that you never miss a thing, between you. I said all along that you would solve it."

20

The following two days passed in a succession of visits from friends and neighbours. The cottage was filled with flowers, homemade biscuits and preserves, and boxes of chocolates, from the kindly, and curious, visitors, all keen to wish them well and hear the story for themselves. Annie, always thoughtful and generous, came over from the Daffodil Tea Shop each morning bearing a dinner and the inevitable cake. Their GP called in to check the men over, to the chagrin of neighbours who claimed they could not get a home visit even if they were at death's door. Most of them knew though that the men were old friends, and that Dr Paul used any excuse to visit them, and the beloved cottage he had sold to them six years earlier. The arrival of Malcolm, the chess club chairman, with Cromwell, his malodorous dog with its insatiable appetite and weapon of a tail, caused Leslie more anxiety than pleasure, and the visitation by Brian Masterson to brag about his prize-winning runner beans was decidedly unwelcome.

By the end of the Tuesday evening Leslie was exhausted, and when the doorbell rang at eight-thirty he uttered a profanity and suggested they pretended they were not at home.

"Alas, you're forgetting we're back in our village;" said Bennett as he ambled towards the front door, "a place where no one can go missing. Everyone knows we're here, and if we don't answer we'll have the police breaking in. Speaking of which," he added as he admitted Detective Chief Inspector Charles Ridgeway, apologising for his late intrusion. As usual, he was passing on his way back from a meeting.

A large plate of cheese and biscuits was produced, under Leslie's strict supervision, and drinks poured, the inspector regretfully confining himself to orange juice due to his prospective drive home. Leslie, no longer weary, quizzed the chief inspector on all the details he had not yet understood, and Ridgeway displayed his remarkable gift for appearing to divulge nothing, while telling the two men everything they wanted to know.

They soon found out that as soon as Jeremy had come to terms with Susan's treachery, he had told the police everything he knew, which was just as well, since he had earlier divulged most of it to Leslie and Bennett. Ridgeway was hoping Susan would talk, but he was not optimistic.

"She must be a psychopath, surely?" said Leslie. "At first I wondered how she thought she could get away with tying me up, and making out I was involved with Jeremy." He grimaced at the thought. "It was madness to think that would work. I know she was acting on the spur of the moment, but it was still madness. But then I remembered her face when she was in that basement, and she really was mad—completely deranged."

"Perhaps, yes. But I doubt she will be declared criminally insane, and formal psychological and psychiatric assessments always take a long time," said Ridgeway, vaguely. "But now, both of you, what put you onto Susan's antics in the first place?"

With a dismissive shrug, which caused a small piece of Stilton to fly from his fork, Bennett said, "Leslie knew straightaway that the relationship between Susan and Jeremy didn't add up, and when Susan's apparent death occurred, he was adamant Jeremy's reaction did not make sense. There was, as he phrased it, something fishy going on. So, in the absence of a corpse, I presumed that the whole thing was a con. There was also a sense of theatre about the event; an unreality."

He paused to take an appreciative sip of port. "I thought Susan was being pursued and perhaps blackmailed by Pete, and that Jeremy was an accomplice in helping her escape from him. I couldn't see quite how they'd pulled it off, but I guessed that some kind of trickery had been carried out."

"That was a reasonable assumption," said Ridgeway.

"I'm afraid I was completely taken in," Leslie interjected, ruefully. "By the death charade, that is." He nibbled a cracker and added, rather defensively, "Jeremy was very lucky that it was Barbara who came back with the news of the so-called death. It seemed unquestionable."

"Quite so; none of you questioned it," said Ridgeway, reassuringly. "Except Bennett."

"Who kept it to himself, as usual," retorted Leslie, with some ascerbity.

Ignoring all these remarks, Bennett took up his glass, and his explanation, again. "There were plenty of clues, once I started thinking about it. That business about Susan's illness, for example. There's nothing easier than reporting fainting symptoms and palpitations to a GP so that it looked genuine if the police made enquiries. The trick was in the timing, to make sure no tests had yet been carried out."

There was a pause while Bennett ate some of his cheese thoughtfully. Ridgeway took the cue and cut himself another great wedge. The man was so thin yet had such a large appetite, Leslie wondered, in passing, if he ever ate anything except when he visited them.

At length Bennett continued. "Another point of interest was the nonattendance of Jean Rook on the course. It caused remark, as did the excuse that Susan had lost touch with her."

"I've been wondering why Susan didn't invent a more convincing excuse," said Leslie. "Anyone would have accepted it if Susan had said she couldn't come on the course because she was visiting a relative, or something like that."

"I wondered that too, at first. But then I realised that it was essential for Susan to completely sever her connection with Jean. Susan knew that in the absence of other friends or family, the police would track down and question Jean for information, following her supposed death. When they caught up with Jean, Jean had to be able to repudiate any current knowledge of Susan."

"Ah," said Ridgeway, "that's probably the most embarrassing aspect of our investigation. One of our officers did locate Jean Rook and had a most pleasant conversation with her which, unsurprisingly, tallied convincingly with what we had been told about her losing contact with Susan. Imagine the officer's mortification when she discovered that she'd been speaking with Susan all along!"

"If it's of any consolation to her," said Leslie, "we were quite taken in ourselves, and Gloria had actually seen Jean the previous year."

"But," said Bennett, "you weren't completely taken in, Les. Despite never having met the woman, you knew that Jean Rook would not behave as she did when she saw you, speeding away in a car."

Turning to Ridgeway, Bennett said, "As soon as Leslie and Gloria were on Jean's trail, I realised that this was more sinister than I'd first thought. The strange circumstances of Jean's house move, the clumsy attempt to impersonate her in writing to her neighbour Marge, and Leslie's sense of deep sadness haunting the whole set up, were disturbing."

"Susan made a big mistake in letting slip that she'd rowed for Cambridge," said Leslie.

"It's the weakness of so many Oxbridge alumni; they can't help dropping it in the conversation. I had the good fortune of having a contact, and another great stroke of luck, if you'll excuse the pun, was that both Susan and Jennifer met in the rowing club, and both were in the photograph which Giles sent me. It didn't take much after that to find out she was really Jennifer."

"Have you managed to find out what happened to the real Susan Gunner?" Leslie asked.

"We're following that up of course," said Ridgeway. "Unfortunately, we're going back to an era when it was much easier to vanish."

Bennett put yet another piece of cheese on his plate and the chief inspector was urged to do the same. As he took the last piece of Stilton he said, "I suppose I ought to rebuke you for not sharing your ideas sooner."

"You're lucky he's told you at all," said Leslie, peevishly. "He didn't let on to me either until it was all over. Some of it I'm hearing for the first time now."

And when Bennett just shrugged, Leslie got up, rather grumpily, to refresh the cheese plate which was now empty except for a few crumbs, and Bennett showed no signs of rousing himself.

Leslie left the room as Ridgeway was mildly chiding Bennett, but he paused just outside the door as Bennett said placidly, "You can hardly accuse me of withholding information; it was merely surmise and I might have been wrong. Then we would all have been on the wrong path. As far as Les is concerned, nearly everything I pick up is from him, through his lens. And, although he doesn't always draw the right conclusion, he sees things I would never see and reads people as I could never read them. I'd ruin that if I put my own construction on things before the right time."

It was rare to hear Bennett attempt to justify himself, and Leslie smiled. He went through to the kitchen, found a fine piece of brie in the fridge, and added some grapes to liven up the plate.

Epilogue

"Me and, if you get this, you," said Bennett.

"What are you talking about?" Leslie replied, rather impatiently.

Ridgeway had finally taken his leave, with an undertaking to arrange a game of chess very soon. He couldn't promise when; it was all subject to the vagaries of the West Country criminal fraternity, not to mention the inexhaustible meetings sprung upon him by the bureaucrats of the police force.

Now the two men were alone in the sitting room, and Leslie was feeling weary.

"Fourteen letters," said Bennett. He wrote the clue on a piece of paper and passed it to Leslie.

"Me: is that ego or I?" said Leslie, after studying the clue for a while. When Bennett shook his head, Leslie gave in.

"Cruciverbalist," Bennett announced.

Leslie, in no mood for Bennett's puzzles, screwed up the paper into a ball and hurled it at Bennett who caught it and tossed it over his shoulder.

Leslie sat back in the armchair and his mind returned to the wretched circumstances of recent weeks. Poor Marge, bereft of her only friend, would probably hear about the crime in due course and be forced to grieve in terrible loneliness; dear Sandra, who mourned the loss of her no-good partner with agonising unconditional love; tragic Jean, looking for happiness and meeting only deception and murder, and then, long ago, the real Susan Gunner. Whatever had happened to her? Leslie hoped the truth would come to light for her too, and justice would be done.

He suddenly realised Bennett was out in the kitchen and went out to see what mischief he was up to, but as he stood up a thought occurred to him. "You know," he said to Bennett as he joined him, "I felt rather aggrieved that I had been mourning the loss of Susan who seemed to have no one else to grieve for her, when she was really alive and up to no good. But I've just realised that the real Susan Gunner does seem to have died unnoticed and unmourned, after all."

Leslie walked over to the window and peered out into the heart of the village. There was no street lighting, but it was one of those nights that never goes completely dark, and the big bulk of the church and the thatched cottages clustered round could easily be made out.

"I sometimes think you couldn't go missing from this village for five minutes without being noticed," he said.

"I expect it could be done if you planned it well enough," said Bennett. "But not as easily as in a town or city."

"I remember once, when I was in London," said Leslie, "seeing a poster up at Kings Cross station, about a woman who had been found dead in the station months earlier. They had mocked up a picture of her and were appealing for anyone who thought they might know her. I was horrified. What could be worse than being missing but not missed?"

"I remember," said Bennett. "You talked about it at the time."

Sighing, Leslie turned round to reply but something on the table caught his eye. Bennett had made a tray of tea and coffee but, noteworthy as this was, it was something particular on the tray which arrested him. As he stared, Bennett lifted a pint of milk and ceremoniously poured it into the milk jug that Leslie was staring at in amazement. It was a small, squat, magnificently grotesque Toby jug bearing the legend: Toby or not Toby. A present from Paignton.

"The Toby jug! Oh, Bennett!" he exclaimed ecstatically. "I can't believe it! I'd given it up for lost. How on earth did you get it?"

"They sent it to me," said Bennett. "Well, to Annie at The Daffodil, actually. She brought it across earlier."

"It's just the most wonderful thing," said Leslie. He looked more closely and noticed that the milk had an unpleasant film of dust floating on its surface from Bennett's failure to wash it out before use. "But I think we'll keep it as an ornament. I'll take my tea with lemon in, if you don't mind."

He went across to the sink, unleashed his arm from its sling and, with great care, rinsed and dried the trophy. Carrying it across to the dresser, he adjusted the existing jugs and placed the Toby jug in the centre. "It will have pride of place in honour of all the forgotten," he said. He stood back to admire it. "Isn't it a monster? I fell in love with it as soon as I saw it in that window; it's so ugly and wonderfully eccentric."

Bennett was standing next to him, holding the mug of tea, to which he had forgotten to add a slice of lemon. "I do realise how lucky I am to have met the only man who could fall in love with something because it's ugly and eccentric," he said, and he carried the tea through to the sitting room.

Postscript

Dear Barbara,

As promised, here are the recipes for the meal we had at Beach Cottage: scallops, salmon and strawberries.

Gloria tells me that you're planning a few days in Devon next month. Do make sure we're on your itinerary as it would be lovely to see you. If you've time, I'll cook a meal and Bennett will get the chess set out.

Best Wishes,

Leslie

Scallops with ginger and spring onion

- 3 fat scallops (with the coral on) per person for a starter patted dry with some kitchen roll
- A bunch of spring onions, prepared and sliced diagonally
- A piece of fresh ginger, grated
- Lemon juice
- Olive oil (or chilli oil for an extra kick)
- Butter (the type with sea salt is nice)

1. Using a nonstick pan, heat a tablespoon of oil and a slice of the butter until very hot.
2. Add the scallops and cook until they just start to brown on each side. This only takes a minute or so each side, and you don't want to overcook them or they go tough. They should be just cooked and soft in the middle.
3. Take them out of the pan and set aside.
4. Add the other ingredients to the pan and cook briefly until the spring onions are just wilted.
5. Return the scallops to the pan to coat them with the sauce.
6. Serve immediately on the shell if you have shells (one shell per person).
7. Season to taste.

Salmon with lemon and watercress sauce

- A salmon fillet per person
- Lemon
- Butter
- Olive Oil
- Watercress to garnish

For the sauce:
- 30g butter
- 1 small onion or shallot
- 1 stick of celery
- 275ml vegetable stock
- 75ml white wine
- Large bag chopped watercress
- 150ml crème fraiche

1. Pre-heat the oven to 160°C fan/gas mark 4.
2. Put a few drops of olive oil in an ovenproof dish to prevent the salmon sticking.
3. Pat the salmon dry.
4. Season with salt and black pepper.
5. Squeeze lemon juice over generously and drizzle with olive oil (I put my thumb over the top of the bottle).
6. Leave to marinate if you like, but you don't have to.
7. Cover with foil.
8. Bake at 160°C fan/gas 4 for about 20 minutes (this depends on your oven, how thick the salmon is and how long you marinate it for). Alternatively, you can prepare the salmon as before and pan fry for about three minutes each side in a little oil and butter instead of baking it.

To make the sauce
1. Melt an ounce of butter in a small pan.
2. Add a very finely chopped small onion/shallot and/or stick of celery and cook until soft.
3. Add the vegetable stock and white wine and simmer for about three minutes.
4. Add a large bag of chopped watercress and 150mls of crème fraiche.
5. Warm through without boiling as it may split.
6. If you have oven-baked the salmon, you can add the juices from the dish to the sauce.

Strawberries with shortbread (Very easy!)

- Fresh strawberries
- Muscavado sugar (about 100g, but will obviously depend on how many strawberries)
- Liqueur or fruit syrup of your choice (a tablespoon or so depending on how many strawberries and which liqueur—I used crème de cassis at Beach Cottage)

For the shortbread (I still like to use my old recipe in ounces for this one)
- 12oz (350g) flour
- 3½oz (100g) sugar
- 8oz (225g) salted butter

1. Cut the strawberries in half and marinate (preferably overnight) in the fridge with muscovado sugar and liqueur/fruit syrup.
2. Reduce the liquid in a saucepan (don't burn it!).
3. Serve warm or leave it to go cold.

To make the shortbread (or buy some nice shortbread instead!)
1. Pre-heat the oven to 170°C fan/gas mark 5.
2. Mix together the butter and sugar until combined but not creamed.
3. Add the flour and mix without overworking it.
4. Roll into a ball then roll out with a rolling pin into the shape of tin you want to use (8 inch circle works, or similar square or rectangle, or cut out individual shapes).
5. Prick with a fork.
6. Bake for 30 minutes 170°C fan/gas mark 5.
7. Sprinkle with extra sugar as soon as cooked.
8. Cool in tin then remove and cool on rack.
9. Serve with whipped cream or ice cream and enjoy.

Dartonleigh Parish Magazine Double Crossword

2 sets of clues (Cryptic and Quick), 1 set of solutions

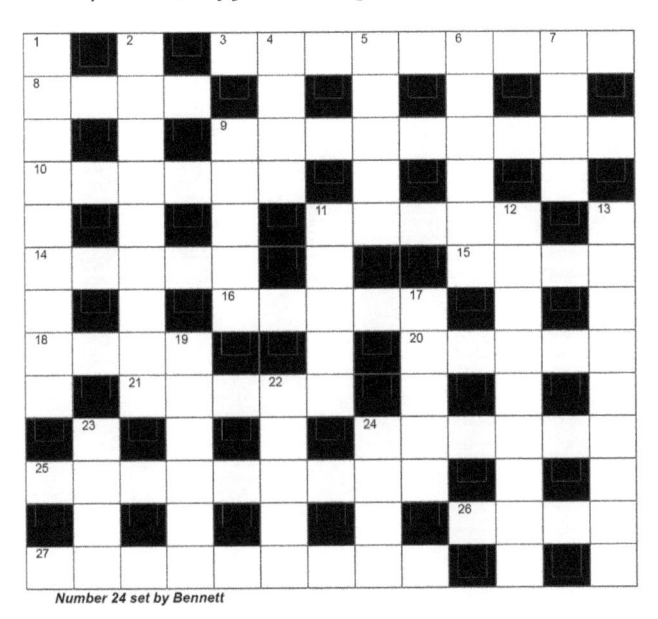

Number 24 set by Bennett

Cryptic Clues

ACROSS

3 Cover John's cakes (9)
8 Bike that works out the thigh muscle (4)
9 Cracked china at horse trials (9)
10 See you inside at the end of prayers? (6)
11 Back to normal when United Nations departs (5)
14 Conquers this creature roundly (and 9 down) (5 & 5)
15 Media in L.A is hot stuff (4)
16 How cricketers are selected (5)
18 East Enders party food? (4)
20 Places to conceal furs (5)
21 Ingredient in the tasty Easter buns (5)
24 A hundred lead the retreat, sticking together (5)
25 This beverage isn't evergreen (9)
26 Something similar is in the making (4)
27 Parlez Francais? (9)

DOWN

1 Argued second best and learner be in the team (9)
2 Friend of the earth has no currency (9)
4 Incline to being thin (4)
5 2 new drivers join the equation at the filling station (5)
6 End a mix-up every year (6)
7 Don't forget it's in your handkerchief (4)
9 Conquers this creature roundly (and 14 across) (5&5)
11 Disquieting setup (5)
12 Mad Larks surround significant places beyond Watford Gap (9)
13 Clairvoyant reordered can sound maritime (9)
17 Somewhere to store minced meat? (5)
19 Each a part of an aromatic quartet (6)
22 Cut and run? (5)
23 A grievance, should this structure you stand on be broken (4)
24 Visit from a bird (4)

231

Quick clues

ACROSS
3 Sweet oat cake (9)
8 Prefix indicating four or fourth (4)
9 Game played with shuttlecock (9)
10 Ability to make wise judgements (6)
11 Common, habitual (5)
14 Defeats (5)
15 Substance of volcanic origin (4)
16 Examines (5)
18 Snake-like fish (4)
20 Conceals (5)
21 Raising agent in baking (5)
24 Cling (6)
25 Having separate sheets of paper (9)
26 Similar (4)
27 Stem of bean plant (9)

DOWN
1 Quarrelled (9)
2 Innately (9)
4 Incline (4)
5 Plimsolls (5)
6 Yearly (6)
7 Fasten or tangle (4)
9 Creature (5)
11 Distressed (5)
12 Recognisable features (9)
13 Ability to predict (9)
17 Ledge (5)
19 Time of the year (6)
22 Divide (5)
23 Femur, for example (4)
24 Cry out (4)

Solutions

Across: 3 *Flapjacks*; 8 *Quad*; 9 *Badminton*; 10 *Acumen*; 11 *Usual*; 14 *Beats*; 15 *Lava*; 16 *Tests*; 18 *Eels*; 20 *Hides*; 21 *Yeast*; 24 *Cleave*; 25 *Looseleaf*; 26 *Akin*; 27 *Beanstalk*
Down: 1 *Squabbled*; 2 *Naturally*; 4 *Lean*; 5 *Pumps*; 6 *Annual*; 7 *Knot*; 9 *Beast*; 11 *Upset*; 12 *Landmarks*; 13 *Farseeing*; 17 *Shelf*; 19 *Season*; 22 *Split*; 23 *Bone*; 24 *Call*

Preview

Stage Effects
The third novel in J Wilcox's *Leslie and Bennett* series.

"Oh, do say you'll do it, Leslie," begged Gloria through a mouthful of fruitcake. She fixed him with her most imploring look. "We're simply relying on you to step in."

When Leslie reluctantly agrees to take a part in Lymeford Amateur Dramatic Society's latest production, he soon discovers there is more drama off stage than on. An obnoxious director, a philandering lead, and a washed-up professional make for high tension. When one of the cast disappears, everyone thinks it's a stunt, but Leslie is suspicious. He decides to investigate, assisted (and sometimes hindered) by the inimitable Gloria.

There are suspects and there are clues, but none of it explains what has happened, or even confirms Leslie's theory that a crime has been committed. Will Leslie's maverick partner, Bennett, step in and help make sense of the plot?